MURDER SERVED COLD

MURDER SERVED COLD

A Langham and Dupré mystery

Eric Brown

This first world edition published 2018
in Great Britain and 2019 in the USA by
SEVERN HOUSE PUBLISHERS LTD of
Eardley House, 4 Uxbridge Street, London W8 7SY.
Trade paperback edition first published
in Great Britain and the USA 2019 by
SEVERN HOUSE PUBLISHERS LTD.

British Library Cataloguing in Publication Data
A CIP catalogue record for this title is available from the British Library.

ISBN-13: 978-0-7278-8852-5 (cased)
ISBN-13: 978-1-84751-976-4 (trade paper)
ISBN-13: 978-1-4483-0184-3 (e-book)

All Severn House titles are printed on acid-free paper.

Severn House Publishers support the Forest Stewardship Council™ [FSC™],
the leading international forest certification organisation.
All our titles that are printed on FSC certified paper carry the FSC logo.

FSC
www.fsc.org

MIX
Paper from
responsible sources
FSC® C013056

Typeset by Palimpsest Book Production Ltd.,
Falkirk, Stirlingshire, Scotland.
Printed and bound in Great Britain by
TJ International, Padstow, Cornwall.

To Aria Eliana Dunnett
with love.

ONE

Langham pulled up outside the Lyons' tea room in Earl's Court just as snow began to fall, large flakes drifting down from a leaden November sky.

He crossed the pavement and pushed open the door beside the tea room. A flight of stairs, with a central strip of navy blue carpet held in place by brass rods, rose to the first floor where the Ryland and Langham Detective Agency had its two-room office. He wiped his feet and hurried upstairs.

Pamela sat behind her desk in the spacious anteroom, tapping away at a typewriter. She looked up and smiled. She really did add a touch of class to the place, with her piled blonde hair, pearl necklace, and pale pink cashmere cardigan.

He removed his overcoat and hung it with his hat on the stand. 'Settling in?'

'Beats the last job,' she said, her cockney accent contrasting with her sophisticated appearance. 'I thank my lucky stars the day Mr Ryland walked in and saved my bacon.'

In August, Ralph had investigated a dodgy character who ran an art gallery in Belsize Park. Pamela had worked there as the receptionist, a girl with personality and obvious intelligence. When the owner was jailed and his business closed down, Ralph had offered her a job.

Langham indicated the door to the inner office. 'Ralph in?'

'With a client, Mr Langham.' She looked at her watch. 'But he's been in there half an hour, so he shouldn't be much longer.'

He perched himself on the corner of the desk and looked around the room. 'You've certainly got this place looking ship-shape. Last week there were boxes stacked to the ceiling.'

The rooms had been rented by a lawyer who'd moved to Holborn in the summer. With dark parquet flooring, polished walnut wall panels and long sash windows, the place was an improvement on their previous office, a grimy single room over a fish and chip shop in Wandsworth. Shelves ran the length of one entire wall, ranked with box-files containing the case notes Ralph had amassed over the years.

Langham's latest novel sat on the desk beside the typewriter. Pamela saw him looking and smiled. 'I'm really enjoying it,' she said, tapping the hardback with her forefinger. 'But there's one thing I don't understand.'

'What's that?'

'The dedication: "To My Darling Maria – Miss Ten Per Cent". What on earth does that mean?'

He laughed. 'Ah – well. You see, as well as being my wife, she also works for my literary agent, Charles Elder. It's something of a joke between us.'

The phone shrilled and Pamela picked up the receiver.

'Good morning,' she said. 'Ryland and Langham Detective Agency. How can we help?'

Langham crossed to the window, smiling at how her accent slipped from cockney to posh in an instant.

The snow was settling. A double decker bus ground along the street, and hunched figures, muffled against the cold, hurried back and forth along the slush-covered pavements.

'Well . . .' Pamela said, 'we don't normally undertake such work.'

Langham warmed his hands on the radiator and watched an old man dragging a stubborn terrier across the road.

'And how long has it been missing? Two days? My advice would be to wait a little longer. Maybe put a saucer of food out tonight – and have you checked your neighbours' outhouses and sheds?'

Langham sat on the radiator and watched Pamela as she wound a strand of blonde hair around her finger and pulled a face at him.

'That's quite all right,' she said. 'Goodbye.'

She replaced the receiver and laughed. 'I know you're not busy at the moment, Mr Langham, but you wouldn't want to investigate a missing cat, would you?'

'We're not quite that desperate, yet,' he said.

The door to the inner office opened and an elderly, stooping gentleman stepped out, dressed impeccably in a Harris Tweed overcoat and trilby, and leaning heavily on a walking stick. He was tall and gaunt, and his melancholic, plum-coloured face suggested a fondness for alcohol. He turned to address Ralph briefly, nodded to Langham, and took his leave.

Ralph watched him go, a thoughtful expression on his weasel face. 'Pam, be a darling and make us a cuppa, would you? Don, I thought I heard your dulcet tones.'

Langham nodded in the direction of the departed gentleman. 'Don't tell me – his cat's gone missing?'

Ralph frowned. 'What makes you think . . .?'

'We've just had a call from an old dear worried about her missing tabby,' Pamela explained. 'Black Earl Grey, isn't it, Mr Langham?'

'Lovely,' he said, following Ralph into the office and closing the door behind him.

'This looks like it might be a nice little earner,' Ralph said, throwing himself into his swivel chair and lodging his winkle-pickers on the desk. 'A stolen painting. And all thanks to your agent, Mr Elder.'

Langham sat down and tipped the chair back against the wall. 'How is Charles involved?'

'That old gent,' Ralph said, pointing a nicotine-stained finger at the door, 'was none other than Lord Elsmere. He's a friend of Charles, who recommended us when he found out that Elsmere had had a painting nicked.'

The door opened and Pamela came in carrying two chipped mugs. She set Ralph's on the desk and handed Langham his.

'You're the best, Pam,' Ralph said. 'We don't want to be disturbed, so no phone calls for a while.'

Pamela smiled her acknowledgment and left the room.

Langham sipped his tea. 'Go on.'

'A week ago Lord Elsmere had his favourite painting taken from right under his nose. One evening it was there, over the fire in the library, and in the morning it was gone. So he got the local rozzers in, and the insurance people – 'cos the painting was worth a bomb – but the theft stumped the police and the insurance bods refused to cough up.'

'Why was that?'

'According to Lord Elsmere,' Ralph said, slurping his tea, 'there was no evidence of a break-in, and no sign of the painting having been stolen – despite the fact that it wasn't where it had been. It didn't help his case that he'd recently had it re-insured for ten thousand quid.'

Langham whistled.

'So the insurance people suspect him of shifty work,' Ralph said, 'the local boys in blue are scratching their heads, and Elsmere is bewildered by a theft he told me was impossible.'

Langham brought his chair down on all four legs. 'Why impossible?'

'The library door was locked, and anyway the door was too small for the painting to fit through. Elsmere said his butler, who has his bedroom right next to the library, is a light sleeper who would've heard any burglars.'

'Evidently he didn't, if indeed the painting was taken,' Langham said. 'What did you make of Elsmere?'

Ralph lit up a Capstan, sat back in his chair, and blew smoke towards the ceiling. 'For a toff, Don, he seemed a decent cove. And he appeared genuinely mystified by the theft.'

'If it was a theft, and not an inside job.'

'But if he did it himself for the insurance dosh, why would he come to us?' Ralph shook his head. 'No, I reckon he was on the level. He seemed more bothered about getting the picture back than getting his hands on any insurance money. Something by Gainsborough. I forget the title. Heard of him?'

'Eighteenth century. Country scenes and portraits, if I remember correctly.'

'This one was a family heirloom, belonged to Elsmere's great-grandfather. He said it was the only thing of value in the whole place – worth more than the ruddy house, he said. His father died back in 'twenty-five, and old Elsmere's been struggling ever since.'

'Death duties have hit the gentry hard,' Langham said. 'It's a wonder he didn't go the whole hog and have the place burned down to collect on the insurance.'

'But he has done something to bring some dosh in,' Ralph said. 'He's divided the house into flats and let them out.'

'Did he say how many are occupied?'

'There are five separate apartments, and four of them are occupied. Along with the gatehouse.'

'So if the theft wasn't an outside job, or an insurance scam,' Langham said, 'there'd be plenty of suspects around the place?'

'So it would seem,' Ralph agreed. 'Anyway, I said we'd accept the case and motor up there this morning. Lord Elsmere has some business to attend to in London this afternoon. He said he'd be back later today, but his son'll be on hand to show us around.'

'Excellent,' Langham said. 'I'm in need of a little country air.'

Ralph looked at his watch. 'Ten o'clock, Cap'n. Let's hop it.'

TWO

They took Langham's Rover and drove from the capital through the worsening snowfall.

'I noticed the Arsenal walloped Bolton last Saturday,' Ralph said as they motored through Epping Forest.

'I missed the game. Maria wanted to go to an exhibition at the National.' Langham glanced at his friend. 'What about Millwall?'

'Drew one-all with Brighton in the Cup and scalped 'em in the replay on Monday night, three-one.' Ralph took a last gasp on his tab-end and flicked it through the window. 'You should've seen Shepherd's goal, a pile-driver from outside the area. I tried to tell Annie how brilliant it was, but she just looked at me funny-like.'

Langham laughed. 'I've stopped trying to interest Maria in the game. As far as she's concerned, it's the one flaw in my otherwise perfect character.'

Ralph chortled. 'She'll live and learn, Don.'

They left the suburban sprawl of London and headed north-east through countryside rapidly turning white beneath a caul of snow. Houses gave way to rolling fields and stark, denuded trees, and soon the snowfall became a blizzard blowing horizontally and reducing visibility to twenty yards. Langham turned up the heater and slowed to thirty miles per hour. Fortunately there was little traffic on the road.

'Reminds me of that time in the Highlands last year,' Ralph said. 'Now, that was one hell of a snowstorm.'

Langham smiled at the recollection. 'I doubt we'll be snowed in this time.'

'If we are, I hope there's a pub in the village. It's a place called Lower Neston, three miles south of where your Mr Elder has his pile.'

'After we've seen our fill at Elsmere's place,' Langham said, 'we could always tootle along to see Charles and pick his brains about Elsmere. According to Maria, Charles is reading manuscripts at home this week.'

'Can't say I blame him,' Ralph said, peering out at the snow-covered fields. 'Here, you sure about moving out to the sticks?'

'Of course. Some quiet village in rural Suffolk with a decent pub and a railway station. It isn't always snowing outside London, you know.'

'As long as you'll still put in a couple of days at the agency . . .'

Langham looked at Ralph. 'Ah, I thought you were a bit quiet when I mentioned house-hunting the other day.'

'Well, you'll no longer be on the doorstep, will you?'

'No, but I have no intention of leaving the agency, all right? I like the work. It complements the writing a treat. And anyway, Maria's keeping on the Kensington apartment.'

'You never told me that.'

'She only made her mind up the other day. Her father insisted on paying the ten-year lease as a wedding present, so we'd be foolish to let it go. We'll use the place as a base when we're in London and spend half the week or so in the country.'

'Best of both worlds.'

'So don't worry yourself that I'm going to do a runner, you duffer. Now . . .' He slowed down as they came to a crossroads, peering through the snow-dappled windscreen. 'Left or right? There's a signpost over there, but I'm dashed if I can make out what it says.'

'Hold on a jiffy. I'll nip out and have a gander.'

Ralph braved the snowstorm and dashed across the road to the fingerpost. He was back in seconds, his teeth chattering. 'Bury St Edmunds to the left,' he said. 'It's twenty miles off, and Lower Neston's five or six miles this side of the town. We're almost there.'

Langham started up and turned left.

A little over half an hour later they came to a collection of thatched cottages, their chimneys trailing pennants of grey smoke. The snow had ceased for the time being, and the village looked impossibly pretty with its whitened village green and iced-over mill pond. A sign next to the church announced Little Nest – the 'on' obscured by the snow-covered branches of a yew tree.

'According to Lord Elsmere, Neston Manor's a mile to the north,' Ralph said.

Langham drove through the village until they came to a fork in the road.

'Now which way?' he said.

To their right, stomping down the garden path of the last cottage in the village, Langham made out the burdened figure of a postman. He wound down the window and called out, 'I say, which way to Neston Manor?'

The aged postman approached the car and peered in at Langham and Ralph. 'The manor, you want?' he said, his nose dripping like a faulty tap. 'Take the lane to the right, then turn right again after fifty yards. I'm going up there meself. Don't suppose I could beg a lift?'

'Of course,' Langham said. 'Hop in.'

The postman climbed in to the back seat and Langham took the lane to the right. 'Foul weather,' he said over his shoulder.

'You said it right,' the old man agreed, 'and you know what always happens in foul weather?'

'Go on.'

'Parcels get heavier and there's always more of 'em. Friends of his lordship, are you?'

'More like acquaintances,' Ralph said.

'Been to the manor before?'

'First time,' Langham said.

'Rum place. Full of odd folk. Artists and foreigners. You see, his lordship likes to collect waifs and strays.'

'Waifs and strays?' Langham said. 'I understood he rents out flats?'

'Aye, that's right, to waifs and strays, leastways that's what

Reg at the Dog and Gun calls 'em. One's a Dutch chap, miserable bloke if you ask me. And some of the women . . . Loose, me missus says. Turn right here, and you'll see the manor between the trees.'

Langham turned down a narrow lane with high hedges on either side. They crawled up a hill, came to the crest, and looked out over a wide vale scintillating with a flawless expanse of snow. The Tudor manor, low and rambling, stood half a mile away between swathes of sinister-looking woodland.

Langham eased the Rover off the lane and approached the manor house down a rutted track, in due course coming to a gatehouse that was built into the high stone wall enclosing the grounds. They drove under the gatehouse's archway and up the drive, around the snow-covered lawn, and halted outside the dilapidated Tudor pile.

'How about I give you a lift back to the village when you've finished here?' Langham asked the postman.

'There's no need. That's me done for the day, and me cottage is just half a mile off through the woods.'

The postman climbed from the car, delivered a handful of letters, then gave a cheery wave and trudged off along the front of the house.

'Artists, loose women, and miserable Dutchmen.' Ralph laughed. 'Must admit, I'm looking forward to this.'

'Typical village mentality,' Langham said. 'All foreigners, artists and fashionable women are suspect.'

'Wonder what they'll make of you and Maria when you move out to the sticks?' Ralph quipped. 'Don't say I didn't warn you. A writer chappie *and* his foreign bride. The locals'll never stop gossiping.'

Langham peered out at the building. The facade was of mellow, honey-coloured brick covered by skeins of ivy, with tiny mullioned windows placed erratically along its length.

The studded oak door swung open and two men appeared beneath a stone lintel inscribed with the date 1565. One was a young man in a tweed jacket and plus fours, while behind him stood a black-clad butler.

Langham climbed from the car and approached the covered entrance.

'Ryland and Langham?' the young man asked. 'I'm Dudley
Mariner. My father rang to say you were on your way. Now,
who's who?'

Langham made the introductions as they stepped into a
cavernous, draughty hallway and deposited their hats and coats
with the butler.

Dudley Mariner was in his late twenties, a small, pot-bellied
man with an unfortunate-looking, lopsided face and receding
ginger hair. He had a hesitant manner and a habit of planing his
cheek with the flat of his hand as if continually contemplating a
knotty problem.

The hall was decked with suits of armour in various states of
repair; many were tarnished and others were missing visors and
gauntlets. Between two such examples stood a tall glass taxidermy
case. Langham was more than a little taken aback to see that it
contained not an exhibit of local fauna but a human skeleton
seated on a dining chair.

'Ah, so you've noticed my great-grandfather. Bit of a story
behind that.'

Langham examined an engraved brass plate on the frame of
the case: *Sir Anthony Edward Mariner, 1805–1880. Bon vivant
and altruist.*

'Old Sir Anthony always joked that he intended to donate
his corpse to the Royal College of Surgeons when he shuffled
off,' Mariner said, 'and when they were finished with it he
wanted to have his skeleton grace the entrance hall. And so it
came to pass. Never fails to amuse visitors.'

'Saved on a funeral bill, I suppose,' Ralph grunted, cocking
an eyebrow at Langham.

'Now, can I get you gentlemen a drink?' Mariner asked.

They settled on tea, and Mariner instructed the butler to serve
it in the library.

'This way, gentlemen. My father asked me to show you the
room from which the painting was taken.'

He led them from the hallway along a dimly lit corridor.

'I came back to help the old man when my elder brother
died in a farm accident five years ago,' Mariner said over his
shoulder. 'Not exactly my line, farming, but I do my bit.'

'What exactly is your line?' Langham asked.

'I worked as an accountant in London. Can't say I miss it, but I do miss the social life. I manage the farm and a couple of workers we have to help, but . . .'

'Your heart's not in it,' Langham finished.

'That's right. The land's not the best – and this place is falling to bits around our ears. As soon as one room is repaired, there's work required in another.'

'Ever thought of selling up?' Ralph asked.

'I've made enquiries to various agents, but to be honest we wouldn't get much for the place. The best we can do is fight damned hard to keep our heads above water. Here we are.'

They came to a tiny, blackened timber door and Mariner produced a bunch of keys. Langham had to duck to enter the long, low, book-lined room which, he thought, warmed by a blazing fire might have been inviting.

'The library is always locked. The keys' – Mariner jangled the bunch – 'are in Pater's possession, and on the odd occasion he leaves the house he gives them to me.'

Langham moved to the vast fireplace and regarded the flock wallpaper above the carved stone mantelpiece.

Ralph stared at the hearth and whistled. 'Look at the size of that! It's bigger than my ruddy kitchen . . . I could stand up in there with room to spare.' And suiting action to the words, he did so.

Langham indicated the wall above the mantelpiece. 'I take it that the painting hung there?'

Mariner nodded. 'That's right, yes. Gainsborough's *Suffolk Pastoral*. Thing of beauty, though I don't go in for art myself.'

On the chimney breast, a bright rectangle of wallpaper indicated the dimensions of the missing painting. 'I don't suppose you have a tape measure handy?' Langham asked.

'Half a mo, I'll rouse Benson.'

Mariner slipped from the room and, watching him duck under the lintel, Langham was struck once again by the tiny dimensions of the door frame.

'Penny for them?' Ralph said, stepping from the hearth.

Langham said, 'The thief enters the room – presumably having made a copy of the key – takes the painting down and removes it from the frame, as the door's too small to admit so large a frame. So what does he do with the frame – dismantle it and take it out piece by piece?' He shook his head. 'But why would he do that? Why take the frame? Why not just leave the dashed thing in here? Dismantling a frame that size would take precious time, not to mention effort – and after all it's the canvas that's the valuable thing.'

'Perhaps whoever wanted the picture also wanted the frame?'

Langham nodded. 'Mmm . . . Possible, I suppose.'

'Or maybe the thieves wanted it to look like an inside job, done for the insurance?'

'That's more likely. If the police came to that conclusion, it'd take the heat off the actual culprits.'

Mariner returned with a tape measure in a leather case shaped like a discus, and Langham and Ryland measured the dust-line across the chimney breast. 'Ten feet six inches long,' Ralph said, 'and six high.'

They moved to the door and measured from the worn floor-boards to the pitted oak lintel. 'Five feet exactly,' Langham said. 'A little more, corner to corner. So the painting wouldn't fit through in one piece.'

He moved aside to allow the butler to wheel a rattling trolley into the room.

Mariner poured three cups of tea and Langham took his before milk was added. He carried it across to a mullioned window and examined the woodwork.

'My father had them repaired five years ago,' Mariner said, 'just before my arrival here.'

Langham sipped his tea. 'We were wondering why the thief would take the frame along with the painting. Do you know if it was especially valuable?'

'I'm sorry, I couldn't tell you. My father would know.'

Ralph consulted his notebook. 'The theft took place on the evening of Wednesday the fourteenth or the early hours of the fifteenth.'

'That's right.'

'Your father's certain on that point?' Langham asked.

'Absolutely. He came here for a book after dinner on the Wednesday evening, around nine o'clock. He would have noticed had the painting been missing.'

'And who discovered it'd gone?' Ralph asked.

'My father. He returned here just before breakfast. The painting had vanished. The old man was beside himself. He loved the daub. Family heirloom and all that.'

Langham sipped his tea and looked around the room.

'Can you tell me who was in the house that evening?'

Mariner rubbed his cheek with the palm of his hand. 'Other than my father, I was upstairs with my fiancée, Esmeralda. Major Rutherford was in his apartment on the ground floor.'

'Major Rutherford?'

'Old friend of my father's, fallen on hard times. So Pater invited him to take a couple of rooms here at a peppercorn rent.'

'And the others? Langham asked.

'Young Rebecca Miles. I say young – she's in her mid-thirties but looks younger. Our resident sloe-eyed beauty. A dark horse, too.'

Ralph looked up from his tea. 'In what way?'

'Well, I ask you. What's a good-looking, educated woman doing hiding away in this neck of the woods, miles from anywhere? Secretive about her past, too.'

'And what *does* she say she's doing here?' Langham enquired. 'I take it you've asked her?'

'Tried, old boy, but she's evasive. Gave me some tale about a small inheritance from her father, and that she wanted to spend some time in the country to get over his passing.'

'But you're dubious?'

Mariner stroked his cheek again. 'Let's just say that I get the impression, and that's all it is, that she's hiding something.'

'How did she come to live at the manor?' Ralph asked.

'Answered the ad my father placed in the local paper. She moved in a few months ago with hardly a stick of furniture to her name, which struck me as odd, too.'

Langham replaced his empty cup on the trolley. 'And that's everyone present on the night in question?'

'No, there was one other – Patrick Verlinden. He lives in the gatehouse. A Dutch chappie in his early thirties, and another odd fellow.'

'Odd?'

'Pathologically shy, I'd say. Traumatized by the war. I didn't like him at first, until I got to know what he'd been through.'

'Which was?' Ralph asked.

'He flew Hurricanes from one of the bases down south. He was shot down in 'forty-two. Lucky to survive. Suffered a nasty scar to his face' – Mariner traced a line from his temple to his lower jaw – 'and walks with one hell of a limp.'

'Does he work locally?'

'He works here. We advertised for a labourer last summer, and Verlinden turned up. He wasn't exactly up to labouring, what with the state of his leg, but my father set him on doing odd jobs around the place. For all my father's bluster, he can't resist a sob story.'

'And the butler, Benson? I understand he was around that night?'

'He knocked off at nine and retired to his room next door.'

Langham returned to the window and stared out. The snow had stopped at last.

He turned to Mariner. 'Whoever took the painting,' he said, 'either obtained the key in your father's possession, or when you had it, or managed to work the lock with some form of skeleton key.'

'I really don't see how they could have come by the key. My father never lets it out of his sight, and I'm scrupulous when he gives the bunch to me. And as for working the lock . . .' He shook his head. 'Just last year my father had a locksmith in and he installed new locks on most of the doors.'

Ralph said, 'I've yet to come across a lock that an experienced burglar can't get round, Mr Mariner.'

Langham looked at the young man. 'How would you account for the theft of the painting?'

Mariner shrugged. 'Well, I suppose it is possible that someone managed to work the lock.'

'One of the residents, perhaps?' Langham asked. 'Is the house accessible from their rooms?'

'Yes. They all have communicating doors.'

'What did the police say?' Ralph asked.

Mariner sighed. 'It was pretty obvious they thought it was an insurance job. I mean, with no obvious signs of someone having broken in . . .'

Langham said, 'Do you think your father would be capable of staging the painting's disappearance, to gain the insurance?'

Mariner turned red. 'Absolutely not! The idea is quite preposterous. My father wouldn't . . .'

Langham raised a placatory hand. 'My question was rhetorical. I don't suspect your father for one moment.'

'I'm happy to hear that.' Mariner hesitated. 'I hope you don't think that *I* . . .?'

Langham was about to reassure the young man when a discreet tap at the door heralded the butler. 'The telephone, sir,' Benson said. 'Your father, from London.'

Mariner excused himself and left the room.

Ralph looked at Langham. 'You don't think it's an insurance job, do you?'

Langham sat down on the arm of an overstuffed chair and slowly filled his pipe. 'Nothing stacks up. If either his lordship or Mariner were behind it, surely they'd have staged a break-in? Jemmied a window – and left the picture frame. They wouldn't have been stupid enough to think the insurance company would pay out with not the slightest evidence of a break-in.'

'So it's down to one of the residents, or an outside job?'

'One or the other, yes. But I won't commit myself until I've had a natter with the residents.'

He was lighting up his pipe when the silence was shattered by a deafening report.

'What the blazes!' Ralph cried, jumping to his feet.

'It sounded to me,' Langham said, blowing out the match and hurrying to the door, 'like a gunshot.'

THREE

He ran from the house and came to a halt in the snow. Ralph, following at speed, almost knocked him off his feet.

'Over there,' Langham said, pointing across to a row of outbuildings standing at right angles to the house.

The central building was a cavernous barn, and in its shadows stood a woman in a long greatcoat. As he watched, she raised a shotgun to her shoulder and took aim. Beyond her, at the back of the barn, was the indistinct figure of a man, his hands pressed to his face.

Ralph was the first to emerge from the paralysis that had gripped them both. 'No!' he cried, sprinting towards the barn.

Langham gave chase, catching up with his friend as the woman swung around and stared at the pair in astonishment. The shotgun dropped, and so did her manly jaw. 'Who the hell are you?'

Langham stared beyond her at the shadowy figure – and what he saw made him laugh with relief.

'For a second there,' he panted, 'we thought you'd . . . that is—'

The figure of the man was nothing more than a statue, thickset and solid, carved from a block of sand-coloured stone.

'It's a statue!' Ralph cried, staring at the woman. 'But why the hell are you shooting at a ruddy statue?'

On closer inspection Langham saw that the chest and arms of the statue were pitted with buckshot. The woman laid the shotgun on a carpenter's bench next to a mallet and a chisel, smiling to herself.

He was aware of someone at his shoulder and turned to see a flustered Dudley Mariner.

'Ah . . . this can be explained,' Mariner said. 'Esmeralda, my sweet?'

The woman looked from Ralph to Langham and inclined her head in grudging assent. She was in her late thirties, tall and somewhat statuesque herself, with a fall of auburn hair cut in a severe coal-scuttle style framing a strong, square face. Her nose and mouth were large, and made her face striking rather than good looking.

For a big woman, she possessed a surprisingly quiet voice. 'Stand back, cover your ears and I'll demonstrate.'

Langham did as instructed. Esmeralda picked up the shotgun, lodged the weapon against her meaty shoulder, took aim and fired. Buckshot ricocheted from the statue along with a spray of powdered stone.

The figure of the stocky man, its hands to its face, was covered in a fresh rash of indentations.

Esmeralda laid the shotgun on the bench and picked up a bottle of milk. What she did next surprised Langham almost as much as her exhibition of marksmanship. She sucked milk from the bottle with a waxed straw, pulled the straw from the bottle, then blew the milk across the pitted torso of the statue.

She repeated the process three or four times, then stood back and admired the results. Rivulets of milk trickled down the stone. She stepped forward and smeared the milk across the statue with a cloth.

'There,' she said. 'That should do the trick. Of course, it would work better in warmer weather. But the end result will be the same.'

She smiled at her audience.

Mariner explained. 'In a day or two the milk will go off and add a patina of mould, like verdigris, to the surface of the statue, giving it an aged appearance.'

'Ah . . .' Langham said.

'It's my response to the political situation between America and Russia,' Esmeralda said. 'My latest sculpture: humanity under fire, covering its face – its intellect – with its hands.'

'I see . . .' Langham said.

She looked from him to Ralph. 'I take it you're the private eyes the old man has brought in?'

Mariner made the introductions, and Esmeralda Bellamy leaned back against the carpenter's bench. 'I must say, you don't much look like detectives.'

Mariner laughed self-consciously. 'My dear, you've been watching too many—'

Esmeralda flashed him a look that reduced him to silence.

'But I suppose your father had to drag them in, for form's sake,' she went on.

'"For form's sake"?' Langham said.

'Oh, come.' She laughed. 'It must be patently obvious what's been going on. Old Teddy is on his uppers and this place is falling to pieces around his ears—'

'My dear . . .' Mariner began ineffectually.

'So he stages the theft of the Gainsborough, sells it on to some pre-arranged buyer and pockets the insurance money. Then everyone, bar the insurer, is happy.'

'My father would never . . .' Mariner began, staring at the ground like a slapped schoolboy.

'If that were the case,' Langham said, 'why didn't he stage it to convince the police, and the insurers, that it was an outside job? The fact that the insurers are refusing to pay up refutes your hypothesis.'

But Esmeralda was shaking her head. 'Not at all, Langham. It was a double bluff he was playing. He's a wily old cove, but in this instance he was *too* wily. Hoist, I think the saying goes, by his own petard.'

Mariner attempted to change the subject. 'And speaking of the old cove,' he said, grinning from Langham to Ralph, 'that was my father on the blower. He's invited you to stay for dinner this evening.'

Langham glanced at his watch. It was not yet three o'clock. He had planned to nip across to see Charles that afternoon – and he saw no reason why he couldn't visit his agent *and* return to Neston Manor in time for dinner, before driving back to London later that evening. He would phone Maria from Charles's to say he'd be late.

He conferred with Ralph, then accepted the invitation.

'Capital,' Mariner said. 'My father's invited all the residents, too, so you'll meet everyone. Mum's the word about the real reason you're here, though.'

Esmeralda sighed and muttered under her breath, 'You do like to play at intrigue like a little boy, Dudley.'

Mariner chose to ignore the accusation.

Langham heard approaching footsteps on the gravel outside the barn.

'What's going on here?' a female voice asked. 'I thought I heard gunshots.'

Langham turned to the new arrival; he guessed that this was Rebecca Miles, the woman Mariner had described as something of a beauty. In that assessment, he thought, the young man was not wrong.

She was in her mid-thirties, petite, raven-haired, and emanated a certain film-star glamour. Her oval face was small, fine-boned, and her eyes were large and brown. She wore a fawn mackintosh belted at the waist, and galoshes.

She looked from Ralph to Langham. 'And who might you be?'

'Ah . . . Donald and Ralph are here from Ealing Studios,' Mariner said, surprising Langham and – judging by his open-mouthed expression – Ralph too. 'They're location scouts. My father suggested that the manor might make a suitable setting for a film.'

The young woman smiled at Langham. 'That's rather a good idea.' She looked at Esmeralda. 'And the gunshots? Did you mistake them for intruders, Esmeralda? Art thieves, perhaps?'

Langham glanced at the sculptress: Esmeralda was staring at the young woman, and if looks could kill . . .

'Esmeralda was merely adding texture to her latest creation,' Mariner explained. 'Oh, by the way, my father has invited everyone to dinner this evening. You will come, I hope?'

'I will, thank you.' Rebecca Miles smiled at Langham and Ralph. 'I'll see you at dinner, gentlemen,' she said, then turned on her heel and strode from the barn.

Langham cast a discreet glance at Esmeralda as the young woman took her leave, and he was in time to see her lips form the quiet but distinct epithet, '*Bitch!*' before she took up the milk bottle and approached the sculpture.

'Now if you'll excuse me,' she said, 'I have work to do.'

Langham murmured a farewell and followed Mariner from the barn.

'I trust you'll excuse Esmeralda. Her social graces are somewhat lacking when she's in the throes of creation. She'll be more relaxed at dinner.'

'I take it that she and Miss Miles don't see eye to eye?' Langham said.

Mariner winced. 'Esmeralda can be somewhat jealous.'

'Of Miss Miles and yourself?' Ralph said.

Mariner looked shocked. 'Oh, I assure you that nothing at all untoward occurred between . . .' he began.

They were crossing the drive to his car when Langham

glanced towards the gatehouse. 'Do you know whether the Dutch fellow, Verlinden, is at home?'

'We could check,' Mariner said. 'Though, come to think of it, I haven't seen him around for a while.'

'I wouldn't mind meeting him before we shoot off.'

They crossed to the gatehouse and Mariner knocked on the door, then opened it. 'He never bothers to lock the place,' he said in explanation. 'Patrick? You in there?' he called out.

They followed him into a small front room that doubled as a kitchen. The most noticeable aspect of the room, after the freezing temperature, was its squalor. A stained sofa and an armchair squatted before an open grate overflowing with ash, and the threadbare carpet was sticky with some unnameable substance. The odour of sour milk pervaded the room. A small bookcase held a selection of assorted paperbacks and a battered hardback edition of Thomas Mann's *The Magic Mountain*.

'Patrick!' Mariner called, moving to a door which opened on to a flight of narrow stairs. 'Patrick, you at home?'

He turned to Langham, indicating the staircase. 'I'll just pop up and see . . .'

He disappeared. Ralph picked up a black and white photograph from a coffee table beside the settee and passed it to Langham. 'Wonder which one is Verlinden?'

The grainy photograph in a cheap Bakelite frame showed half a dozen smiling fighter pilots standing before the barracuda nose of a Hurricane.

Mariner returned, shaking his head. 'No sign of him. I thought he might be in bed, sleeping off a hangover.'

Langham passed him the photograph. 'Which one is Verlinden?'

'Third from the right. The tall blond fellow, though he's lost a bit of weight since then. He's almost unrecognisable, now. This was before his accident, of course.'

They left the gatehouse and Mariner pulled the door shut behind them. 'He's most likely down at the pub,' he said, 'drinking to drive away the demons.'

Langham shook hands with the young man, said they'd see him at dinner that evening, and crossed to his Rover.

'Interesting . . .' Ralph said, slipping into the passenger seat and lighting up a Capstan.

They drove back through the village and headed north to Charles Elder's stately home three miles away on the outskirts of Meadford.

FOUR

From the journal of Major William Arthur Rutherford.

I've not been quite the ticket for the past week or so, and have been remiss in attending to my journal. The old emphysema has been playing up and two days ago I came down with a shocking head cold which laid me low. I'm feeling a little better this evening and shall endeavour to record the somewhat startling events of late.

On the 12th I rose at eight, breakfasted on toast and strong tea, and then made my customary, if slow, trek around the drive. It was one of those bright frosty mornings when one does not begrudge the winter its grip on the land. The air was crystal clear, the sun scintillating, and the frosted ground as hard as iron. It's the rain I cannot abide: the damp gets into my old bones.

Esmeralda was up and about, attending to her sculpture in the barn which she calls, somewhat affectedly, her studio. Her latest offering to the world of art is a monstrous figure with its face hidden behind its hands. Last week she took time to explain the symbolic meaning of the piece, but I must admit that it all rather went over my head.

A light was burning in the front room of the gatehouse, and through the uncurtained window I made out young Verlinden, drinking tea from a big mug before he started work. I waved my stick at him, but if he saw me he gave no sign. However, a couple of minutes later, just as I was rounding the drive towards the woods to the east, I heard footsteps on the gravel and turned to see Verlinden waving at me as he limped along.

He's a curious individual, I must say, and a most unlikely war hero. He is tall and thin to the point of seeming malnourished, with a sunken chest and rounded shoulders. I sometimes wonder how he fitted himself into the cramped cockpit of the Hurricanes he flew during the war. His most distinctive feature, however, is the weal that disfigures the left side of his face. There are some scars that add character to a man's physiognomy – the duelling scars of Regency Bucks, for instance – and ones which serve only to disfigure: Verlinden's is one such. The puckered cicatrice pulls down his eye so that it appears half-closed and twists his lips into what can only be described as an ugly sneer. It lends the young man a most unfortunate appearance.

My feelings for Patrick Verlinden, I must admit, were until that day somewhat ambivalent: the soldier in me admired the bravery he must have exhibited during the war, and yet I found his shifty, diffident manner somewhat off-putting. I use the phrase 'that day' as our ensuing conversation, and our later exchange, coloured my opinion of the young man.

I shall endeavour to record our subsequent conversation as faithfully as I can, given that some time has elapsed since that morning.

'Major!' Verlinden called, limping up to me with his peculiar stumping gait.

'Young Verlinden,' said I. 'A fine morning.'

'I do not like the cold,' he stated bluntly. 'I would like a word with you.' He speaks like this, in short declarative sentences.

I continued walking, and he fell into step at my side. 'Fire away, young fellow,' I said.

'I have been to London,' he said. 'It was last week.' He shot me a shifty glance, one eye wide, the other half closed. His English is good, if heavily accented. 'There I met a mutual acquaintance.'

'My word, you did?'

'A fellow named Carter, Colonel Douglas Carter. He said he knew you many years ago.'

'That's right,' I said. 'And how the devil did you bump into old Carter?'

He gave an odd smile, which struck me as ingratiating and yet supercilious. 'I had . . . certain business at the Carstairs Club.'

'Business?' I said. 'At my club?'

I thought that highly unlikely. The Carstairs is a members-only military club, and we don't admit fliers. They have their own establishment – on Piccadilly, I believe.

'A little matter I needed to sort out,' he went on.

We crunched around the drive. I stared at the frozen ground.

'And you got chatting to Carter, hm?'

'That is correct.'

Truth to tell, I've never much liked Colonel Douglas Carter. Ex-Signals, for one thing. Ruddy chap never saw real action – sitting well behind the front line as he did – but he talks as if he were in the thick of it. In fact, listening to him, he'd have you believe that he and his men defeated the Nazis single-handedly.

'And what did he have to say for himself?' I asked.

'Oh, he told me some interesting things, Major Rutherford.'

I didn't like the chap's tone, I must admit. The way he glanced at me, from the corner of his eye, reminded me of a cunning rat eyeing up its prey.

'Is that so?' I said.

'He said he knew you very well.'

'I wouldn't say that,' I blustered. 'Not "very well" at all. Passing acquaintance. Member of the same club, that's all.'

I shot him a glance. He was smiling to himself. I didn't like that smile one bit.

'That is not what Colonel Carter said,' he went on.

I didn't rise to the bait. I strode on, increasing my pace. The manor beckoned, and the first drink of the day. I decided I'd take a little whisky, with hot water and honey, to combat the cold. Later, after lunch, I'd see if Teddy were around and we'd have a peg or two in my room.

'Colonel Carter told me what happened to you a few years ago,' Verlinden said.

'"What happened"? You're being rather vague, young man.'

'He mentioned why you had to leave London.'

I stared straight ahead, my heart pounding. I admit it, his words shook me, but I was damned if I'd let him know this.

'Don't know what on earth you're driving at. Now, if you'll excuse me . . .'

I turned left along the drive and hurried away. Thankfully he made no move to follow me. I reached the manor and the refuge of my room, poured myself a stiff one – beggar the hot water and honey – and sat before the open fire, brooding.

Carter was a blabbermouth – I knew that – but I'd no idea he was aware of what'd happened back then; and I was sure Fat Boothby wouldn't have spilled the beans. Of course, others knew about the affair – those on the Carstairs's committee – so perhaps Carter had winkled it out of them.

But what I didn't like was why Patrick Verlinden should bring it up, and I didn't care for his insinuating tone. Why mention it at all, unless he had some ulterior motive?

I had another whisky and did my best to forget about him. If he tried to threaten me, he'd live to regret it.

I made myself a bite of lunch – anchovies on toast – and then at two o'clock young Miss Miles popped in to check on me. I assured her I was in tip-top form and said I was about to seek out Teddy for a little drink. She stayed and chatted for ten minutes or so, then asked if I wanted anything from the village.

That's what I like about this place, the sense of community. Verlinden aside – and perhaps excepting Esmeralda, who's something of a martinet – the others, Teddy, young Mariner, and Miss Miles, are made of sound stuff and would do anything for anyone.

That afternoon Teddy and I put the world to rights over a peg or two, railed at the government for not standing up to the ruddy Russians in Hungary, and agreed that we should have remained in Egypt. 'I voted for Macmillan and the Tories so they could show that Britain still had some backbone!' Teddy declared.

I admit I was a little merry by the time Teddy left. The Scotch had slipped down a treat and I was contemplating another when someone knocked on the door. I thought it was Miss Miles with my shopping, but when I opened the door, who should I find standing there, hunched in the low passageway, but Verlinden.

My good mood evaporated pretty rapidly at the sight of his lop-sided smile. 'What do you want?' I snapped.

'Just a little chat,' he said.

'I'm busy now.'

'It will not take long. A little minute. You see, I know one or two things about you, Major Rutherford.'

That did it. Enraged, I slammed the door and turned the key. He knocked again, calling out that he would like a little word. I told him in no uncertain terms to beggar off or I'd take my service revolver to him. That did the trick; off he went.

I did have another whisky – well, several stiff ones, in fact – and wondered what the blazes the young fiend wanted.

I thought I'd left all that behind when I moved from London . . . But evidently not.

Another large one before bed, methinks. I'll continue this entry another day.

FIVE

hat one must remember about Lord Elsmere,' Charles Elder said, 'is that the man is as honest as the day is long.'

Langham's literary agent and old friend was ensconced upon a two-seater settee before the blazing fire in the library of Elder House. He was decked out in leisure wear: dark green velveteen breeches, a pale green silk shirt and a mauve cravat, and his bulk filled the space between the arms of the settee with little room to spare. On the wicker table beside him was the thick manuscript he'd been perusing and a decanter of brandy; it was obvious from the flushed aspect of his fleshy countenance that he'd been helping himself liberally to the Courvoisier.

He'd greeted Langham and Ralph, a little earlier, like travellers returned from an Arctic expedition, ushering them into the library, throwing more logs on to the open fire, and sending Albert to make a pot of coffee.

Langham wallowed in an armchair across from Charles, anticipating the hot drink and luxuriating in his friend's company. Charles Elder had the skilled host's ability to make his guests feel as if his existence had been enhanced by their arrival.

'How long have you known his lordship?' Langham asked.

Charles tipped his head back so that his snowy coiffure rested against the antimacassar. 'Now let me think. It must have been back in 'thirty-five, shortly after the death of my father, when I decided to move from London and take up residence here. Elsmere had been a friend of my father's, and as I recall he dropped by to give me advice about certain repairs the house required. He knew all the best tradesmen, you see.' He hesitated. 'I must admit I feel sorry for the old fellow.'

Ralph stretched out his legs. 'Sorry?'

'Teddy suffered a double tragedy a few years ago,' Charles said. 'He lost his wife to some terrible wasting disease in the summer of 'fifty-one. It knocked him all of a heap – they were a devoted couple. And then, later that year, his eldest son Jeremy died instantly when his tractor overturned while ploughing a field. Teddy bore it like a trooper, but close friends could see that his son's death, coming so soon after Vera's demise, knocked the stuffing from the old chap. But as I was saying, Teddy's as straight as a die: calls a spade a spade and his word's his honour.'

'So you don't think,' Langham asked, 'that he would have staged the theft of the painting for insurance purposes?'

Charles's huge red face wore a pantomime display of mock-outrage. 'What? Teddy? Stage the theft? Of course not! The thought's preposterous.' He hesitated. 'Between you, me and the four walls, though, I wouldn't say the same about his son.'

Ralph glanced at Langham and raised an eyebrow.

'Why's that?' Langham asked.

Charles laced his plump fingers, bedecked with rings, across his ample stomach and looked from Ralph to Langham. He nodded sagely, warming to his theme. 'Young Mariner,' he pronounced, 'is a bit of a black sheep.'

'Tell me more,' Langham said, sinking deeper into the armchair.

'Mariner elected not to follow his brother into farming, though after the war Teddy offered him a job developing the estate. Instead he took up accountancy and worked for some investment firm in the City. However, after his brother's accident, he returned to take up Jeremy's position managing the farm and the estate in general.' Charles leaned forward, straining over his stomach. 'Word soon got around the village, however, that his return was not occasioned by any altruistic impulses or the desire to assist his doubly bereaved father, but on account of his being caught massaging, shall we say, the assets of the company that employed him. In short, he'd siphoned off a few thousand pounds into his own account. The word was that Lord Elsmere was approached by the company, on the quiet, and rather than see his only son prosecuted and jailed, agreed to pay the monies owing. Yet another burden for the old chap to bear.'

'That's *very* interesting,' Langham said.

'I wouldn't trust the young scallywag as far as I could throw him,' Charles said. 'Which is a crying shame, seeing as he hails from fine stock.'

'One can never tell,' Langham said.

Charles stared at the flames. 'Odd thing is, as you said earlier, Donald, if it were an inside job, why didn't the perpetrator – Mariner, let's say – make it look like a burglary? He might sail close to the wind, but the lad is anything but stupid.'

He sat up as the door opened at the far end of the room. 'I do believe this is Albert, bearing comestibles.'

Charles's young companion carried a tray bearing a silver coffee pot and a huge fruitcake. He set the tray on a small table and poured the coffee.

'I always think,' said Charles, hoisting the brandy decanter, 'that in weather such as this, with gales blowing without and snow lying six inches deep, the addition of brandy to one's coffee is a necessity. Albert, if you would be so good . . .'

Grinning, the young man splashed a generous measure of the spirit into each cup.

Albert Harker was a tall, thick-set fellow, built like a light heavyweight boxer with a raw-boned face, craggy good looks and huge hands. He worked as Charles's valet, chauffeur, handyman and general factotum, and was devoted to his employer.

He sliced thick wedges of fruitcake and passed them round, then took a seat before the fire.

Langham glanced at Ralph, who was eyeing Albert with some reservation. He'd noticed Ralph's odd regard of the young man back in August, when they had first met at Charles's London garden party. Afterwards, Ralph had buttonholed Langham and whispered, 'I know Albert's *like that*, Don – but what I want to know is what does he see in Charles?'

Langham had replied that he thought Charles represented the father Albert had never had.

'We were discussing, Albert, the theft of Lord Elsmere's Gainsborough. Donald and Ralph have been hired to look into the affair.'

Albert took a huge bite of cake, pointed at Langham with the remaining chunk, then said, still chewing, 'Know what they're saying down the Dog and Gun, Don?'

'I'm all ears.'

'Word is one of the guests did it.'

'Albert,' Charles explained, 'enjoys the occasional pint at the Dog and Gun.'

'Beats the ale they serve at the Plough in Meadford. The landlord at the Dog keeps a fine stout and he sells decent pies.'

'Have you met any of the folk from the manor?' Ralph asked.

'Most of 'em over the past few months. Mariner, the son, comes in occasionally but he keeps hisself to hisself, and his fiancée is a bit stuck-up. Some kind of artist, they say. When

Mariner isn't sucking up to her she's tearing him off a right
strip. Has a nasty tongue on her, that bitch, excuse me French.
And she likes to, you know . . .' He blushed. 'She's liberal with
her favours, as I read in one of your books, Charles.'

'She has affairs?' Ralph said.

'I'll say. Two years back she hadn't been at the manor a
month when she was seen with Mr Escott, who farms up at
Budbury. Didn't last long before she took up with Mariner. And
the rumour is she's seeing someone up Bury St Edmunds way.'
He paused. 'And then there's Rebecca Miles—'

'Surely she doesn't go to the Dog and Gun alone?' Langham
asked, taking a mouthful of brandy-laced coffee.

'I saw her just the once when she was waiting for the Dutch
chap, and I got talking to her. She seemed a nice woman. Told
me she were writing a book, so I said I worked for a literary
agent and I'd put in a good word when it was done.' He
shrugged his huge shoulders. 'I don't think she believed me,
though.'

'Do you think Miss Miles and Verlinden were . . .?'

Albert frowned. 'I wondered about that. I saw them later,
when he'd arrived, but they didn't seem intimate. Just talking
together quietly, no holding hands or anything.'

Langham asked, 'And the Dutch fellow? What do you make
of him?'

'Doesn't say much. Just nods and takes his pint into the
corner. In there a lot. Reg says he has five pints, talks to no
one, then staggers home at throwing-out time. Has a nasty scar
down his cheek, and he's badly lame on account of a flying
accident in the war. Flew for the RAF, he did. I'd like to talk
to him about it, but I don't think he'd be that keen.'

Langham finished his cake. 'Then there's another resident
up at the manor, a fellow called Rutherford. A military historian,
by all accounts.'

Albert shook his head. 'Don't know anything about him,
Donald. He don't venture down the Dog.'

Charles said, 'I've met Major Rutherford on a few occasions,
when dining with Teddy at the manor. He struck me as a crusty
old duffer, plagued by gout and some respiratory problem. Old
school, still regretting the fall of the Empire. Spends most of

his time keeping a journal, he told me. He got wind that I was
a literary agent and bent my ear about his life story – runs to
over fifty volumes, for heaven's sake!'

'So let's rule out the major,' Ralph said, 'if he's a semi-
invalid. And that slip of a thing, Miss Miles. I doubt she
could've lifted the painting off the wall.'

Langham regarded Albert. 'What's the word in the Dog and
Gun?'

Albert shrugged. 'Rumour is that Esmeralda's a gold digger,
hitched herself to Mariner for all she can get. So she might've
fancied getting her mitts on the painting. Word is that the
Dutchman is up to no good, but that's just talk.'

'"Let's pin it on Johnny Foreigner", hm?' Charles grunted
into his coffee.

Langham sighed. 'It's a pretty puzzle, and I'm not sure we'll
get to the bottom of it any time soon.'

'Then how about,' Charles began, struggling upright in his
chair and pointing across at Langham and Ralph, 'I have you
up tomorrow for a long weekend? Bring Maria, why not, and
we can indulge in a spot of house-hunting. Albert will drive us
around a few villages in the locality so that you can recce the
lie of the land. And in between times you can nip along to
the manor and do your sleuthing.'

Langham saluted the idea with his cup. 'That sounds like a
civilized plan. I'm all for it. Ralph?'

The cockney frowned. ''Fraid Annie has something planned
for Saturday, Don. But I might pop up meself at some point
and have a poke around.'

'In that case,' Charles said, 'do drop by for a meal, or at
least a drink.'

Ralph smiled. 'Grand. I'll do that, Charles.'

Langham looked at his watch. 'Crikey, it's after five. We'd
better be pushing off if we're to be back at the manor for dinner.
Oh, could I possibly phone Maria to tell her that I'll be late
back tonight?'

Five minutes later, having told Maria to expect him around
midnight – but sweetening that pill with Charles's invitation
– he and Ralph took their leave.

Langham eased the Rover from the drive of Elder House and

turned right. The road was covered with snow and darkness was descending.

He looked across at Ralph and laughed. 'Annie has something planned for Saturday!' he scoffed. 'More like you're off to watch Millwall, right?'

Ralph had the good grace to look sheepish. 'Much as I'd like to get me knees under the table back there, Don . . .'

Smiling to himself, Langham slowed down and turned along the lane that led to Little Neston.

SIX

Neston Manor, with snow covering its pitched roofs and warm orange lights glowing in its many mullioned windows, suggested that a cheery welcome awaited within.

'Looks like something from a Christmas card,' Ralph said as they climbed the steps to the front door.

'Which reminds me,' Langham said. 'What are you, Annie and the boys doing on Boxing Day?'

'Millwall are at home to Swindon, but Annie said I can't go.'

'And I should think so too!' Langham laughed. He banged the iron knocker in the shape of a knight's visor. 'Maria suggested you come over for lunch. It'll be nice to have the boys around – that's what Christmas is all about, after all: children.'

'Won't be long before you're cursing your own little perishers.'

'Later rather than sooner, as far as I'm concerned,' Langham said.

The door swung open on creaking hinges and the butler appeared. 'Lord Elsmere will see you for sherry in the library. If I might take your coats?'

Divested of their overcoats, they followed Benson along the narrow passageway to the east wing. He opened the library door and announced their arrival.

A log fire roared in the hearth and thick, claret-coloured curtains were drawn across the windows. A tall figure rose with arthritic caution from a wingback chair beside the fire as they entered the room.

Lord Elsmere stood well over six feet tall, though his stature was diminished somewhat by his pronounced stoop. His face was thin and highly coloured, and he had a full head of iron-grey hair. His pouched eyes spoke of the tragedies that had visited him over the years.

'Mr Ryland, pleased to meet you again,' he said, shaking the detective's hand. 'Mr Langham, welcome to Neston Manor. You'll be needing a drink, no doubt?' It was evident from his breath, and the whisky bottle on a table beside his chair, that he had been indulging himself in that department already.

He indicated a sideboard beside the hearth, an array of bottles and crystal glasses scintillating in the firelight. 'Sherry, or would you prefer whisky?'

They opted for sherries; Lord Elsmere did the honours, then topped up his own glass with whisky.

'You come highly recommended, gentlemen. No lesser authority than Charles Elder sings your praises.'

'That's very kind of him,' Ralph murmured.

'Thing is,' Elsmere said, 'I've been hearing scurrilous rumours around the village.'

Langham sipped his sherry, finding it excellent. 'Rumours?'

'Known Elder for years. Salt of the earth. Shoulder to cry on when my wife passed on . . . But' – he shuttled a look from Ralph to Langham – 'that young chap he employs . . . Word is, and I won't beat about the bush, that Elder's a fruit and young Albert does more than act as his valet. Scurrilous gossip, what?'

Ralph looked uncomfortable, and Langham said quickly, 'That's right, sir. Nothing more than gossip.'

'That's a relief, Langham. That's what I wanted to hear. Thought so meself, but one can never tell, can one? Especially in this day and age.'

Langham murmured an equivocal agreement; Lord Elsmere indicated a pair of buttoned leather armchairs before the blazing fire.

'I often came in here,' he said, easing himself into his chair, 'to admire the Gainsborough. It kept me company.' He waved a hand at the vacancy above the mantelpiece. 'Now I feel as if a part of me has been ripped away.'

'I can understand the feeling,' Langham said.

'Dudley mentioned you had a poke around earlier; don't suppose you came to any conclusions?'

Ralph said, 'Only that the insurance company is wrong for not coughing up, sir.'

'That's good to hear, I must say. What with the bod from the insurers and Inspector Montgomery from the local constabulary making suspicious noises, I was beginning to think I'd gone gaga and done it meself.'

'Inspector Montgomery?' Langham echoed.

'That's right. You know him?'

'I worked on a case with him last year.'

'Thing is . . .' Elsmere fell silent, his rheumy eyes gazing at the flames. 'Thing is, if you don't think I did it, do you suspect one of the guests?'

Ralph glanced at the old man. 'That's always a possibility, sir, and one we can't rule out at this stage.'

'Thought as much,' Elsmere muttered. 'Well, you can rule out Major Rutherford for starters. Known him donkey's years. The old fellah can hardly walk, never mind filch a ruddy great canvas. Same for the girls: might be able to walk, but they're women, after all, and as weak as kittens.'

Langham smiled to himself; he doubted if Esmeralda Bellamy, with her strapping physique, could be dismissed so easily.

He said, 'That leaves only the Dutch fellow, Patrick Verlinden.'

Elsmere's grim smile gave his face the expression of a death's head. 'It does, but I hope Patrick wouldn't stoop so low. I'm a good judge of character, gentlemen, and I know a sound chap when I see one.'

'So if it wasn't one of your guests,' Ralph said, 'it must've been an outside job.'

Elsmere pointed at him with a crooked forefinger. 'That's what I'd like you to prove. And the sooner you do, the sooner I can get my painting back.'

'We'll do our very best,' Langham assured him.

'And I'm sure you'll do a good job; after all, that's what I'm paying you for.'

Langham said, 'One thing I was wondering, sir – why did the thief take the frame as well as the canvas? It would have been far easier just to have taken the latter. Unless, of course, the frame itself was valuable.'

Elsmere shook his head, his lips pursed. 'I'm afraid I can't enlighten you there,' he said. 'My father had the thing re-framed donkey's years ago, when I was still in knickerbockers.'

He was silent for a time, sipping his whisky and gazing across at Ralph. 'Ryland, Ryland . . .' He said at last, his eyes narrowed as if in speculation.

Ralph blinked. 'Sir?'

'Do you know, when Charles Elder mentioned your name, I did wonder . . .'

Ralph looked non-plussed. 'Wonder, sir?'

'I thought, could it be? Then I saw you at your office and thought the resemblance most striking. Was your father one Desmond Ryland, by any chance?'

Langham looked across at Ralph and was surprised to see that his friend's face had turned beet-red. Ralph nodded minimally, staring at the fire. 'That's right, sir.'

'Good Lord! The world's a small place.'

Langham said, 'You knew Ralph's father?'

'I'll say! I was in politics before the last war, in a small way. Funded some people in a couple of elections down Bermondsey way. This was when I *had* funds to indulge my whims! Your father, Desmond, was secretary of the South London branch. Splendid fellow. I addressed them once or twice. I say, how is Desmond these days?'

Ralph was still staring at the fire, his expression frozen. 'My father died just after the war, sir. Heart attack.'

'Oh, I say. I'm sorry to hear that. Fine fellow, Desmond. My commiserations . . .' Elsmere peered drunkenly at a grandfather clock across the room. 'My word, it's almost six! They'll be gathering like vultures in the great hall. What say we join them?'

Langham glanced across at Ralph for an explanation, but his friend avoided his gaze as they followed Lord Elsmere from the room.

*   *   *

PROCEEDED

They processed from the library, Elsmere leaning heavily on his stick, and along the crooked corridor illuminated by the occasional oil-lamp. Langham wondered if the manor was wired for electricity.

'A side of beef, roast potatoes and gravy,' Elsmere said. 'What's a meal without a good gravy, is what I say. And a fine claret, what? Comes to something,' he went on, 'when what one looks forward to in life is the meal at the end of the day, hm?'

'Oh, I don't know,' Langham said, taking the old man's elbow and assisting him up a couple of steps as they moved from the east wing to the main body of the building. 'I've always appreciated good food.'

'Trencherman, eh? That's what I like to hear.'

Elsmere pushed open a heavy oak door with his walking stick to reveal a long, beamed dining hall lit by a blazing fire and an array of oil-lamps. Langham made a mental note to ask his lordship about the electricity, or lack of.

Elsmere's guests had gathered at the far end of the room, warming themselves before the fire: Dudley Mariner and his fiancée Esmeralda Bellamy, Rebecca Miles and Major Rutherford, the major being the only resident he had not yet met. Notable by his absence was the Dutch flyer, Verlinden.

Conversation ceased, and all eyes regarded them as they approached.

'Don't know who you've met,' Elsmere said, waving his stick in airy dismissal of protocol, 'so I won't stand on ceremony; my guests are Ralph Ryland and Donald Langham: Ralph, Donald, here we have my son, Dudley – who you've met – Miss Rebecca Miles, Esmeralda Bellamy, and my old friend Major Rutherford.'

After the handshakes were completed, Mariner said to the major, 'Ralph and Donald are location scouts for Ealing Studios.'

Lord Elsmere looked astonished for a second, then cottoned on. 'Ah, yes. That's right. Thought I might put the manor up as a possible film location.'

The butler replenished their drinks and murmured that dinner would be served in ten minutes.

Elsmere looked around the little gathering, frowning. 'Still no sign of Patrick?'

Major Rutherford, whose thin lips, craquelured facial flesh and bald pate gave him the appearance of a benign tortoise, wheezed, 'Fellah's vanished. No one's had sight nor sound of the chap for days.'

Esmeralda said, 'No doubt gone on a bender.'

Miss Miles sipped her wine, her eyes sparkling in the firelight, and Langham thought she bore a distinct resemblance to the actress, Audrey Hepburn. She wore a peach-coloured cashmere cardigan with the sleeves pushed up, and a small gold watch sat high on her left forearm. He wondered if wearing it like this was the latest fashion. She saw him looking and, rather self-consciously, pulled down her sleeves.

'Verlinden goes to London from time to time,' she said. 'He's probably there now.'

'But he left his front door unlocked,' Ralph said.

'I can't say I'm that surprised,' Esmeralda said. 'Have you seen the dump? There's nothing in there worth stealing.'

Lord Elsmere looked worried. 'How long would you say he's been gone?'

'I last saw him about a week ago,' Mariner said.

Langham asked Lord Elsmere, 'Did he mention he was going away?'

'Not a word,' his lordship said. 'But then he often goes AWOL for a few days, then turns up looking sheepish and says he had business in London.'

Benson struck a reverberating gong and announced that dinner was about to be served. They crossed the room and took their places at the table, Lord Elsmere at the head, and Langham seated between Miss Miles and Major Rutherford. Across from him sat Ralph, Esmeralda, and Mariner.

'Tell me,' Esmeralda said, with a sly glint in her green eyes, 'what is it that film people look for in a location?'

Ralph lowered his soup spoon and looked across at Langham. 'Don?'

'Ah, well . . .' Langham said, delaying his reply with a mouthful of wine. 'The principal attribute of a setting is, of course, authenticity, and atmosphere. And from what I've seen so far, I'd say that Neston Manor has both in bushel-loads.'

'So will you be recommending the place as a suitable location?' Miss Miles asked.

'It is certainly a strong possibility,' he said. He then changed the subject and murmured, 'A little bird tells me you're a writer?'

'Strictly amateur, I assure you.' She smiled. 'But how did you know I wrote?'

'We have an acquaintance in common – Charles Elder.'

She frowned, her pale forehead wrinkling slightly. 'Well, I have met his friend, Albert. He said that he'd mention my manuscript to Charles when I was happy with it.'

From across the table, Esmeralda said, staring icily at the woman, 'I would have thought that the life story of someone barely out of their twenties would have limited appeal, my dear.'

'Who said I'm writing my life story, Esmeralda?'

The sculptress moved her jaw sideways, which gave her long face an expression of wry amusement. 'Didn't you once tell me something about Becky's book, Dudley?'

The young man looked more than a little discommoded as he tore at his bread and dunked it in his soup. 'Did I, dear? I don't recall.'

Langham glanced at Elsmere and the major; the old men were spooning their parsnip soup in happy ignorance of the sudden icy atmosphere that had settled over the table.

Roast beef followed, and the meal proceeded with no further contretemps. The wine flowed – the major and Lord Elsmere leading the way – and the former told a rambling but ultimately humorous tale about his schooldays when a prefect had smuggled a quart of Bénédictine into the dormitory, with disastrous results.

'That was back in eighty-five, would you believe?' The major looked around the gathering, his eyes twinkling. 'I can see you trying to work it out. I was ten back in eighty-five, so that makes me eighty-one this year.' He hoisted his glass in acknowledgement of the polite expressions of disbelief that passed around the table.

A little later, as Benson was serving spotted dick and custard, Miss Miles murmured an excuse and slipped from the table. A minute later Esmeralda followed suit and left the dining hall.

The atmosphere around the table seemed to thaw by several degrees.

Five minutes later, when neither women had returned, Langham asked Lord Elsmere the direction to the bathroom, dabbed his lips with a napkin, and excused himself.

He heard voices almost immediately in the shadowy corridor leading to the hallway. Evidently the women were in a passageway that ran at right angles to the corridor. Langham approached the corner soundlessly, then paused and listened.

'And why the hell should I believe that?' Esmeralda asked.

'You can believe what you like—'

'You're nothing but a scheming little witch!' Esmeralda spat. 'I know all about you.'

'What did you say?'

'That comes as a shock, doesn't it? I said I know all about you,' Esmeralda went on, 'and your little secret.'

Rebecca replied in a low voice, of which Langham caught only, '. . . at least I don't run after men just because they're—'

'Why you little . . .!'

Langham heard the sound of a scuffle, then Rebecca's, 'Let go of me!' – followed by a resounding slap.

He cleared his throat and rounded the corner, affecting surprise when he saw the women all but wrestling each other. 'I say, I'm sorry—'

Esmeralda gave a strangled cry and pushed past him, pressing a hand to her slapped cheek. She crossed the passage, opened a concealed door, and disappeared up a narrow staircase.

He touched Rebecca's forearm. 'Are you . . .?'

She avoided his eyes, murmured, 'I'm perfectly all right, thank you, Mr Langham,' and moved off down the corridor towards the dining hall.

He continued on to the bathroom, waited a minute, then retraced his steps to the great hall.

As he resumed his seat, he cast a glance across the table at Rebecca Miles; she blushed and looked away.

Mariner, sensing that not all was as it should be and alerted by his fiancée's absence, excused himself soon after and left the dining room. By this time the major had drunk himself senseless, and Rebecca said she'd fetch his bath chair and take the old man back to his room.

Lord Elsmere was reminiscing, as he swirled the port in his glass. 'I remember those days before the war. They were heady times. And what a coincidence, my knowing your father . . .'

Ralph looked at his watch, flustered. 'Hope I'm not being rude, sir. But it's high time we were pushing off. Got to get back to London tonight, see?'

'Not at all, Ryland. Don't fancy such a long drive myself in weather like this.'

They thanked Lord Elsmere for the meal, and Langham said they'd be back in the morning. As they stepped out into the freezing night and crossed to the Rover, he turned to Ralph. 'Now what on earth was all that about?'

'All what?' Ralph muttered.

Langham opened the car door and slipped in behind the wheel. He waited until his friend had settled himself in the passenger seat, then said, 'All that business about Elsmere and your father?'

Ralph sat very still and stared ahead into the darkness. At last he sighed. 'I'm not proud of this, Don.'

'Go on.'

'My father . . . back in the thirties. He was involved with Mosley's mob, wasn't he? The Blackshirts. Like Elsmere said, my old man was the secretary of the Bermondsey branch. But I don't like talking about it.'

'I see.'

Langham started the engine, then rolled the car down the drive and through the archway of the gatehouse. He glanced across at his friend, who remained silent, and he knew better than to press him.

A little later, he said, 'Well, Lord Elsmere's being a Mosley-ite is a bit of a turn up . . . though in a way I suppose I shouldn't be surprised. Half the damned aristocracy in England was hand in glove with—'

'Like I said, Don, I don't like talking about it.'

Langham nodded, gripping the wheel. They drove on through Little Neston in silence, then turned on to the London road.

Ralph changed the subject. 'So what's the plan for tomorrow?'

'I think I'll drive into Bury St Edmunds and talk to Inspector Montgomery in the morning,' Langham said. 'Then how about we meet back at the manor around noon and have another gander at the library?'

'Let's do that.'

As they drove on through the night, they discussed the theft of Elsmere's painting, and Langham described the exchange he'd overheard earlier that evening between Rebecca Miles and Esmeralda Bellamy.

'Mark my word, Ralph, there's something going on there, and I'd like to know more about it.'

They fell silent; Langham concentrated on the road and, much later, the lights of London appeared in the distance.

SEVEN

Langham left the city immediately after breakfast on Friday, accompanied by Maria. He dropped her off at Charles's just before ten, then motored on to Bury St Edmunds. No further snow had fallen during the night, but a hard frost had stolen over the countryside and made the roads treacherous.

An intense, low sun dazzled across the undulating farmland, illuminating the rooftops of villages and the occasional church spire. He found himself admiring the stark beauty of the landscape and wondering what life in the country might be like.

At ten thirty he pulled up outside the police station, a dour red-brick Victorian building, and asked at reception if Detective Inspector Montgomery was available.

He flashed his accreditation, said it was in connection with the theft of the art work at Neston Manor, and was duly ushered into an office at the rear of the building.

'As I live and breathe,' exclaimed the small, balding man, rising from his seat behind the desk and offering his hand. 'Langham, what are you doing in this neck of the woods?'

'Would you believe I'm looking into the purloining of Lord Elsmere's Gainsborough?'

Montgomery swore. 'Thanks for reminding me about that!'

The little man, impeccably attired in a dark suit and black tie, looked more like an officious town clerk than an officer of the law. He'd struck Langham as brusque to the point of rudeness when they'd first met last year, but, over the course of the investigation into the murder of Vivian Stafford, the little man had thawed and become almost friendly.

'I don't suppose you have a quick half hour to talk about the case?' Langham asked.

'I reckon I owe you one after the affair at the Chase,' he muttered. 'You're a Fuller's man, I recall?'

Taken aback, Langham said, 'I wouldn't say no to a pint.' He looked at his watch. 'But at this hour?'

Montgomery took his coat from the stand. 'Whenever did the licensing laws keep a copper from his pint, Langham? The Lion along the street keeps a decent bitter.'

Two minutes later Montgomery was hammering on the postern door of the public house, and in due course they were admitted by a cleaner with a mop and bucket.

'Don't get Vic out of bed,' the inspector said. 'I'll serve myself.'

They entered the darkened taproom and Montgomery moved behind the bar. Langham found a seat and filled his pipe. 'One of the perks of the job?' he called out.

'Vic often calls last orders well after midnight,' Montgomery said, 'and I turn a blind eye on account of the information he slips me.'

He rounded the bar bearing two foaming tankards and settled himself beside Langham. 'Now, what do you want to know?'

Langham puffed his pipe into life. 'Lord Elsmere thinks you suspect him of stealing his own painting,' he said.

Montgomery took a draught of bitter. 'My initial feeling was that Elsmere was behind it, for the insurance,' he said. 'But that didn't stack up, to my way of looking at it. If his lordship wanted to make it look like the painting was stolen, he'd have made damn sure there was evidence of a break-in.'

'That's exactly what I thought.'

'So I came to the conclusion that the painting was nabbed by one of the residents. They had all night to accomplish the theft, and they simply took the painting apart, rolled the canvas, and ferried it from the manor.'

'But why go to the effort of taking the frame?'

Montgomery paused with his pint halfway to his mouth. 'Why not, if they had the time? Do you know how much frames cost these days, especially hefty, gilded frames like that one? You wouldn't get much change from fifty nicker, young sir.'

'Very well . . . But if it was taken by one of the residents, who do you suspect?' He paused. 'Patrick Verlinden?'

'I had quite a chat with him, and he didn't seem the type to bite the hand that feeds. Quiet, retiring type – and grateful for his lordship giving him work and a place to kip.' Montgomery paused. 'But you think Verlinden might've been behind it?'

'I'm not sure – but it doesn't look good that he's gone missing.'

'Missing?'

'Hasn't been seen for a while.'

'And there I was, wondering if Esmeralda Bellamy might've had a hand in it. The boys in the Smoke have a file on her as long as your arm.'

'Esmeralda?' Langham sounded surprised, even to himself.

'That's the woman, face like a shocked horse. Mariner's fiancée. Before she reinvented herself as a sculptor, she worked as a secretary in a solicitor's office in London. While she was there, she used some information on one of their clients to . . . extract monies, let's say. Or call it blackmail.'

Langham whistled. 'She gives the impression of being part of the county set, pearls and tweeds and rides to hounds.'

Montgomery laughed into his pint. 'She pulled one over on you, then. Nothing posh about our Esmeralda. And her name isn't even Esmeralda Bellamy – she was born Mavis Jones in Bow, daughter of a tannery worker.'

'I don't suppose Lord Elsmere or Mariner is aware of this?'

'Pretty sure his lordship is in the dark, but as for Mariner . . .' The inspector took a long drink and smacked his lips. 'We have information that Mariner and Esmeralda got together several years ago, while they were both in London, and not two years ago when she moved up to the manor as he claims. Young

Mariner, for all his pedigree, is a bit of a shady character. He was drummed out of his job in the city for "appropriating funds". If you want my opinion, Esmeralda might even have put him up to that. Easily led, our Mariner.'

'That's interesting. I was aware that Lord Elsmere extricated him from a probable jail sentence.'

Montgomery nodded. 'Poor old geezer deserves better than a son like Mariner. I did wonder if he and Esmeralda might've been behind the theft of the painting – the woman providing the brains and Mariner doing the donkey work. I don't know if you noticed, but the woman has him like this' – the policeman made a gripping gesture with his fist – 'by the veritable short and curlies.'

'It hasn't escaped my attention,' Langham said. 'But do you have any proof they were in it together?'

The inspector's thin, pale face creased into a frown. 'That's the thing, Langham. Not a shred. I've had men follow the pair to London, and I've had someone sift through their bank records. Nothing. No meetings with shady fences, and no evidence of thousands being paid into their accounts.'

'So you've swept the case under the carpet?'

Montgomery sighed. 'Let's say it's on the back burner, until I've followed up a few more leads. But I'm glad his lordship had the sense to get you in. Any thoughts so far?'

Langham contemplated the last inch of his pint. 'Well, with Verlinden having skedaddled . . .'

Montgomery looked superior, like a headmaster bestowing the benefit of his knowledge on a dim pupil. 'Take my advice and forget Verlinden,' he said. 'Concentrate on Esmeralda and Mariner, and you'll do all you should.'

They chatted about the theft for a while, then Langham raised his empty glass. 'Thanks for the drink. Oh,' he went on, 'were you aware that Lord Elsmere was involved with Oswald Mosley and his motley crew before the war?'

Montgomery raised his eyebrows. 'That's news to me – but then he is a toff, so I'm hardly surprised.' He finished his pint. 'Right, back to it. Would you believe I'm investigating the theft of a herd of Gloucestershire Old Spots at the moment?'

'A copper's lot is never a happy one,' Langham commiserated.

Laughing, they left the pub by the back door.

EIGHT

Ralph Ryland was already at Neston Manor, leaning against the frame of the barn door and smoking a Capstan, when Langham passed beneath the gatehouse and parked up.

He crossed to the barn. 'Been here long?'

'About an hour,' Ralph said. 'Learn anything useful from Inspector Montgomery?'

'Only that he pulls a decent pint, and one or two other things.'

Ralph gave him a quizzical look, and Langham murmured, 'Later, OK?'

At the far end of the barn, Esmeralda and Mariner were in the process of crating up the woman's latest work of art. They'd swaddled the statue in old blankets, secured by lengths of washing line, then constructed a timber box around the figure.

At one point, Esmeralda shot Langham a suspicious glance; he wondered if it was due to what he'd overheard in the corridor last night, or the fact that Esmeralda knew he and Ralph were private investigators. Could her guilty conscience be catching up with her?

Mariner was busy nailing a front panel to the crate. A block and tackle hung from a beam above the crate, and when the box was nailed up, Esmeralda and Mariner fastened a thick rope around it and, little by little, tipped the crate backwards so that it lay on its side on a long timber palette.

'Due to be transported to London this afternoon,' Ralph explained. 'A gallery has commissioned it, apparently, along with a companion piece.'

Langham said under his breath, 'The sculpting lark must pay better than blackmail.'

Ralph shot him a glance. 'Come again?'

He ensured that Esmeralda and Mariner were preoccupied with lowering the crate, then told Ralph what Montgomery had said that morning.

'But why would Mariner nick his old man's painting?' Ralph objected.

'Exactly. The inspector seems to think he's being led astray by Esmeralda. Anyway, for what it's worth, my money's on Verlinden, especially since he seems to have done a runner. I want to search the gatehouse later, see what we can find.'

He filled his pipe and sucked it into life.

'Oh, I had a natter with the major earlier,' Ralph said. 'He saw me drive up and dragged me into his place for a cuppa. I don't think he has much company.'

'Did you mention the theft?'

'I got the subject round to that, but he was more interested in telling me all about his various ailments. Christ, what *isn't* he suffering from! Emphys-something-or-other, a bad ticker, gout . . . Then he told me he had a cure, and asked if I'd like to know what it was?'

'Don't tell me: a bottle of sleeping pills?'

'You're on the right track. There we were, sitting in his comfy den, when he pulls out his service revolver and tells me that when push comes to shove, he'll put a bullet through his brain.'

'What did you say?'

'What could I say? I gave him a sickly smile and said I hoped that wouldn't be for a good while yet.'

'Did he say anything about the theft?'

'Nothing of substance. "Terrible business, bad show, poor old Teddy", that kind of thing.'

Across the barn, Esmeralda and Mariner regarded the crate resting on its palette and Mariner dusted his hands together. They crossed to Langham and Ralph.

'Come for another shufti?' Esmeralda said, looking down her equine nose at Langham.

'Something like that,' he said, then addressed Mariner. 'We'd like another look around Verlinden's gatehouse, if that's all right?'

Mariner waved. 'By all means. Help yourself. The door's open, as you know. Come inside for a spot of tea when you've done.'

'What do you think you'll find in there?' Esmeralda asked.

'I've absolutely no idea.' Langham smiled. 'But I'm sure we'll know when we find it.'

'So you think Verlinden was behind the theft?' she went on.

'Let's just say that we're keeping an open mind, shall we?'

'Don't be influenced by the fact that he's vanished,' she said. 'He's always going off like that. Could be gone for days on end. I understand he frequents Soho brothels from time to time. Come, Dudley.'

She strode off towards the house, Mariner skipping along to keep up with her.

They stared after the pair. 'Wonder if she made it her business to know about Verlinden,' Ralph said, 'with an idea to blackmailing him?'

'I wonder . . .' Langham said. 'What she said last night, to Miss Miles: "I know all about you . . ." It makes you think.'

'A pretty can of worms we've uncovered here, mate,' Ralph said as they crossed to the gatehouse.

Langham pushed open the door and stepped inside. The room was just as bleak as he recalled, but the reek of soured milk was even stronger. 'We'll start down here and work our way upstairs. I'll take the kitchen.'

'You're welcome to it.' Ralph moved into the sitting room area. 'I take it we're not looking for the painting?'

'He would've been a fool to hide it here. I'd like to find out more about the man himself.'

They began a thorough search. Langham went through the tiny kitchen drawer by drawer, examining the scant contents of the larder and finding only two tins of peas, a box of stale porridge oats, and three cracked eggs. He pulled a curtain aside and looked under the sink: a mouldy plunger, a rusted tin of Brasso, and an empty tin of brown Kiwi shoe polish.

Finding nothing of interest, he joined Ralph in the sitting room and pulled cushions from the armchair and settee, then sorted through the magazines stacked beside a big Baird radiogram. There was nothing of note among old copies of the *Radio Times* and the *Picturegoer*, and nothing much to indicate Patrick Verlinden's character. Even the paperbacks in the bookcase were an eclectic mix of titles, from thrillers to war stories.

They stood and surveyed the room. 'Not a single letter, official or otherwise, and no photos other than that.' Langham pointed to the photograph of the airmen.

'Let's take a look upstairs,' Ralph said.

Langham followed him up the narrow flight of steps to a room which ran the length of the archway. An unmade single bed and a vast Victorian wardrobe stood at one end of the room, and at the other a door gave on to a tiny, mould-infested bathroom. A cursory search uncovered a cutthroat razor, an old tablet of soap and a few damp towels. The room, like the rest of the place, was freezing. Patrick Verlinden had lived a spartan existence.

Langham was stepping from the bathroom when Ralph called out, 'Bingo!'

He crossed to where Ralph was examining something on the bed.

'Found this on top of the wardrobe,' he said.

He unbuckled a canvas wallet the size of a paperback book and unfolded it across the rumpled sheets. Half a dozen long keys were slotted into serried pockets.

'If they're what I think they are, Ralph . . .'

'A nice set of skeleton keys, pride of any self-respecting locksmith. Bloody hell, Don, you were right when you thought Verlinden was our man.'

'He just might be.'

Ralph returned the keys to the top of the wardrobe. 'What now?'

'I'd like a quick word with Mariner about Verlinden,' Langham said, leading the way downstairs.

They crossed the drive to the house and found Mariner and Esmeralda in the dining room, eating toasted crumpets before the open fire. Esmeralda looked up and did her best not to scowl. 'Oh, it's you.'

Mariner smiled. 'Please, join us. Plenty of these.' He pointed to the plate of crumpets. 'Pull up a pew.'

'We won't, thanks. I'd like to ask you a couple of questions about Patrick Verlinden, if I may?'

'Fire away,' Mariner said.

Langham leaned against the chimney breast while Ralph affected an interest in a set of hunting prints on the wall. 'You said that Verlinden was employed by your father as an odd-job man?'

Mariner wiped butter from his chin. 'That's right, yes.'

'Do you know if Verlinden was up on the roof around the time of the burglary?'

'Let me see . . .' Mariner stared into the fire. 'The theft took place on the Wednesday evening.' He rubbed his cheek, thinking. 'It wasn't the following day, the Thursday, that I saw Verlinden up on the roof, but the Friday. My father wanted Patrick to fix a leak in the major's place. Verlinden was up there, bobbing about like a monkey. He seemed reluctant to come down, but my father was adamant that the leak needed seeing to.'

'Do you know if he was also up there *before* the painting went missing?'

Mariner frowned in concentration. 'Sorry, don't recall. Of course, he could have been, but I didn't particularly notice. Why—?'

Langham swept on. 'Now, the lighting in the manor.'

At this, Esmeralda turned to him and snorted, 'What lighting?'

'It's a bit of a bugbear with Esmeralda,' Mariner said. 'You think Pater should shell out for electricity, don't you, my love?'

'It would make the place a damned sight more comfortable,' Esmeralda said. 'But your father is nothing if not a miser.'

'I take it that the only lighting in the house is provided by oil-lamps?' Langham asked.

'That's right.'

'And are they kept burning all night?'

Esmeralda laughed. 'What? And waste valuable fuel? As I said, his lordship . . .'

'Is nothing if not a miser,' Langham finished for her. 'So I take it that the house is in darkness during the night, with not even candles burning?'

'We have candles to hand if we need them,' Mariner replied, 'but ordinarily, no.'

Langham smiled. 'That's what I wanted to know.'

Esmeralda looked at him. 'Would you mind explaining what all this is about, Mr Langham?'

'In the fullness of time,' he said, turning to Mariner. 'Now, just one more thing. Do you happen to have a torch handy?'

'In the top drawer of the old bureau in the hallway,' Mariner

said. Langham thanked him and left the room, pursued by
Ralph.

They came to the entrance hall and Langham found a heavy
rubber torch in the bureau. He passed it to Ralph and said,
'Wait for me outside the library. I won't be a tick.'

'What're you up to, Don?'

'I'll tell you in a second,' Langham said, and hurried outside.
He moved along the facade of the manor until he came to the
windows of the passageway leading to the library, then closed
the shutters one by one.

He returned inside and made his way along the darkened
corridor. Up ahead, outside the library, Ralph directed the torch's
beam towards him.

Langham said, 'So here we are. It's some time after midnight,
and Verlinden – if he is our man – is working by torchlight
only. He gets into the library and takes down the painting,
dismantles the frame and rolls the canvas. Then he proceeds to
take it, bit by bit, from the library and along the corridor by
the light of the torch . . .' He shook his head. 'I don't think it
could be done without making one heck of a racket. Moreover,
I think Verlinden would've realized this and wouldn't even have
attempted it. The canvas alone, yes – but not the frame as well.'

Ralph frowned. 'But why take the frame? Why not simply
cut out the canvas and skedaddle?'

'As Inspector Montgomery pointed out this morning, the thief
probably wanted the frame as well. They don't come cheap,
apparently.'

'So . . .' Ralph said. 'What are you driving at?'

'Simply that our thief decided *not* to take the frame from
the library. Which means it's still in there.'

Langham opened the library door and they stepped into the
room.

'In here?' Ralph looked around in puzzlement. 'You're joking,
right?'

'Give me the torch,' Langham said, and crossed the room to
the fireplace.

'Don?'

Langham ducked beneath the mantelpiece and peered up into
the darkness.

'And where,' he asked, his voice echoing cavernously in the chimney breast, 'might our thief have thought to conceal the frame and, perhaps, even the painting?'

He switched on the torch and directed its dazzling beam up the chimney.

Ralph joined him. 'See anything?'

In the wavering light of the torch, Langham made out sooty brickwork and a ledge about six feet above his head – but no sign of the dismantled painting. 'Dammit. Nothing visible. But perhaps it's lodged further up.'

'Lodged? But how would he have got it up there?'

'Pulled it up on a rope from the roof?' Langham suggested.

'At *night*?' Ralph sounded sceptical.

Langham pulled his diary from his jacket pocket and riffled through the pages until he came to Wednesday the 14th of November. He showed it to Ralph. 'Almost a full moon,' he said. 'We should get up there and take a look, on the off-chance. Let's find Mariner.'

They left the library, negotiated the passage by torchlight, and found Mariner seated alone by the fire in the dining hall.

'We need the ladders Patrick Verlinden used to gain access to the roof,' Langham said.

'They're in the storeroom next to the barn,' Mariner said. 'I'll show you.'

Mariner led the way across the drive to a cavernous chamber next to the barn, filled with all manner of rusting junk including an ancient tractor, a ploughshare that would have graced a farming museum, and what to Langham's unpractised eye looked like a thresher.

'Is your father around?' Langham asked.

'Driven into Bury St Edmunds with the major, to fetch a case of wine from his merchant. He should be back in an hour or so.'

Plenty of time, Langham thought, to do what they had to do. He just hoped that the outcome was successful.

Mariner indicated a long ladder and a shorter one with hooks on one end. Between them they carried the ladders from the barn and across to the east wing.

Langham stood back and gazed at the chimney stack

positioned above the library; it was set back, in the valley
between two pitched roofs, and he could make out only its
flat-topped summit.

'See anything?' Ralph asked.

'I thought I might be able to make out a rope emerging from
the top, but maybe Verlinden concealed it on the far side of the
stack.'

As Langham set the long ladder against the eave, Mariner
asked, 'Mind me asking what the devil you're up to?'

'Attempting to retrieve your father's painting. Of course, we
might find nothing at all up there.'

'My word!' the young man exclaimed as Langham lodged a
foot on the first rung.

Ralph said, 'Perhaps I should do it, Don. I mean, you and
heights . . .'

'I'll be fine. After scaling that cliff face in Cornwall in the
summer, I'm up – excuse the pun – for anything.'

'Maybe I should go first?'

'No, I'll be fine. I'll take it easy – and if I slip, then you'll
be there to cushion my fall.'

Ralph gave an ironic salute.

Langham climbed up the ladder, concentrating on the ivied
brickwork and not looking down. Once at the top, he called out
to the two men, 'Now, if you'd pass the short ladder . . .'

Between them, Ralph and Mariner passed the hooked ladder
up to Langham, who pushed it up the incline of the snow-covered
tiles until it bumped over the high ridge and the hooks took
hold.

He proceeded to climb carefully over the guttering and lodge
himself at the bottom of the short ladder, and then peer up the
incline. The tall chimney stack was positioned in the cleft of
the closest pitched roof and the one beyond: it would be a case
of ascending to the ridge, hauling the short ladder after him,
then descending the other side to the base of the chimney stack.

Ralph climbed up after him, his thin face appearing over the
gutter like a weasel investigating the lie of new territory. On
all fours, they climbed up the second ladder then crouched
on the ridge cap, buffeted by a freezing wind.

Langham peered across at the chimney stack, then pointed

in triumph. 'Bingo, Ralph – as you so eloquently put it in the gatehouse.'

A rope emerged from the top of the chimney and was tied around the stack much lower down. 'Now you see how the resourceful Verlinden suspended the frame, and with luck the canvas, in the chimney?'

'Well, I'll be . . .'

They pulled the short ladder up after them, see-sawed it over the ridge, and laid it down the incline.

Langham led the way down the ladder and stepped carefully over the lead flashing towards the chimney stack, its summit some three feet above his head. Ralph joined him and touched the knotted rope.

'So Verlinden sneaks into the library at some point during the night of Wednesday the fourteenth,' Langham said, 'takes the painting apart and attaches the four lengths of the frame, and hopefully the rolled canvas, to a rope already in position. Then he returns outside, climbs up here, hauls the ropes so that the frames are concealed high up in the chimney breast, and secures the rope.' He patted the knot.

'Then on the Friday following the "theft", he returned up here to retrieve his haul – but if you recall, his lordship called him down to fix a leak.'

'And he can't have had time, after that, to return up here and grab the booty.' Ralph shook his head. 'But where the heck is he? I assumed he'd hopped it with the painting.'

'That's a mystery we can worry about later.' Langham regarded the knotted rope. 'Of course, there is a more pessimistic scenario.'

'Go on.'

'Verlinden concealed the frame up here as we've said but skedaddled with the rolled canvas.'

'How would he have got the painting down from here?'

Langham thought about it. 'Wait until everyone in the house was elsewhere then let it down into the hearth? Or, more likely' – he pointed along the rooftop to where, fifty yards away, a ragged hole showed in the old tiles – 'perhaps he intended to pull the painting up the stack and then stash it in the loft-space through there, until all the brouhaha died down?'

He hesitated, looking at his friend. It was as if both men were reluctant to proceed, for fear of finding only the dismantled frame at the end of the rope.

'Right,' Ralph said. 'How're we going to do this?'

'It'll be far easier to let it down than to haul it up,' Langham said. 'You return to the library, then I'll unknot the rope and let it down little by little.'

'Give me a couple of minutes to get down, Don. I'll shout up the chimney when I'm in place.'

Langham watched Ralph scramble back up the ladder, pull it back over the ridge, then disappear over the peak.

He examined the rope; it was fastened in a simple reef knot, for quick release. Verlinden had thought of everything. He smiled to himself when he imagined the look on Lord Elsmere's face when he set eyes on his treasured painting . . . If the canvas *was* concealed up the chimney.

Ralph's muffled voice called out, 'Ready when you are!'

Taking a grip on the rope above the knot with his left hand, he loosened the knot with his right, taking all the weight as the knot came free. He held on with both hands and felt the full weight of the suspended frames. Hand over hand, he let the rope out.

The rope slackened and Ralph called out, 'Got 'em, Don! Now what've we got here . . .?'

Langham waited, heart thumping; it would be a terrible anti-climax if Patrick Verlinden had absconded with the canvas. He imagined having to break the news to Lord Elsmere.

He heard the scrape of the short ladder as it was pushed up the tiled incline; then he saw the hooks drop over the ridge, followed by Ralph's beaming face.

'Well?' Langham asked, staring up.

'Looks like we're in luck. The frames, *and* something wrapped in a length of oilcloth.'

'Just the ticket!'

Reaching *terra firma* minutes later, Langham hurried after Ralph into the house and along the corridor to the library.

Mariner was already there, standing before the fireplace with his right hand to his cheek, staring at the floor.

Laid side by side on the polished floorboards, still attached to five lengths of washing line which were in turn secured to the rope, were four separate pieces of a gilded frame and a long cylinder of black oilcloth.

Langham gestured to Mariner. 'Perhaps you should do the honours?'

The oilcloth was bound by half a dozen strips of insulating tape. Mariner knelt and pulled at the strips one by one. In due course the last of the tape came free, and Mariner pulled back a flap of oilcloth to reveal a length of rolled canvas.

They carried it to the centre of the room, pushed back a settee and an armchair, and proceeded to gently unroll the painting.

The pastoral scene, with vivid greens and a sunlit summer sky, filled the gloomy room with life and light.

Mariner murmured, 'It appears to be undamaged. My word . . .' He shook his head as if in wonder. 'I don't know how to thank you. My father . . . Why, he'll be beside himself.'

'All in a day's work.' Ralph laughed. 'Ain't that right, Don?'

'Well, I must admit it's the first time I've helped recover a work of art,' Langham admitted.

He moved to the frame and examined the individual pieces. At the end of each length, a brass screw-plate overhung the mitre. 'If you can rustle up a few half-inch screws,' he said to Mariner, 'then we can assemble the frame and have the canvas in place and hung before your old man gets back.'

'What a surprise that will be!' Mariner exclaimed, hurrying from the room.

They made further space on the floor and laid out the frame. Ralph took his handkerchief and dusted the gilded scrollwork, sooty from the fire his lordship had had made the other day. If Verlinden had hung the canvas any lower, Langham reflected, it would have been in danger of going up in flames.

Mariner returned with a handful of assorted screws and a couple of screwdrivers, and they fixed the frame together and carefully stretched the canvas in position.

Then, with Langham at one end and Ralph at the other, and Mariner directing the operation, they took the painting's considerable weight and eased it on to the double mountings on the chimney breast.

'Excellent!' Mariner declared as they stood back and admired

their handiwork. 'The look on Pater's face when he walks in
. . . Now, I think this calls for a drink. Will you join me,
gentlemen? Whisky?'

They were admiring the painting a little later, drinks in hand,
when the quiet of the winter afternoon was interrupted by the
sound of a car engine.

Mariner moved to the window. 'His nibs! I'll pop out and
collar him on some pretext. Prepare yourself to witness one
very surprised, and grateful, Lord of the Manor.'

He disappeared through the tiny door and Ralph laughed.
'All's well that ends well, eh?'

Langham raised his glass. 'If only all our cases went as
smoothly as this one.'

Ralph drained his drink. 'I don't think they'd object if we
had another quick one for the road, do you?'

'In the circumstances, I think we could drain his stock and
come back for more.' Langham finished his tot and Ralph refilled
his glass.

They were sipping their drinks when the door creaked open
and Lord Elsmere limped in, grumbling, 'Don't see what's so
urgent, m'boy. I was just about to lay a few bottles down for . . .'

He caught sight of Langham and Ralph and nodded.
'Afternoon, Ralph, Donald.' Then he looked up. 'What the . . .!'

Langham was watching him as he halted in his tracks as if
pole-axed, staring at the painting above the hearth. His eyes
popped and his jaw dropped, and he almost staggered. 'Lord
bless my soul!' he exclaimed. 'Upon my word . . .'

Langham gripped his elbow and assisted him into a nearby
armchair. The old man sat down heavily, gripping the arms of
the chair with his claw-like hands and goggling at the
Gainsborough.

'But how . . .? I mean, where . . .? And who the blazes?'

Mariner poured him a generous measure of whisky and thrust
it into his father's hand. Elsmere drank, smacked his lips, and
gave what Langham described to Maria, later, as a war whoop.

'Good God, you did it! Must admit, I never thought I'd see
the thing again. But c'mon,' he said, his rheumy gaze shuttling
from Ralph to Langham, 'don't just stand there like a couple
of cats who've got the cream! Out with it!'

Ralph pointed. 'It was Don's bright idea.'

'We worked as a team,' Langham corrected, 'and it was Ralph here who found the skeleton keys in Patrick Verlinden's bedroom.'

'Verlinden?' Elsmere exclaimed.

'It does look as if he was behind this,' Langham said.

'And he got in here using skeleton keys, eh?' Elsmere grunted.

'What we thought might have been difficult,' Langham went on, 'wasn't so much how he got in here, but how he managed to spirit the painting, frame and all, from the room.'

'And how did he, young man?'

'He didn't. He disassembled the whole shooting match *in situ* and hid the lot up the chimney at the end of a rope. He was in the process of retrieving it, that Friday, when you called him down to fix a leaking pipe.'

'Bless my soul, so I did!' Elsmere exclaimed. 'Well, what do you know?'

'If not for that burst pipe,' Ralph put in, 'he might've got away with the painting scot-free.'

'How fortunate indeed that Elder put me on to you two.' Elsmere's expression clouded over as he went on, 'But hang it all, what the deuce happened to young Verlinden? I can understand him doing a bunk *after* he'd got his hands on the painting, but the blighter hasn't been seen since . . .' He looked at his son. 'How long, Dudley?'

'The last time I saw him was on the Friday, when you called him down from the roof.'

'So why the blazes has the young reprobate gone to earth?' Elsmere asked. 'It doesn't make the slightest bit of sense.'

Mariner topped up his father's glass. 'The main thing is that you have the painting back.'

'Yes, you're right at that, and good riddance to Mr Verlinden!'

The library door opened and Esmeralda Bellamy stepped into the room. Langham watched her as she took one look at the painting, appeared momentarily astonished, then turned on her heel and hurriedly left the room.

'Esmeralda!' Mariner called after her. 'Darling, the most

wonderful news . . . Excuse me,' he said over his shoulder, scurrying after her. 'Esmeralda, you'll never guess . . .'

Lord Elsmere watched him go. 'Spent years wondering if he'd ever find himself a match, and when he does, look what he ends up with. I do wish he wouldn't run about after the silly woman as he does. Now, you two' – he went on in a business-like tone – 'I'm going to see that you're amply rewarded for your sterling service. Young Ralph, send me your bill and add fifty guineas for a job well done, hm?'

'It's been a pleasure working on the case,' Ralph said.

'You'll stay for dinner, won't you? I'll crack open a nice bottle of claret. I've had one waiting for just such an occasion.'

Langham demurred. 'My wife and I are dining at Charles's tonight – in fact, we're spending the weekend with him.'

'You are, are you?' A calculating look entered his lordship's watery eyes. 'Tell you what, how about you and your little lady, and you too, Ralph, come over for Sunday lunch? I'll give Charles a bell and get him over, too, as a little thank you for putting me on to you two.'

'That would be splendid,' Langham agreed.

'So it's agreed then, noon for one o'clock. I'll have Cook rustle up one of her specialities.' Elsmere chuckled to himself. 'Don't get much cause these days to celebrate, so one must grab the bull by the horns when one can, what?'

Langham agreed, then looked at his watch and said he must be pushing off.

'You don't mind if I don't see you out, do you?' Elsmere said. 'I think I'll remain here, pour meself another snifter, and admire the painting.'

They left his lordship sipping whisky and gazing at his Gainsborough.

Langham led the way from the library, along the still darkened passageway, and from the manor.

As they crossed to their respective cars, Ralph said, 'Not too sure we'll be able to make it on Sunday. Annie mentioned something about visiting her mother. Give his lordship my apologies, will you?'

'I'll do that. See you at the office next week.'

'So long, Cap'n.' Ralph ducked into his car.

Langham was crossing to his Rover when the front door opened.

'Oh, there you are, Mr Langham,' Rebecca Miles called out. 'I thought I'd missed you.'

She stood at the top of the steps, dwarfed by the dimensions of the entrance. She wore a black dress that clung to her slim figure and matched her jet-black hair. On her small feet were a pair of quaint, fur-topped boots; she hugged herself and shivered in the freezing wind.

'I hope you don't mind,' she went on, smiling, 'but I wonder if we might have a quiet word?'

Thinking that she might want to explain her contretemps with Esmeralda last night, Langham nodded. 'Not at all.'

She hesitated, then gestured behind her. 'If we could speak in my room . . .?'

He followed her into the house and along a corridor to the west wing. They climbed a small set of three steps and turned right along another passageway, the walls becoming more warped and the ceiling lower as they progressed. Floorboards creaked, signalling their passage.

Miss Miles came to a pitted oak door, unlocked it, and led the way into a comfortably appointed sitting room, with chintz furniture, colourful rugs, and a fire burning in the hearth. Two mullioned windows looked out over the snow-covered drive.

She crossed to the fire and turned to Langham. 'Congratulations on recovering the painting. I've just seen Dudley and he told me all about it. And . . .'

Something in her eyes – a twinkle of barely suppressed mischief – told him that she knew he and Ralph were not the location scouts Mariner had claimed they were yesterday.

'Go on,' he said, returning her smile.

'I knew who you were all along,' she said. 'You see, I overheard his lordship on the phone to your agency earlier this week. He was in the hall, and as he was speaking rather loudly, and I was passing . . . I hope you don't think I was eavesdropping?'

He laughed. 'I'll take your word for it.'

'Thank you.' She looked relieved. 'Anyway, congratulations on finding the painting.' She hesitated. 'Can I get you a drink?'

'I was about to push off. In fact . . .' He made a show of glancing at his watch.

'Of course. I'm sorry.' She looked uncertain, as if wondering where to begin.

'Look,' he said, 'if it's about what I might have overheard last night—'

'It did have something to do with that,' she began. She indicated an armchair and sat down on a sofa beside the fire.

'How can I help?' Langham asked, seating himself.

She pressed her slim legs together, angling them like a downhill skier, and stared at her hands folded in her lap. She murmured, 'What exactly did you hear, Mr Langham?'

'Not much. A few muttered words. I heard Esmeralda call you a name and claim to know something about you. And that's all.'

'She's a witch!' the young woman said. 'I don't like myself for saying this, but she is. A scheming, money-grubbing witch. She . . .' She stopped suddenly.

Going on a hunch, Langham took a gamble. 'Is she blackmailing you, Miss Miles?'

She appeared startled, whether at the accuracy of his query or otherwise, he could not tell.

'How on earth did you know?'

He shrugged. 'Let's just say it was an educated guess.'

'I . . . I'm not even sure that you *can* help me,' she said in a small voice. 'But I need your advice.'

She stood quickly, moved across the room to a small bureau, and took something from a drawer. It appeared to be the folded front page of a national newspaper. She hesitated, staring down at the quartered sheet, then crossed to him and dropped it on his lap.

As she resumed her seat, Langham picked up the paper and stared at the photograph under the banner headline: *Husband Slayer Freed.*

The picture showed a young woman, identical to Rebecca Miles, being escorted by two uniformed policemen.

Langham looked from the paper to Miss Miles, then began reading the story beneath the headline. 'Janita Gerson, thirty-three, was released yesterday after serving a three-and-a-half-year sentence for the manslaughter of her husband . . .'

He checked the newspaper's dateline: July 16, 1956 – just four months ago.

He looked up at her. 'You?' he asked.

'No!' she cried. 'That's the terrible thing, it *isn't* me. But Esmeralda found the newspaper, saw the picture, and jumped to the wrong conclusion. Oh' – she waved at the paper dismissively – 'I grant it certainly looks like me – the resemblance is uncanny. But I assure you that woman is *not* me. Try telling that to the hateful Esmeralda, though.'

'I see,' Langham said, 'and Esmeralda is threatening to tell . . . someone . . . if you don't agree to pay her to keep quiet?'

Silently, staring down at her clenched hands, she nodded.

'How much?'

'She asked for fifty pounds.'

'And you said?'

'I said I need time to collect that much.'

'When was this?'

'Just this morning. But she mentioned something yesterday afternoon, said she wanted to see me. I could tell by her tone she was planning something malicious . . . That's what our little confrontation last night was all about. This morning she came knocking at the door with the newspaper.' She looked up and smiled at him. 'What should I do, Mr Langham?'

'Who do you fear Esmeralda might tell?'

'His lordship, the villagers, the few friends I've made locally. Lord Elsmere has been so good to me, and I'm so settled here . . .'

He sat back and regarded her. 'If I were you, Miss Miles, I'd tell Esmeralda to mind her own business.'

'But—'

'Hear me out. She has no proof that you and this Janita Gerson are one and the same person, just a somewhat grainy photograph of someone who looks like you.'

'But if she told his lordship . . .'

'Then you'd simply show Elsmere your passport – I take it you have one?'

'I have. But what if Esmeralda claimed that, as someone

released from jail to start a new life, I'd been issued with a new identity?'

He shook his head. 'I understand your fear, but . . .'

Into his mind's eye then flashed the image of Esmeralda's face as she entered the library and caught sight of the restored painting. She had looked astonished – or shocked. He had a sudden idea.

'Listen,' he said, 'stall Esmeralda if she approaches you. Tell her you'll go into town and collect the money next week.'

'But . . .'

'As I've been invited to lunch with Lord Elsmere on Sunday, I'll have a quiet little word with Esmeralda and warn her off.'

She regarded him, nipping her bottom lip between perfect white teeth. 'Do you think it will work? I don't want beastly rumours spreading about me.'

'Of course you don't, and I'll do my very best to prevent Esmeralda doing that.'

'Thank you. Oh, you don't know what a relief it is just to tell someone.'

'I can imagine,' he said, climbing to his feet. 'Just leave it to me, Miss Miles, and I'll see you again on Sunday.'

'Thank you again, Mr Langham.'

'I'll see myself out,' he said, left the room and made his way back through the house.

As he eased his Rover under the archway of the gatehouse and motored through the village, Langham considered the viper's nest of jealousy and intrigue that was Neston Manor.

Then he wondered what might have happened to Patrick Verlinden.

NINE

On Saturday morning Langham blinked himself awake to find Maria, her face propped on her palm, watching him.

'You do look funny when you've just woken up, Donald.'

'I do?'

'Your hair is a haystack and your face always looks a little gormless.'

He laughed. 'Thank you, my darling. I wonder how it is that, first thing, you happen to look like a perfect vision?'

She leaned forward and kissed him. 'You're so sweet.'

He stretched and yawned. 'My word, but I enjoyed last night.'

They had taken aperitifs in the library at six, then enjoyed a first-rate dinner cooked by Albert. The wine had flowed, and Langham had regaled Charles and Albert with how he and Ralph had recovered Lord Elsmere's Gainsborough.

'I thought the drink was slipping down rather easily,' Maria said. 'How do you feel this morning?'

He did a quick inventory. 'Mouth a trifle dry, head surprisingly clear, vision a little bleary.' He rubbed the offending optics. 'There, that's better.'

She stroked his cheek. 'Are you looking forward to driving around a few villages, Donald?'

'I'll say. All the more for having got the painting business out of the way. You?'

'I never thought I'd be so excited at the prospect of leaving London, but I think it's the right thing to do.' She squinted at him. 'But you won't miss the city?'

'I've lived there long enough. I feel in need of a change; country living will be an adventure. And it isn't as if we'll be *really* leaving London, if we keep the Kensington place on.'

'The best of both worlds.'

She jumped out of bed, washed in the adjacent bathroom, then returned and dressed. As she was rolling on her stockings, she looked at him and said, 'I'm looking forward to lunch at Neston Manor tomorrow and meeting the people you described.'

'Odd crowd. My father used to say that there's "nowt as queer as folk". He was right. Look under the surface, and everyone has their secrets.'

'Even you?'

He thought about it. 'Well, I don't tell everyone about my active service in Madagascar. You?'

She made an attractive moue of her rose-coloured lips. 'I once stole a friend's toy dog – when I was five. I felt so bad about it for a week, I threw it over her garden wall on the way to school. Luckily she found it.'

He laughed. 'Never had you down as a thief, Maria.'

'Speaking of thieves,' she said, 'I wouldn't be surprised if Lord Elsmere asked you and Ralph to consider tracking down this Verlinden fellow.'

Langham scratched his head. 'It is intriguing. Where the devil is he? Why did he vanish like that, leaving the booty hanging, as it were? It doesn't make much sense, if you ask me.'

'I'm intrigued by the sculptress, Esmeralda. I've never knowingly met a blackmailer before.'

'She's a strange one, and no mistake.'

When recounting the case over dinner last night, he had said nothing about his suspicion that Patrick Verlinden might have had an accomplice, and that that accomplice just might have been Esmeralda Bellamy: her expression of shock when she had seen the picture returned to its rightful position had made him wonder.

'Now are you going to get up?' Maria said, throwing a pillow at him. 'Charles said breakfast is at nine, and it's five past already.'

They enjoyed an excellent breakfast of bacon and eggs and the obligatory devilled mushrooms – Charles's favourite – served by Albert, who joined them and recounted his plan for the day ahead.

'Charles said you want to see all the likely villages in the area, so I've made a list of places.' He spread a map of Suffolk on the table and indicated half a dozen locations ringed in pencil.

'Albert is nothing,' Charles declared, 'if not thorough.'

'All these,' Albert said, 'have what's vitally important – a decent public house and a station on the Ipswich line a short drive away.'

'Well done,' Maria said, peering at the map. 'Oh, I love the funny names! Copley Spruceton, Ingoldby-over-Water, Spankington Wallop . . .'

Langham scrutinized the map. 'You made that last one up!'

She pulled a face at him. 'Well, I'm sure there's a Spankington Wallop somewhere in England.'

'And we'll end up here,' Albert said, stabbing the map with

his forefinger, 'Little Neston. How about a pint later at the Dog and Gun?'

'I've never willingly refused the offer of ale,' Langham said. 'I'll be able to quiz the locals about Mr Verlinden.'

Charles pointed to a pile of newspapers on the chesterfield. 'I've been scanning the property pages for suitable houses, and there are two or three candidates you might like. We'll drive by and you can see what you think.'

Maria squeezed his hand. 'You're a treasure, Charles!'

They set off just after eleven, Albert driving the Daimler and Langham and Charles occupying the back seat. Maria bagged the job of navigator and sat in the passenger seat with the map opened out on her lap.

'These,' Charles sang as they motored down the narrow lanes, 'are my favourite winter days of all: with frost in the air and bright sunlight radiating its beneficence. The world looks made anew and the very freshness of the air seems fortified with an elixir that engenders confidence.'

Albert laughed and called out, 'I don't understand a word you're saying, mate – but I take it that days like these make you happy?'

'You take it correctly, my boy. To quote Clare, "The winter comes; I walk alone, I want no bird to sing; To those who keep their hearts their own, the winter is the spring" . . .'

Like this, with Charles waxing lyrical and Albert laughing with him, they bowled along the country byways. The snow had thawed and was now but a thin encrustation on the higher ground; bare oaks dripped with diadems of meltwater and the winter sun's reflection scintillated from puddles.

Albert slowed down as they came into the village of Copley Spruceton, a collection of tiny red-brick thatched cottages huddling around a Norman church. 'I've heard tell the Five Jolly Butchers serves a decent pint,' Albert said, 'and the town of Middleford a couple of miles away has a railway station.'

Charles consulted a folded newspaper. 'The cottage next to the church – over there – is for sale at seven hundred. Three bedrooms, a spacious sitting room and a small garden.'

They passed the cottage at a crawl and Maria peered out. 'Oh! But it's lovely, Donald.'

'And big enough.'

'A study each, and a garden so you can grow vegetables.'

'And what's more,' Charles said, 'well within your budget.'

They drove on, and the day progressed, and it seemed to Langham that each village was prettier than the last, and each advertised house and cottage just what they had been looking for – at least in terms of appearance.

A little after three, Albert steered them down a familiar lane and presently they approached Little Neston and parked outside the Dog and Gun. They took a turn around the green to stretch their legs, then repaired to the oak-beamed snug. A small fire blazed in the hearth and a platoon of Toby jugs with gurning faces hung from a low beam above the bar.

Half a dozen locals, farm labourers and the ancient gnome Langham recognized as the postman he'd given a lift to on Thursday, nodded taciturn greetings and returned to the silent observation of their respective pints.

Langham bought a round, bitter for himself and Albert, a gin and tonic for Maria, and a sweet sherry for Charles. They sat around a small table of beaten copper, and once again Charles read aloud the particulars of the houses they had viewed, as if declaiming poetry.

Charles and Maria dissected the various merits of the candidates, while Langham sat back and enjoyed his beer. He wondered if there could be any state better than that attained in a country pub with a pint of fine ale and a roaring fire adding somnolent warmth to an otherwise frosty winter's day.

At one point Albert bought a round and remained at the bar, chatting to the publican, a man of such corpulence that he had trouble reaching the beer pumps. They were joined by the locals, and the conversation grew animated. Eavesdropping, Langham heard, 'Done a runner, by all accounts,' and 'Wouldn't trust him an inch!' and 'Scarlet woman, she be . . .'

Albert returned, belatedly, with the drinks, smiling to himself. 'Village is agog,' he murmured. 'Word's got out that his lordship's painting's been found, and the Dutch chap has vamoosed. I didn't let on that we had the man hisself who found the picture!' He accounted for half of his pint and went on, 'And something else . . .' He leaned closer to his friends. 'Old Roger was in here the day before the painting went missing, and who should he see at the corner table, as thick as thieves . . .?' He paused dramatically, eyeing the trio.

'Go on, my boy,' Charles said, 'you have us in suspense!'

'None other than the Dutch chap, Verlinden, and that woman you were telling us about last night, Don – the sculptress, Esmeralda Bellamy.'

Langham lowered his pint. 'Verlinden and Esmeralda? The day before the theft, you say? You're sure about that, Albert?'

'Well, old Roger is. Says they were huddled over the table, whispering secretive like.'

'You don't think, Donald,' said Charles, touching Langham's forearm, 'that the Dutch fellow had a co-conspirator in Esmeralda, do you?'

'It's certainly a possibility,' Langham allowed.

A little later Albert suggested one for the road, and the motion was passed.

Later that evening as they were preparing for bed, having enjoyed yet another fine meal conjured by the ever-resourceful Albert, Maria paused in the process of removing her earrings.

'I think now, Donald, I am looking forward more than ever to lunch at the manor tomorrow, are you?'

'Not half,' he said. 'It should be . . . interesting, to say the least.'

'But if Esmeralda and the Dutchman were in it together,' she said, 'what might have happened to him?'

It was a question that kept him awake as moonlight shone through the drawn curtains and somewhere far off an owl gave its plaintive hoot.

TEN

At noon on Sunday, Albert drove Charles, Langham and Maria the three miles to Neston Manor along twisting country lanes. It was one of those resplendent sunny November days which might, in a forgetful moment, be mistaken for spring. The warmth of the sun had banished the snow and the breeze was mild.

Albert dropped them at the manor. He'd make a splash, he said, by parking the Daimler outside the Dog and Gun, and then enjoy a couple of pints while he waited to pick them up at four.

'That's the only trouble with calling Albert my valet,' Charles murmured to Langham as they climbed from the car and approached the covered entrance. 'One can hardly insist that one's valet be invited to dinner, can one?'

Across the drive, the barn door was open and Esmeralda Bellamy could be seen within, bending over the carpenter's bench.

Benson opened the heavy oak door, announced that the other guests were in the drawing room, took their coats and led the way through the house.

Maria took Langham's hand. 'I see what you mean about the lighting. It's positively medieval. You think he'd be able to afford electricity, wouldn't you?'

'I think Lord Elsmere runs the place on a shoestring,' he said. 'Though I'll give him this, he doesn't stint on food or drink if the last meal was any indication.'

In the drawing room, Lord Elsmere was installed before the blazing hearth, toasting his rump and holding forth. Mariner stood beside him, a glass of sherry in hand, while Major Rutherford occupied a high-backed chair. Beside the major stood Rebecca Miles. She looked up and smiled brightly at Langham as he crossed the room.

'The man himself!' Elsmere called, limping forward. 'I was just singing your praises, Langham. And Charles, how good to see you again!'

'You're looking well, Teddy,' Charles said.

Langham introduced Maria, and Lord Elsmere kissed her hand and presented her to the company.

He looked beyond Langham and frowned. 'And what about the little chap, Ryland?'

'I'm afraid he had a prior engagement,' Langham said. 'He sends his apologies.'

'No matter. I'll have to catch up with him in London at some point – dine you both at my club, what?'

Langham concealed his smile at the thought of Ralph's reaction to being invited to a gentleman's club. 'I'm sure he'd be delighted.'

Benson appeared with a tray of sherry and they helped themselves.

'You did me a favour when you recommended Ryland and Langham, Charles. God bless my soul,' Elsmere went on, mopping his brow, 'and to think, I had Benson build a fire in the library the other day. The whole shooting match might've gone up in flames if I'd added another log!'

Rebecca Miles smiled at Maria. 'What is it like to be married to a successful detective?'

'It is strange,' Maria replied, 'but I don't think of Donald as successful at anything but his writing. You see, he works as a private investigator only part-time.'

Rebecca looked at Langham, surprised. 'You're a writer?'

Charles said, 'Of successful thrillers, might I add. And Donald's star is set to rise even higher, as Hollywood is about to film one of his early books.'

Langham shifted uneasily. He wondered when someone would increase his discomfort by mentioning that he'd shot a man dead during the war.

Maria said to the woman, 'Donald told me that you write.'

'Not seriously,' Rebecca murmured, evidently reluctant to discuss the matter.

Dudley Mariner said, 'You seemed pretty serious about it when you were telling me the story not so long ago – tale of derring-do set in the war,' he explained to the company.

Rebecca blushed and took a sip of sherry.

'Don't get me talking about the war,' Major Rutherford said. He struggled from his chair and stood to attention. He wore a brown quilted smoking jacket and a mustard-coloured cravat, and Langham thought that he looked even more like a tortoise than ever.

'Three of 'em!' the major went on. 'The Boer War, the Great War, and the Second – not that they let me get a crack at the Hun in the last one,' he complained. 'Had to make do with commanding the Highgate Home Guard.'

'You served King and country even so, Major,' Elsmere said.

'And one day, when I release me journals, everyone'll read about it.'

Rebecca changed the subject. Perhaps, Langham thought, she wanted to steer the old soldier off the topic he'd bored her with too often in the past. 'I wonder what the aftermath of the Suez debacle might be?' she enquired.

While Lord Elsmere gave his opinion on Egypt – he decried what he called Britain and France's ignominious retreat – Langham glanced through the window. He saw that Esmeralda was still in the barn, busy at the bench.

Mariner noticed the direction of his gaze. 'She gets so absorbed in her work . . . I'd better go and remind her we're dining at one.'

'Would you mind terribly if I went out and spoke to her? I need a quiet word anyway.'

Mariner hesitated, then acquiesced. 'Of course. If you could ask her to join us for drinks while you're at it.'

Langham murmured an excuse to Maria and slipped from the room.

He left the house, tramped through the slush to the barn, then cleared his throat as he came up behind the woman.

She turned quickly, surprised. 'Oh, it's you.'

She wore a waxed hunting jacket whose boxy shoulders made her appear even more mannish than usual. She clutched the stub of a pencil in her large right hand, and on the bench behind her was the sketch of what might have been her next project. Beside the curling draughtsman's paper, which was weighted down with a hammer and a couple of chisels, the shotgun lay where she'd placed it the other day.

'Well, Langham, did you come here to stare at me or are you going to say something?'

He smiled to himself and made an even more leisurely job of filling his pipe. Not until he'd puffed it into life did he speak. 'Dudley asked me to remind you that we're dining at one. But before that,' he went on, 'I'd like a little word.'

She tossed the pencil on to the bench, where it rolled and fetched up against the shotgun's stock. 'About?'

'About the theft of Lord Elsmere's painting,' he said.

She sighed. 'Not here, Langham,' she said, sweeping past him.

She led the way from the barn, around the house, to a large, square garden at the rear, where long gravel paths ran between half a dozen flowerbeds with precise, geometric formalism.

Striding along a path, she thrust her hands deep into the pockets of her jacket and pressed her square jaw to her chest. Langham caught up with her.

'Well,' she snapped, 'what about the theft?'

He removed his pipe and said, 'Do you have any idea where Patrick Verlinden might be?'

She appeared surprised. 'Verlinden? What makes you think . . .?'

'I just thought that, as you know him rather well, you might have some idea as to his current whereabouts.'

'In that case you're mistaken.' She gave him a penetrating look. 'And what makes you think I know him "rather well"?'

'You deny it?'

'I know him as a fellow resident at this dump, that's all.'

'A fellow resident you met at the Dog and Gun from time to time, and with whom you planned the theft of Lord Elsmere's painting.'

She stared at him, open-mouthed. At last she found her tongue. 'I don't know where the hell you got that idea.'

'It struck me that you might be the brains behind the heist and put Verlinden up to it.'

'I did nothing of the kind!' She stared ahead, at the bare trees on the horizon, and would not, or could not, meet his gaze.

'You had the bright idea of hiding the painting, frame and all, up the chimney, until such time as Verlinden – who went up on to the roof as a matter of course – had the opportunity to retrieve it.'

'You have absolutely no proof—'

'The look of shock on your face yesterday afternoon, when you saw the painting back in its rightful place, was eloquent enough.'

'This is downright slander!' she snapped. 'And anyway, the painting is back in Elsmere's possession, isn't it? There hasn't, technically, been a theft.'

He smiled. 'That's an interesting point that the police could ponder when they're in full possession of the facts. Namely, who was responsible for the painting's removal, the investigation of which occasioned considerable police time, as well as money. I think they'd take a very dim view of who was behind the act, don't you?'

She stared back at the house.

He went on, 'But what really puzzles me is why Patrick Verlinden should have vanished as he has. It just doesn't make sense. Why would he up and off like this, and draw attention to himself, when the sensible thing to do would be wait until the police investigation blew itself out?'

He detected something in her eyes: it appeared that she was as mystified as he was.

Avoiding his gaze, she said quietly, 'There's no need to inform the police, or Lord Elsmere, of your suspicions. He has the painting back, after all.'

Langham pursed his lips, considering the point.

'Well, you see, as an upright law-abiding member of the public – and as a private detective, after all – I'm not at all sure that withholding vital information like that would sit easily on my conscience. However . . .'

She looked at him sharply. 'What?'

'In a way, you're right. His lordship does have the painting back. But . . . the detective in me likes to have all the i's dotted and t's crossed. It would take *some* inducement to make me keep schtum.'

'Why, you scheming—'

'I think it's you who's the scheming player in all this.' He watched her as he went on, 'Lay off Miss Miles, Esmeralda. Forget all about threatening to reveal her supposed identity and I might see my way to keeping silent on the subject of your part in the theft.'

'I don't know what you're talking about. What's the little bitch been claiming now?'

'You forget: I overhead you the other evening. What did you say? Something about knowing all about her little secret?'

'So the woman has got her evil claws into you!' she sneered.

'It's a simple deal, Esmeralda. Forget about blackmailing Miss Miles, and I won't say a word to Inspector Montgomery

. . . who'd certainly be taking a good look into *your* past if I gave the word.'

'Why you—!' the woman began.

He was turning to go when a figure appeared around the side of the house. Dudley Mariner hurried across to them.

'Oh, there you are. We're about to go into dinner, Langham – and, darling, my father has an important announcement to make. He said he'd tell us after dinner. You know what he's like with these theatrical declarations. He was on the phone for a long time yesterday afternoon. I think something big is in the offing.'

'Something big?' Langham said.

'We'll find out soon enough,' Mariner said, and led the way back to the house.

They were just in time to tag on to the tail end of the procession as Lord Elsmere led everyone into the dining hall. Langham fell into step beside Maria.

'What was all that about?' she murmured. 'I saw Esmeralda storming from the barn – she looked annoyed.'

'I'll say. I'll tell you all about it later.'

They seated themselves, Elsmere taking his place at the head of the table. Rebecca Miles looked across at Langham with a slight frown of enquiry. He gave the merest nod to indicate that all was in hand.

The quality of the fare lived up to Langham's expectations, and he could see that Maria – a vocal critic of English cuisine – was quietly impressed. Onion consommé was followed by traditional roast beef, potatoes and Yorkshire pudding with a rich ale gravy.

At one point Lord Elsmere cleared his throat, and Langham assumed that he was about to make the announcement Mariner had foretold. However, his lordship fixed Langham with a smile and raised his glass.

'This little dinner, indeed the gathering, is my small way of giving thanks to the sterling work of Langham here, and the regrettably absent Ryland, in returning my picture. Estimable detective work, old boy. To Langham and Ryland!'

Everyone echoed the sentiment and drank, though Esmeralda

looked as if she were imbibing poison. Langham busied himself
by refilling his glass while this was going on and responded
with a few murmured platitudes.

Conversation, as the meal progressed, turned to other matters,
and at one point Major Rutherford asked Charles how he'd
come to know Lord Elsmere.

'Ah, now thereby hangs a tale,' Charles declared, his baritone
ringing down the table. 'It was back in the thirties, when my
father died and I moved up to Elder House. Teddy rode to
hounds in those days and kindly invited me to join his hunt.
Sadly, or perhaps not so sadly, though I name many sedentary
pursuits among my accomplishments – I can inhabit a sofa with
the best of them – I find it impossible to remain upright in the
saddle for more than thirty seconds. Something to do with my
shape, I think. Teddy suggested I follow the hunt in my motor
and join him for a drink at day's end. Thus a firm friendship
was forged in the hostelries of the county over many a fine
claret and the occasional single malt.'

'Those were the days,' Elsmere said.

Langham looked from Charles to Lord Elsmere and wondered
if Charles knew anything of his lordship's political past. It had
certainly changed his own opinion of the man.

Talk turned to horsemanship, and Major Rutherford said, 'I
rode into battle at Diamond Hill, South Africa, would you
believe? And that was over fifty years ago!'

Maria smiled across the table at Mariner and Esmeralda. 'Do
you ride?'

'Hate the animals,' Esmeralda said shortly.

Mariner added, 'Pater gave me lessons when I was knee high,
but we sold the horses years ago.'

Lord Elsmere said, 'Part of the steady erosion of the estate,
m'boy. Costs a packet to stable good horses, and to employ
staff to look after 'em.'

Mariner said, 'I know; I'm not complaining, Father.'

Elsmere muttered something, eyeing Esmeralda, and took a
draft of wine.

The major said, 'Do you ride, Rebecca?'

The young woman smiled. 'I think that, like Charles, I
wouldn't last thirty seconds in the saddle.'

The major patted her hand. 'Pity, young Rebecca – you'd look spiffing in jodhpurs and riding jacket.'

Later, when Benson had cleared away the crockery and returned with port and stilton, Lord Elsmere prepared to make his announcement. He cleared his throat and tapped his empty glass with a silver teaspoon until he had everyone's attention.

'Thought I'd better mention this, and there's no time like the present.' He looked around the table. 'We've been muddling along pretty well over the past few years. The old place hasn't yet fallen to pieces – at least, not all of it – and what repairs we've had to make, we've managed to do without breaking the bank. However—'

Looking aghast, Major Rutherford interrupted, 'You're not going to sell the manor, Teddy!'

'Perish the thought!' Elsmere chuckled. 'Sell up? I couldn't leave the ruddy place, at least not while I'm living. Carry me out of here feet first, they will. No, I have absolutely no plans to sell Neston Manor. But looking to the future, and taking everything into consideration, I realized that things couldn't go on as they have been. What with the house falling steadily into disrepair, and the cost of maintenance ever increasing . . .' His rheumy gaze raked the diners. 'Something had to be done.'

'And what,' asked Mariner, 'was that "something"?'

'Earlier this year I had an interesting offer. Seemed too good to be true. I was approached by a company of . . . they call themselves "property speculators", from Norwich. I had my solicitor look into them, and he assured me they were *bona fide.*'

'Property speculators?' the major said, suspicious. 'What did they want?'

Lord Elsmere sipped his port, taking his time before replying. 'They made me an interesting offer. Been on the blower to them over the past few months, discussing the finer points . . . Long and short of it is, they've agreed to take an eighty per cent share of Neston Manor, with myself retaining the balance.'

Mariner leaned forward. '*Take?*'

His lordship sighed. 'Dudley, the sad reality is that the manor, our family seat, is a liability. Do you have any idea of the duties you'll have to stump up when I shuffle off? You'd be faced with the prospect of having to sell the ruddy place, and no one wants that.'

'Or setting fire to the pile,' Esmeralda muttered.

If Elsmere heard the remark, he chose to ignore it. 'So Carnaby and Wentworth, the speculators, will take an eighty per cent share of Neston Manor, and in doing so will be legally bound to effect all repairs, alterations and improvements to ensure that the entirety of the place – including those parts of it so far uninhabitable – is fit for purpose. I have their assurance that the present tenants will remain *in situ*, and that your rents will remain fixed, as we've agreed previously, for the next five years.'

'And . . .' Mariner began, tentatively, 'what might happen when – that is, when . . .'

'What he's trying to say,' Esmeralda interpolated, 'is what'll happen to the manor when you, as you said earlier, "shuffle off"?'

'All that is in hand,' Elsmere said. 'In the event of my death, my twenty per cent share in the place will pass on to you, Dudley, along with your suite of rooms and thirty per cent of the land we currently own. The rest of the manor will pass into the hands of Carnaby and Wentworth.' He looked around the table. 'But we can all go into the details, with our individual solicitors, when the time comes to examine the contract that Carnaby and Wentworth's people are drawing up.'

'It seems, on the face of it,' Major Rutherford said, 'the best of a bad job. Suits me, speaking personally, as I don't think I'll be around for another five years anyway.'

'Nonsense, Major,' Rebecca said, 'you're good for another decade.'

He patted her hand. 'You're too kind, m'girl.'

Langham sipped his port and looked across at Mariner and Esmeralda. He wondered how Mariner was taking the news; the young man's expression was non-committal. Esmeralda stared down at her glass, a calculating look in her eyes.

Lord Elsmere was saying, 'You see, the alternative doesn't bear thinking about. We go on as we have been doing, and the place falls gradually into an appalling state of disrepair until the point is reached where nothing can be done for it. Then I meet my maker and leave you, Dudley, in the proverbial pickle, saddled with death duties *and* an uninhabitable shell. You do see my reasoning?'

Mariner dabbed at his lips with a napkin. 'Of course, Father.'

Elsmere was about to add something further when he looked up, over Langham's shoulder, and stared through the French windows.

'What the blazes . . .?' he began.

Langham turned in his seat and followed his host's gaze. Staggering towards the house was the postman Langham had given a lift to on Thursday, incongruous in his Sunday best. His haggard face wore a vacant expression of shock.

Langham pushed himself from the table, crossed the room and opened the French windows. The postman cried something incomprehensible; he was followed by a huge brindled lurcher with soiled paws and an even muddier muzzle.

The old man leaned against the door frame and stared at Langham with tear-filled eyes. 'His lordship! I need to see . . .'

'I'm here, man. What is it?'

Elsmere assisted the old man inside. Langham pulled up a chair and the postman sank on to it.

Elsmere snapped over his shoulder, 'Someone get the man a brandy!'

Charles obliged, ferrying a balloon glass across to the stricken local.

'Now in your own time, Cedric,' Elsmere urged.

The postman took the glass in both hands and swallowed a mouthful. 'In . . . in the woods . . . I were passing through, like I do Sundays, shortcut from the Dog. Had Baldwin with me . . .' He indicated the lurcher, which now sat obediently at his owner's feet. 'And it were the dog that found it.'

Elsmere gripped the man's shoulder. 'Found what, for heaven's sake?'

Cedric's eyes grew wide. 'Found the body, sir. Baldwin dived into the undergrowth and began scratting around. Wouldn't listen to me when I called him off. Thought he'd found a dead fox, I did. I called again, then when he wouldn't come I stepped off the path and saw . . .'

'Easy, man, have another swallow.'

Cedric nodded. 'Ah . . . that's better. That's a drop o' good stuff, that is.'

'A body, you said?' Elsmere prompted.

'Aye, a body – lying there half-buried under some leaves.'

'Do you know who it was?' Langham asked.

The old man shook his head. 'I only saw the chest and a bit o' leg. But . . . but there were a bloody great hole in the chest. Saw the ribs, I did, all bloody and broken . . . Thought I were back at the Somme!'

Langham turned to Mariner. 'Ring the police,' he said. 'Get through to the station at Bury St Edmunds and ask for Detective Inspector Montgomery. Insist that Montgomery comes out here, even if it interrupts his Sunday roast.'

Mariner hurried from the room.

Langham turned to the old man. 'Are you up to showing us what you found?'

Cedric took another mouthful of brandy and nodded resolutely. 'Aye, sir. Just let me gather me wits. Nice drop of brandy, this.'

'Top him up, Charles,' Elsmere said.

In due course, with another couple of fingers fortifying the old soldier, Langham took Cedric's arm and assisted him from the dining hall and across the drive, ensuring that the lurcher remained in the room.

With Lord Elsmere leading the way, leaning heavily on his stick, the trio took the path along the front of the east wing towards the leafless woodland.

'Bit of a shock, it was, sir. Don't come across things like that every day.'

'I'll say, Cedric. Good show. You're a brave man.'

'Just on me way back from the Dog, I was. Didn't expect to see what I saw . . .'

They entered the woods, a mixture of oak, sycamore and elm. A well-worn path wound through the trees, littered with old leaves and fallen branches. A hundred yards into the woodland, Cedric paused and pointed a dithering finger towards a stand of ferns growing beneath the slanting bole of an elm.

'Just beyond them ferns, it is, sir. You don't mind if I . . .?'

'Of course not. Stay here, old boy. Won't be a jiffy. C'mon, Langham.'

They approached the ferns and Lord Elsmere parted the fronds with his stick.

'My God!' the old man gasped.

The dog had uncovered the corpse's shattered ribcage and its left leg, though the face was still concealed beneath a pile of leaves. Half a dozen shattered ribs stood out starkly against congealed, blackened blood and the minced remains of a lung.

'Better not get any closer,' Langham said. 'Don't want to disturb any possible footprints.'

Elsmere looked at him. 'Gunshots, d'you think?'

'Looks like it. From pretty close range, too, by the look of it.'

'Christ a'mighty!' Elsmere said. 'A ruddy shooting, and on my own patch at that! You don't suppose it was self-inflicted . . .?' He trailed off.

Langham shook his head. 'No, it's murder, sir. I've never heard of a suicide successfully concealing himself under a pile of leaves.'

'Of course not . . .' Lord Elsmere leaned forward, peering more closely at the body. 'Good God!'

'What is it?'

'That boot, Langham. I recognize it – the damned thing belongs to young Verlinden.'

Langham peered at the hobnail boot protruding at an angle from the leaf mould. 'You're sure?'

'Certain. Never saw the chap in anything else, summer or winter. It's Verlinden, all right. But who in God's name would have done this?'

As he looked away from the corpse, Langham asked himself the same question.

'How long d'you reckon it's been there?' Elsmere asked.

'Going by the look of the flesh, I'd say a good few days,' Langham said. 'I think we'd better get back to the house and wait for the police. I don't know about you, but I could do with a drink.'

'Never a truer word spoken, young man.'

Langham examined the ground around the stand of ferns, but

the earth in the shade of the fronds was dry and had not taken footprints. The muddy path was another matter entirely, churned by the boots of many a passer-by.

They made their way back to the manor, Langham assisting old Cedric by the elbow.

Mariner met them at the front door. 'I got through to a desk sergeant who rang Inspector Montgomery. Said he'd be here in half an hour.'

'Good man,' Elsmere said.

'Everyone's in the drawing room,' Mariner went on, leading the way.

Maria and Charles looked up when they entered, then hurried over to Langham.

'Patrick Verlinden,' he murmured. 'The body was hidden under leaves in the woods. Shot in the chest, at least twice. Been there a while.'

'Whisky, Langham?' Elsmere called out.

'A stiff one, thank you.'

'Coming up.'

Elsmere passed him a tumbler of Scotch, then attended to old Cedric, who was recounting his experience to Mariner in rather incoherent terms.

Langham was making inroads on his second whisky when a black Humber pulled into the driveway, followed by a scene of crime van and a squad car.

The diminutive figure of Detective Inspector Montgomery, in a tight-fitting suit and a trilby perched on the back of his head, climbed from the car and approached the house.

Langham crossed the room with Lord Elsmere and met Montgomery on the threshold.

'Ah, Langham, wondered if you'd still be around. M'lord . . .' The detective doffed his hat. 'I understand the body was discovered by one' – he referred to a notebook – 'Cedric Hardaker?'

'You'll find him in the drawing room, a little shaken after the experience,' Elsmere said.

Montgomery introduced a young, portly man in a grey raincoat as Detective Sergeant Halliday, then instructed his subordinate to take a statement from Mr Hardaker.

'If you'd be so kind as to show me where the body was discovered, m'lord.'

Elsmere led the way across the drive and into the woods, trailed by Montgomery and Langham. A police surgeon, two policemen in boiler suits, and a photographer brought up the rear.

They came to the stand of ferns, and Langham and Elsmere stood back as the inspector and the surgeon trod carefully through the undergrowth, then knelt to examine the corpse.

Montgomery called over his shoulder, 'Any idea who it might be, m'lord?'

'It's Patrick Verlinden, my odd-job man. I recognize the boots, y'see.'

Montgomery spoke in hushed tones to the surgeon, who opened his bag, took something from it, and leaned forward. The ferns hid from view what he might have been doing to the corpse.

Montgomery said, 'We'll require a formal identification, m'lord, so we're uncovering the chap's face.'

The inspector rose to his feet, frowning as he stared down at what was revealed. He looked across at Elsmere. 'I'm sorry, but I'll have to ask you to take a quick look, just to ascertain that it is the chap in question. I must warn you . . . he was shot in the face, as well as in the chest.'

Lord Elsmere braced himself and stepped forward. The police surgeon parted the fronds so that Elsmere could get a better view, and in those few seconds Langham caught a brief glimpse of half a face, its flesh green-tinged and rimed with frost. The other half had been blasted away with the impact of the shot.

Lord Elsmere stepped back, shaken. 'That's him, poor chap. Recognize the scar on the cheek . . .' He moved off a little way and leaned against a tree.

In due course the surgeon stepped away from the ferns and the police in boiler suits took over, taping off the area. The photographer took a dozen shots of the corpse, his flash illuminating the trees like localized lightning.

The surgeon, a huge man with a vast moon face made to seem even larger by a bald pate, gave his assessment. 'I won't be able to say for definite until I've examined the corpse extensively, but it looks to me as if he's been dead between . . . I'd say a week and ten days. Three shotgun wounds, two to the chest and one to the right side of the head. At pretty close range, I'd say, too.'

'How close?' Montgomery asked.

'Certainly no further away than six feet, and probably closer. I'll be more exact after the post-mortem.'

'And death was pretty damned quick, I hope?'

'The first two shots would have done for him. I suspect the third shot was administered when the victim was on the ground.'

'And it happened here?' Montgomery asked. 'Or elsewhere, and the corpse was brought to its resting place?'

'I've yet to ascertain that. I'll have forensics comb the area.'

Inspector Montgomery asked Lord Elsmere, 'When did you last see Verlinden alive?'

'I spoke to him the day after I discovered the theft of my painting.'

'So that would be Friday the sixteenth?'

'He was up on the roof, repairing something or other. I called him down to fix a leak in Major Rutherford's kitchen.'

'What time was this?'

'Around four.'

'So it was getting dark?' The inspector considered this. 'I suspect he didn't die that night, then. This was a daylight shooting. Whoever did it would hardly have apprehended him in the woods, carrying a torch.'

The surgeon nodded. 'That would make the approximate time of death between Saturday and Sunday, sir.'

'Very good,' Montgomery said. 'Right, back to the house and I'll have a word with whoever was around at the time.'

With the police photographer's flash illuminating the twilight, Lord Elsmere led the way from the woods. As they emerged on to the drive, Montgomery slowed his pace and touched Langham's elbow.

'You've been kicking around for a couple of days, Langham. You've spoken to the residents of the place. I take it you've been keeping your eyes peeled?'

'Do you mean, do I have any idea who might have . . .?'

'You're a bright chap. You must have a suspicion or two.'

'I have one or two ideas, yes. I wonder . . . Could I have a quiet word with you in the library?'

'Don't see why not,' Montgomery said. 'Will ten minutes do?'

'That should be plenty.'

ELEVEN

As they entered the house, Montgomery said, 'M'lord, if you'd be good enough to send Detective Sergeant Halliday along to the library in ten minutes.'

'Will do, Inspector. Oh, and help yourself to drinks. I had Benson light the fire earlier, so the room will be warm.'

Elsmere shambled off down the darkened corridor and Langham led the way to the library.

'Good to have you on the case, Langham. Bright chap like you . . . I remember when I was your age. Didn't miss a thing.'

'And now?' Langham asked, opening the library door and ushering Montgomery into the room illuminated by the fire's dancing flames.

'Still pretty sharpish, if I say so myself. "No flies on Montgomery", as they say back at the station. I don't miss much.'

'That's good to know, Inspector. Drink?'

He led the little man across the room to where a row of bottles and glasses stood on the sideboard.

'A nip of whisky would go down a treat on a day like today, young sir.'

Langham poured two measures and passed one to the inspector. He gestured to the settee and they sat down.

'Now,' Montgomery said, 'what've you noticed?'

'First, Inspector,' Langham said, doing his level best not to smile, 'what have *you* noticed?'

'Me? Why, I've hardly set foot in the place.'

Langham sat back and gazed up at the oil painting gracing

the chimney breast. 'I was referring to anything you might have seen in this room, Inspector.'

'In this room?' Montgomery scratched his head and looked around him. 'Can't say I notice anything out of the ordinary.' He stared at Langham. 'Just what are you driving at, lad?'

'I mean,' Langham said, indicating the painting with his glass, 'that.'

Montgomery looked up and his jaw dropped. 'Good God! Well, I'll be . . . The painting! Lordy, how the ruddy hell did that get there?'

Langham shrugged modestly. 'Oh, a little bit of detective work, Inspector. I kept my eyes peeled, as it were.'

'You young scallywag!' Montgomery barked. 'You're taking the blessed Mickey!'

'As if I'd do that, Inspector.'

Montgomery had the good grace to laugh, then saluted Langham with his glass. 'Well done, sir. Now, out with it. How on earth did you find the thing?'

He told Montgomery about Ralph's discovering the skeleton keys in the gatehouse.

'It would've been dashed hard to carry the four lengths of timber frame along the corridor without making a hell of a din and waking anyone, so I wondered if Verlinden decided against taking the painting from the room. Perhaps he concealed it in here?'

'In here?' Montgomery looked incredulous. 'But where?'

Langham pointed to the fireplace. 'Up the chimney.'

'You're having me on!'

'Scout's honour. That's where we found it, frame, canvas and all, hanging from a rope tied to the chimney stack on the roof.'

'But, dammit, Langham – I checked up there myself and didn't see a thing.'

'It was high up, concealed by a ledge. We had to get up on the roof, where we found the rope.' He described the discovery in detail.

'Well, I'll be . . .'

'Verlinden was up there on the Friday, no doubt attempting to retrieve his haul. He would have, if Lord Elsmere hadn't called him down.'

'And at some point on Saturday or Sunday, someone shot him dead.' Montgomery sampled his whisky. 'Question is, are the two connected? Did the theft, or rather the *concealment*, lead to his murder?'

'It's something we can't discount, Inspector.' Langham contemplated his drink. 'As to the theft, I did wonder if Esmeralda Bellamy might have had a hand in it.'

'Go on.'

'The look on her face when she walked in and saw the painting back on the chimney breast . . . She did her best to conceal her shock, but it was pretty evident. Also, some locals saw Esmeralda and Verlinden together in the Dog and Gun the day before the theft, talking conspiratorially. Thick as thieves, you might say.'

'Those two things, in themselves, don't conclusively prove she had anything to do with it, though.'

'That's true enough,' Langham conceded, 'but there's something else. Esmeralda's been up to her old tricks.'

Montgomery shot him a glance. 'Blackmail?'

'Rebecca Miles confided in me the other day. Apparently Esmeralda picked up the wrong end of the stick when she found a photograph in an old newspaper . . .' He recounted what Miles had told him about Esmeralda Bellamy's threat.

Montgomery stared up at the painting. 'Which is all very well,' he said at last, 'but does that link Esmeralda Bellamy with Verlinden and the theft?'

'After my conversation with Miss Miles, I buttonholed Esmeralda and confronted her with what Miles had told me. I said I suspected she was in on the theft, and that if she went to Elsmere with the story about Miss Miles, then I'd inform the police about my suspicions concerning her and Verlinden.'

'What did she say?'

'That's what I found very interesting. She denied it, of course, called my accusation slanderous. But she looked more than uneasy when I said that Elsmere, and the police, would be very interested in my theories. Then I told her that I'd keep quiet if she lay off Miss Miles.'

'And her response?'

Langham smiled. 'Again, angry denials, but her anger told

me I'd hit the nail on the head. I reckon she was the brains
behind the theft. She had the idea of concealing the painting,
and Verlinden had the wherewithal to carry it through.'

'So if Esmeralda and Verlinden were in it together . . .' He
looked at Langham. 'If you're right,' he went on, 'where does
this leave us as regards Verlinden's killing?'

'It makes you wonder . . .'

'Go on.'

'I'm speculating here – but what if Esmeralda, exhibiting the
greed she's shown in her previous blackmail attempts, decided
she'd rather not share the proceeds with Verlinden?'

'And bumped him off?'

Langham shrugged. 'It's a possible motive that needs looking
into. Also, she owns a shotgun.' He told Montgomery about the
weapon she used as an aid to her sculpting.

A tap sounded at the door and the bulky Halliday ducked
into the room. 'Sir, I've corralled everyone in the drawing room.'

Montgomery finished his whisky. 'Good man. Bring Esmeralda
Bellamy along for a little chat, Halliday, and have your notebook
ready.'

The detective sergeant saluted and left the room.

Langham said, 'Mind if I sit in on the interview?'

'After what you've fed me,' Montgomery said, 'I could hardly
tell you to scarper.'

Langham finished his whisky, replaced the glass on the sideboard, and took up an unobtrusive position leaning against the
chimney breast.

'How do you intend to play this, Inspector?'

Montgomery passed a hand over his balding head, arranging
the scant strands of dark hair. 'Steady as we go. Routine questions and see how she responds. I'll keep our suspicions to
myself. Might come in useful later.'

He pushed the settee back, rearranged an armchair so that it
was facing him, and resumed his seat.

In due course Halliday ushered Esmeralda Bellamy into
the library, the big woman having to duck to avoid hitting her
head on the lintel above the door. She advanced with a set
expression.

Montgomery indicated the armchair. 'If you'd care to take a seat, Miss Bellamy.'

She sat down with her brogues placed side by side and her big hands clasped on her tweed-clad lap. She flicked a glance at Langham, but her steely expression suggested nothing as to what she thought of his presence.

Before Montgomery could say anything, she asked, 'Is it true, Inspector, what old Cedric says – that Mr Verlinden has been shot dead?'

Seated on a dining chair behind the woman, Halliday wrote something in his notebook.

Montgomery nodded. 'I'm afraid it is true. Terrible business.'

She shook her head. 'Do you know if he took his own . . .? That is—'

The inspector interrupted. 'I'm afraid he was murdered, Miss Bellamy.'

She looked up at Langham, something like alarm in her eyes.

'I'm going to ask you a few routine questions,' Montgomery said, 'the same as I'll be asking all the other residents.'

She inclined her head to indicate that she understood.

'First of all, how long have you known the deceased?'

'He arrived here six months ago. Lord Elsmere took him on as an odd-job man and gave him the gatehouse to live in.'

'Did you know him well?'

'Hardly at all.'

'But you met him from time to time?'

She shrugged. 'In the course of daily business around the place, then yes.'

'You conversed with him.'

'We spoke.'

'And what did you make of Mr Verlinden?'

She shrugged, then asked, 'Can I smoke?' and when Montgomery gave his assent, lit a Pall Mall with a small mother-of-pearl lighter. Langham noticed that her hand was shaking.

'He was very quiet,' she replied. 'His English was good, but he was taciturn. I think he was very self-conscious about his injuries, his scarred face and limp.'

'Intelligent?'

'He was no fool. He was a pilot during the war, after all. Why do you ask?'

'I'm simply trying to build up a picture of the deceased,' Montgomery replied. 'How often did you speak with him, would you say?'

She shrugged. 'On a dozen occasions, perhaps.'

'Did you go for a drink with Mr Verlinden in the Dog and Gun?'

'We . . .' She hesitated, her eyes darting to Langham. 'I was in the public bar on one occasion, as far as I recall. He came in, and quite naturally we spoke.'

'About?'

'I'm afraid I can't remember.'

Montgomery slowly lit his own cigarette. 'Do you know if Mr Verlinden got on with the other residents of the manor?'

'I've no reason to believe that he didn't. You'd have to ask them about that.'

'Now . . . the theft of Lord Elsmere's painting.' The inspector pointed at the oil with his cigarette.

Esmeralda drew nervously on her cigarette. 'What of it?'

'I was wondering if you had any idea who might have taken it?'

She made a split-second calculation, then said, 'Really, I don't know why we're playing these silly games, Inspector.'

'Games?' Montgomery echoed, sitting back and regarding the woman through the smoke drifting up from his cigarette. 'And to what games might you be referring?'

'This charade,' she said with a passion missing from her previous demeanour. She nodded towards Langham. 'He thinks Verlinden and I were in cahoots and planned the theft between us. I've no doubt he's told you all about his little theory.' Her right hand, as she raised the cigarette to her mouth, was trembling.

Montgomery said, equably, 'And you would deny the charge?'

'Of course I bloody well would! I had nothing to do with the theft, or rather the painting's concealment. The idea . . .' She flashed Langham a venomous look. 'The very idea is preposterous.'

Montgomery smiled and sat back in his chair. 'Now, I understand that you own a shotgun?'

'That's correct.'

Montgomery drew on his cigarette. 'Where do you keep it?'

'It's in the barn—'

'Securely locked away?'

'I . . . Not at the moment, no.'

'So any Tom, Dick or Harry could have walked in and helped themselves?'

She shrugged. 'I suppose so.'

'And I understand that you keep the weapon to . . . let's get this right . . . to give texture to your sculptures?'

'That's correct.'

'Where do you keep the cartridges you use?'

'I don't. That is, I don't use that many, so I take what I need from Elsmere's gunroom.'

Montgomery nodded. 'You're a good shot? Do you hunt?'

'No, I don't. And the only things I've ever shot are my sculptures.'

He finished his cigarette and stabbed it out in a chunky glass ashtray balanced on the arm of the settee. 'Can you account for your movements from Friday the sixteenth to Sunday the eighteenth?'

She considered the glowing tip of her Pall Mall. 'On the Friday I was working on my latest sculpture all day. I didn't leave the place.'

'Not even for a walk in the woods?'

'Not even for a walk in the woods.'

'And on the Saturday?'

'I drove into Bury St Edmunds with Dudley at midday. We did a little shopping at the market and got back around five. And no, neither before going into town, nor after, did I take a walk in the woods.'

'And on the Sunday?'

She shrugged. 'I seem to recall that I woke late, pottered about my apartment, then worked in the afternoon.'

'And went nowhere near the woods?' Montgomery failed to hide a smirk.

'That's correct, Inspector.'

'Very well, Miss Bellamy. That will be all for now.'

'I can go?'

'On your way.'

She rose from the armchair with the air of someone mustering dignity, shot Langham an unpleasant look, and strode from the room.

Montgomery looked from Halliday to Langham. 'What did you make of that, gentlemen?'

'Hard as nails,' the detective sergeant said.

'I'm convinced she was lying about the theft,' Langham began.

'And the murder? Do you think she might have done it?'

Langham blew. 'I honestly don't know.'

'Right,' Montgomery said, nodding to Halliday. 'How about we have young Miss Miles in here?'

Halliday vacated his seat and left the library.

Montgomery said, 'I spoke to Miss Miles last week about the theft. Lovely girl. Bit of a looker, too.'

'I'll say.'

'This business about the resemblance between her and this released killer . . .?'

'Go on.'

'Nothing in it, do you think?'

'I assumed not at the time,' Langham said. 'But we'd be as well checking, just in case.'

The door opened and Rebecca Miles entered the room, smiling from Montgomery to Langham.

TWELVE

'I'm just going to ask you a few questions, Miss Miles. It's the routine we must go through in these situations.'

'I understand perfectly, Inspector.'

She sat upright in the armchair, leaning forward a little, her slim back arched. She wore a grey checked skirt and a thin navy-blue cardigan with a gold necklace glinting in the firelight. On her feet were the little fur-topped boots that Langham had found so fetching the other day.

He noticed that Halliday had shifted the position of his armchair so that the woman could see him, and she gave him a small smile as he took up his notebook.

Montgomery said, 'Could you tell me how long you've been resident here, Miss Miles?'

'A little over three months.'

'Would you mind telling me why you came to live here? It is an out-of-the-way place, after all.'

'That's exactly what I was looking for. My father had passed away a month or so previously – I nursed him during his final illness – and I wanted to get away from London. The sale of the family home, and a small inheritance from my father, meant that I could live well within my means if I found somewhere not too expensive. Neston Manor fitted the bill perfectly.'

'How did you find out about the room?'

'I was staying in Bury St Edmunds for a weekend when I saw Lord Elsmere's advertisement in a local paper.'

'And you're settled here?'

'Very.'

'I understand you're a writer?'

She blushed becomingly and stared down at her fingers. 'I wouldn't call myself that, until I'm published, Inspector – if ever I am. At the moment I'm writing a rather poor novel, I fear.'

Montgomery lit another cigarette, waved out the match, and asked, 'And your fellow residents? How do you get on with them?'

'Very well, in general. Lord Elsmere is kindness itself. And Major Rutherford is altogether sweet. Dudley is personable, if a little distant.'

'Did you ever have much to do with Patrick Verlinden?'

'Very little. He once asked me out for a drink at the Dog and Gun.'

'And you accepted?'

'I thought it might be seen as rude not to.'

'And how did it go?'

Miss Miles shrugged her slim shoulders. 'Patrick was some-what tongue-tied and shy. We had very little in common, it transpired. He tended to avoid me, after that. He was of a practical mind-set – he liked fixing things – and I am more inclined to the arts.' She gave a small laugh. 'I do hope that doesn't sound pretentious.'

'Not at all,' Montgomery murmured. 'Now, the theft of his lordship's painting . . . I recall from my notes, when I interviewed you over a week ago, that you had no idea who might be responsible, though you did wonder if it was one of your fellow residents.'

'That's correct, yes. Lord Elsmere keeps the house very secure. It's one thing I noticed on moving in. All the doors have the latest locks fitted, and the same is true of the main entrance.' She shrugged. 'I could see no way a burglar might have entered from outside and stolen the painting.'

'At the time you wouldn't venture just which one of the residents might have been responsible—'

'That's because I had no idea who might have done such a thing.'

'And have things changed in the interim to suggest a culprit to you?'

A frown buckled the perfection of her forehead. 'Lord Elsmere informed the major and me that the painting had been discovered, by Mr Langham and his partner, concealed in the chimney breast. It did occur to me if Verlinden might have been behind the theft, as he's the only person with any reason to be up on the roof. He's called upon to repair leaks from time to time.'

Montgomery smiled. 'Quite the detective, Miss Miles. I'll see if there's a vacancy on the force.'

The young woman blushed again and regarded her fingers. 'Also, the fact that he went missing shortly after the theft is suspicious.'

Montgomery nodded. 'It certainly is. Now . . .' He consulted his notebook. 'Did you happen to see Mr Verlinden around the place on the Friday, Saturday or Sunday, Miss Miles?'

'On Saturday afternoon I saw him leave the gatehouse and walk past the east wing towards the woods. I assumed he was going down to the Dog and Gun, where he spent much of his time.'

'Can you recall if he was accompanied by anyone?'

'No, he was alone.'

'And did you happen to see if anyone followed him, or if anyone else was outside at the time?'

She shook her head. 'No, I saw only Verlinden.'

'Do you recall what time this was?'

'I'd just switched on the wireless to listen to the four o'clock news. I was making myself a cup of tea when I looked through the window and saw him. So it must have been just before four.'

'I don't suppose you heard gunshots not long after that?'

She made a moue of her lips and shook her head. 'I'm sorry, no. I had the wireless on rather loud, you see.'

'Quite.' Montgomery gently broke a length of ash from his cigarette into the ashtray. 'Now, you having been here three months . . .'

'Yes?'

'I was wondering if, in that time, being an aspiring novelist and no doubt having observed the characters of your fellow residents, you've noticed any . . . animosity, let's say, between them and the deceased?'

'Not at all. Mr Verlinden had very little to do with the other residents. He kept himself to himself.'

Montgomery nodded, sucked the last scintilla of nicotine from the tab-end of his cigarette, then stabbed it out in the ashtray. 'I noticed, in answer to my earlier question about how you got on with your fellow residents, that you omitted mention of Esmeralda Bellamy.'

He watched Miss Miles carefully.

She glanced up at Langham, considered her words, then said, 'As a matter of fact, Esmeralda tried to extort money from me. Fifty pounds. You see, she mistakenly thought I resembled someone . . .' She went on to explain the situation.

'How did you respond to her demand?'

'I said I needed time to raise the money.'

Montgomery took his time over lighting another cigarette. 'I hope you don't mind me observing that something strikes me as a little odd.'

'Odd?'

'When Miss Bellamy threatened you, why didn't you simply tell her – and pardon my phraseology – to go to hell?'

The young woman sighed. 'I suppose it does seem strange, doesn't it? But you see, I didn't want the seeds of doubt sown in the minds of the people I've come to know here – Lord Elsmere and the major, and my friends in the village. The resemblance between me and the woman is remarkable, I admit, and I knew that if Esmeralda let it be known . . . then tongues would wag. And I really didn't want that. I hope you can see the situation from my point of view?'

'Quite,' Montgomery said. 'And I hope that you see why I must ask these seemingly intrusive questions. Now, just one more thing: do you happen to know if Patrick Verlinden and Esmeralda Bellamy were on speaking terms?'

She gave a tinkling laugh. 'Forgive me, I shouldn't laugh. But the phrase, "speaking terms" . . .' She looked from the inspector to Langham and back again. 'Why, I had the impression they were lovers.'

Montgomery appeared surprised. 'What made you think this?'

'I saw them in each other's company quite often, and they always seemed secretive, furtive.' She hesitated, then went on. 'To be honest, considering her behaviour, I don't understand what Dudley sees in her – she leads him a merry dance and treats him appallingly.'

'Do you know if Dudley was aware that his fiancée and Verlinden were . . .?'

'He must have been blind if he wasn't.'

Montgomery nodded. 'I think that will be all for the moment, Miss Miles. Thank you for your time.'

She smiled at him, then at Langham and Halliday, rose gracefully and left the room.

'Do you think,' Montgomery said as the door closed behind her, 'that what she said about Esmeralda and Verlinden was just her being catty and getting even?'

'I'm not so sure about that,' Langham said. 'I've heard rumours about Esmeralda's inclination in that department. But as for Verlinden and Esmeralda being involved romantically . . . Perhaps they were planning the theft, and Miss Miles got hold of the wrong end of the stick?'

'That's a possibility,' the inspector said. 'I wonder what

anyone sees in Esmeralda Bellamy? As far as I'm concerned she's about as attractive as a bag of sprats.'

'Perhaps it's her forceful personality,' Langham said. 'I've heard that some men like to be . . . subjugated, I think the word is.'

Montgomery laughed. 'Enough of the amateur psychology,' he said. 'Right, Halliday, go and fetch Dudley Mariner, will you?'

Mariner entered the room, looking nervous and rubbing his cheek as if he were suffering from toothache. He nodded at the three men and took the armchair before Montgomery.

The inspector went through his reassuring spiel about routine questions, then said, 'Can you account for your movements from Friday the sixteenth of this month to Sunday the eighteenth?'

Mariner replied that he'd spent the Friday supervising various work around the farm until well after five. On Saturday he'd driven into Bury St Edmunds with Esmeralda.

'And what time did you return?'

'Five-ish? Around then, anyway.'

'And Sunday?'

'I got up late and had breakfast around eleven. I spent the rest of the morning reading the papers. The afternoon? Esmeralda was working in the barn, so I must have taken her a cup of tea at some point and stayed for a chat. In fact, I seem to recall I did just that.'

'And when was the last time you saw Patrick Verlinden?'

Mariner stroked his cheek. 'Must've been the Friday afternoon, when Pater called him down from the roof.'

'Are you sure you didn't see him after that?'

'Pretty certain, to be honest.'

'Do you know if any of the residents might have harboured a grudge, a resentment, against Verlinden? Disliked him in any way?'

Mariner thought about it and shook his head. 'Can't imagine anyone taking against him. He was a quiet enough chap. Pretty nondescript, for all his pilot-hero stuff and war wounds. Snake in the grass, he turned out to be, though.'

'You didn't suspect that it was Verlinden who'd stolen your father's painting?'

'Far from it. I assumed it was an outside job. Wasn't till Langham here did his stuff that the penny dropped. I assume Verlinden resented my father for what he thought of as his wealth and decided to help himself to a bit of it.'

'How was your own relationship with Patrick Verlinden?'

'Can't say that I had a *relationship*, as such. He worked for my father around the place, so I found myself giving him the occasional job on the farm.' He shrugged. 'He was competent enough, didn't complain and got the job done. We didn't socialize, as such.'

'Now, your fiancée . . . How did Esmeralda get on with Verlinden?'

Mariner frowned. 'Didn't have much to do with the chap. Only time she spoke of him was when he rolled home drunk one night and lost the key to the gatehouse – came hammering on the manor door. Esmeralda called him a drunkard, as far as I recall.'

'And your relationship with Esmeralda?'

Mariner blinked. 'We're engaged to be married.'

'And was it love at first sight?'

The young man looked uncomfortable. 'Well, certainly attraction. I know she isn't every man's idea of beauty – and I've heard the rumours.'

'Rumours?'

He sighed. 'Down at the Dog. Someone buttonholed me a while back and claimed that Esmeralda was seeing a chap up St Edmunds way. I brought it up with the old girl and she assured me it was nothing but a tissue of lies.'

'And you were happy with that?'

Mariner smiled, and Langham's sympathy for the chap went up a notch or two. 'Esmeralda wouldn't do anything like that. She loves me, though sometimes she has a dashed odd way of showing it. You see, she knows she's on to a good thing here. Rooms at a peppercorn rent, and when we're eventually married a stable enough living, even though I won't come into a fortune like the scion of some of the landed gentry.'

'Ah, yes,' Montgomery said, 'I understand that your father's in the process of doing a deal with a firm of property speculators . . . How do you feel about that?'

'Pater found himself caught between a rock and a hard place, Inspector. I'm thoroughly behind his decision.'

'And Esmeralda?'

'I think she sees the sense in it, too.'

'She wasn't disappointed that the man she's going to marry wouldn't be inheriting a fortune?'

Mariner laughed uneasily. 'I'd like to think not, Inspector.'

The young man caught Langham's eye and smiled, and Langham found himself nodding with what he hoped was convincing agreement.

Montgomery said, 'Thank you, Mr Mariner. That'll be all for the time being.'

'Not at all. It's been my pleasure.'

When Mariner had left the library, Montgomery said, 'Any thoughts?'

Langham sighed. 'I just wonder how anyone can be so dashed blind . . .'

'I wonder,' Halliday began, and both men looked at him.

'Go on,' Montgomery said.

'I don't know . . . It just struck me that perhaps he's not as daft as he appears. What if he does know his fiancée's been playing the field – having a bit of how's your father with this Verlinden chappie? Mariner finds out, takes the shotgun, and lets him have it.'

'I suppose that can't be ruled out,' Langham said. 'Even though Miss Miles last saw Verlinden on Saturday afternoon, and Mariner and Esmeralda were in town at the time, it isn't written in stone that Verlinden died on Saturday. He might have been killed on the Sunday at some point.'

'We'll have a better idea of just when he bought it when the surgeon's done his stuff.' Montgomery looked at his watch. 'Four thirty. Let's get this over with, shall we? Get old Rutherford in here, followed by his lordship, then I can toddle off home and get some tea.'

Halliday left the room and returned with the major.

THIRTEEN

Major Rutherford shuffled into the room, clutching a glass of whisky, and sank into the armchair across from Montgomery. 'Terrible business, what?' he wheezed. 'Bad luck to be shot in peacetime. I can understand it in battle, but when you're minding your own business on the way to the pub . . .'

He lifted his glass with a palsied hand and took a long drink. If he wondered at the presence of an Ealing Studio's location scout at the interrogation, he gave no sign; Langham thought the old man was probably too sozzled to note the fact.

'Young Mr Verlinden,' the major murmured, shaking his head, 'shot three times, according to Teddy. Who could've done such a thing?'

'That's what we're here to ascertain, Major. I'd like to ask you a few routine questions, if I may?'

'Fire away, young man.'

'First off, what did you make of Patrick Verlinden?'

Major Rutherford peered at the policeman. 'Must admit, didn't have much to do with the chap. He was on the quiet side, nodded once or twice but kept quiet most of the time, knew his place. He fought the Nazis in the war, so there's that to his credit.'

'Do you know how he got on with the rest of the residents?'

'Can't say as I do. Saw him once or twice hobnobbing with that awful Esmeralda woman. Can't see what Dudley sees in her, if you ask me,' he said, going off at a tangent. 'Hasn't a good word to say to anyone – she's only here by the good grace of his lordship, and because she's getting herself hitched to Dudley.'

'Quite,' Montgomery said. 'But back to Patrick Verlinden. When was the last time you saw him?'

The old man screwed his eyes half shut. 'Now that's a poser,

sir! Let me think . . . Yes, I have it. The day after Teddy's daub
– that one there,' he said, raising his glass to the chimney breast,
'the day after that was nabbed. Teddy sent him along to fix a
leak in my kitchen. Burst pipe. Chap had it done in a jiffy.
Offered him a drink, I remember, but he declined.'

'That was the Friday, and you didn't see him again after
that?'

'That's right, but there's nothing unusual in that. Often didn't
see the fellah from one week to the next.'

Montgomery lit a cigarette. 'What do you make of your
fellow residents, Major?'

'What do I make of 'em?' he growled. 'Told you what I think
of that Esmeralda woman. Hard-faced, uncharitable harridan,
she leads young Dudley a merry dance.'

'A merry dance . . . In what way?'

'I might not get out much, but I notice things, Inspector.
Esmeralda's a flighty piece. Heard rumours and seen her driving
off to meet her fella.'

'A lover?'

'So I've heard. Can't recall his name. Some bigwig on the
Bury St Edmunds town council, so I've heard.'

'And Rebecca Miles?'

At the sound of her name, Major Rutherford's pale blue
eyes seemed to melt. 'Ah, Miss Miles. Now there's a gal. If
only I were fifty years younger . . . beauty *and* brains. The
perfect package. And kind, too.'

'Do you know if she had any dealings with Mr Verlinden?'

'Dealings? What do you mean, "dealings"?'

'Was she friendly with him, would you say?'

'She once told me she found him remote, that's the word.
But she wouldn't say anything against the chap, not Miss Miles.
Never a bad word to say about anyone, that gal. Brightened my
life up no end when she moved in.'

'How long have you been resident here, Major?'

'Coming up to five years this January. Bit of a life saver, I'll
tell you that.'

'In what way?'

'Between you and me, I was a bit down on me uppers. A bit
of bad luck with some shares. I was living at me club at the

time, the Carstairs just off the Strand. Been there since the end
of the war, but the living wasn't cheap. I had to have most of
me things put into storage, all the volumes of me memoirs, me
books. And then me stocks and shares went pear-shaped and I
found meself facing the poorhouse. Awful prospect. It wasn't
the Carstairs I'd miss so much, but me friends there, y'see. Fat
Boothby and one or two others.'

'What happened?'

'Old Teddy stepped into the breach. Offered me a place up
here. Said he was converting a few rooms, and how would
I like me own? Plenty of room for me journals and books. I
jumped at the chance, almost bit his ruddy hand off! That was
back in 'fifty-one, and I've been here ever since.'

'I take it that you and Lord Elsmere go back a fair bit?'

'I'll say! Met in the Great War, 1915 it'd be. He served under
me in the Lancers. We hit it off from the very start. Fine fellah,
Teddy. And brave. Doesn't mention his Military Cross, does
he? Not the type to shoot off at the mouth. But he stormed a
Hun machine-gun post single-handed at Ypres and saved the
life of half a dozen Tommies in the process. That's the kind of
stuff he's made of, Inspector. Salt of the earth.'

He took another mouthful of whisky and soda and went on
reflectively, 'Deserves a better hand than what Fate's dealt him,
and that's a fact.'

'Ah, his wife and eldest son . . .'

'And before that, his first wife.'

Montgomery looked up from his notes. 'I didn't know he'd
been married twice.'

'Got hitched back in the early twenties. Gloria Heaton, her
name – daughter of the Norfolk Heatons. I was happy for him,
at the time. Match made in heaven, or so I thought. And young
Teddy was taken with the woman, I'll tell you that.'

'What happened?'

'Gloria turned out to be less than glorious. Two years into
the marriage, the woman met an American millionaire –
Samuel Dowling, his name was – and off she goes, ups sticks
and takes herself and her young son off to Paris. Teddy was
distraught. Well, y'would be, wouldn't you, if some floozy
absconds with your son and heir? Hit the bottle. I was there

for him, mind, but there wasn't much I could do in the circumstances.'

Montgomery leaned forward. 'But I thought . . . I understood that Mariner was his lordship's only remaining son, and stood to inherit the title and this place?'

Major Rutherford was shaking his head. 'Apparently – and I don't know the details, as Teddy never speaks of it, which is understandable – Gloria and the son were killed during the war. So Mariner *is* the sole heir of Teddy's somewhat diminished estate.'

'I see,' Montgomery said. 'So the poor chap's had a hard time of it, all in all.'

'I'll say. Bad enough that old Vera, his second wife, passed on as she did . . . but then Jeremy was killed in a bloody stupid accident. I'd just moved in here when it happened. Hell of a shock all round. But I'll give Teddy this, it could've been the ruin of a lesser chap, tragedy piled on tragedy. But he's not one to give in to self-pity. Grieved like a man and got on with it.'

Montgomery stubbed out his cigarette. 'Thank you for that, Major. You've been very informative.'

'Any time, Inspector. Any time.'

'Halliday, be a good chap and see the major back to the drawing room, and if you could ask his lordship if he'd care to join us . . .'

Halliday assisted the old soldier from the room and Langham warmed himself before the fire.

'What a life!' Montgomery said. 'Some people get dealt a dud hand, and no mistake. Little wonder he looks like an undertaker most of the time.' He laughed. 'And added to that, his remaining son is hitched to a money-grubbing floozy.'

Presently the door opened and Halliday stepped aside for Lord Elsmere to enter.

'I'm sorry to have to trouble you with this, your lordship,' Montgomery said as Elsmere settled himself in the armchair. 'Just a few questions to establish the facts, then we'll be on our way.'

'Whatever it takes to clear up this dreadful business, Inspector.

But first, would you mind awfully pouring me a drink?' He pointed to a bottle on the sideboard, and Halliday leapt to it.

Drink in hand, Elsmere turned his lugubrious face to Montgomery.

'You mentioned, back in the woods, sir, that the last time you saw Patrick Verlinden was on Friday the sixteenth, around four o'clock. You asked him to fix a leak in the major's room.'

'That's right, yes.'

'And you're absolutely sure that you didn't see him after this date?'

'Absolutely. He usually works on Saturday mornings, but as I'd asked him to do this extra job when it was knocking-off time, I told him to take the morning off.'

'Do you know if he was on bad terms with anyone in the village?'

'Y'mean, someone who would've wanted to shoot him dead?' Elsmere shook his head. 'I can't imagine young Patrick offending anyone. Meek as a mouse. Liked his pint down at the Dog and Gun, got on with his work here . . .'

Montgomery hesitated. 'Now, regarding the theft of your painting . . .'

At this, Elsmere smiled. 'The painting which young Langham here so ably recovered,' he said, a challenging twinkle in his eye as he regarded the inspector.

'Quite,' Montgomery said.

'Well, it looks as though it were Verlinden, what? Skeleton keys found in his room, and he was up on the roof after the theft.'

Montgomery nodded, taking a long draw on his cigarette. 'Do you think that the theft of the painting and Verlinden's death might be linked?'

'I gave this due consideration,' Elsmere replied, 'and it did occur to me that it might be connected.' He smiled, ironically. 'But I am not a detective, Inspector. I shall leave that in your capable hands.'

Montgomery returned the smile. 'Moving on . . . Now I understand that Dudley is your sole heir?'

'That's correct.'

'But you had – and I hope you don't think it indelicate of

me to mention – you had a son with your first wife, back in the twenties?'

Elsmere smiled. 'The major mentioned that, did he? The old chap does let the drink run away with his tongue. But yes, Inspector, you're correct. I had a son and heir in James Edward.'

'And I believe both he and your first wife passed away in Paris during the war.'

Elsmere inclined his head. 'That is so, though I only heard about it in 'forty-six, and though I've attempted to ascertain the details, they seem pretty thin on the ground. Apparently they were killed in an air raid on Paris in 'forty-four.'

'I'm sorry.'

'To be perfectly honest, Inspector, the passage of time served to numb me somewhat to the shock of the news. It'd been over twenty years since my wife ran off, though I did consider my son from time to time. I would have liked to meet him at some point, but since there was no contact between Gloria and myself, I didn't dwell on the matter. So when I heard, belatedly, of their deaths . . .' He shook his head and took a draught of whisky.

Montgomery thanked him for his time. 'I'll have a constable stationed here tonight, your lordship, and my team and I will be around the place over the course of the next few days. We'll be doing our level best to get this business wrapped up just as soon as possible.'

Elsmere inclined his head. 'I would appreciate that, Inspector.'

He rose slowly to his feet and limped from the room.

Montgomery sighed and moved to the fire, warming his hands. 'If you'd transcribe all that, Halliday, and get it on my desk by morning, there's a good chap. Oh, I take it you questioned the butler?'

'That's right, sir,' Halliday said, referring to his notebook. 'Benson was away from the manor on Saturday, visiting his sister in Newmarket, and he didn't get back till well after nine. He was here all Sunday.'

Montgomery nodded and looked at Langham. 'What are your plans? Sticking around for a day or two?'

'I'll have to consult with my better half,' Langham said. 'We're staying with a friend in the area, and I had planned to push off in the morning. But this has thrown a spanner in the works.'

'If you do stay put and learn anything, you know where to find me. Right,' he went on, 'I'll have a quick word with the surgeon then get off.'

Montgomery and Halliday left the library, and Langham made his way through the house to the drawing room.

Maria and Charles stood with their backs to the blazing fire, smiling at something Major Rutherford was telling them. They'd been joined by Albert. Tall and raw-boned in a tight-fitting grey suit, he looked like a young soldier in mufti with his short-back-and-sides and upright stance, the sherry glass in his big right hand reduced to the size of a thimble.

Of Mariner, Esmeralda and Rebecca there was no sign. At the far end of the long room, Lord Elsmere was conferring with the butler.

Langham took Maria's hand. 'I'm sorry about that, rather left you hanging. It all took longer than I thought.'

'Don't be so silly, darling. The major's been entertaining us with his war stories.'

'And risqué some of them were, too.' Charles laughed.

'And there's plenty more where those came from!' the major wheezed.

Maria turned to Langham. 'How did it go?' she murmured.

'I'll give you all the gen over dinner.'

'I thought I'd better come up here,' Albert said, 'before I got too drunk to drive, and then when I get here, Mr Mariner insists I come in and have a sherry. Can't say I care for the stuff,' he added. In a quiet aside to Langham, he went on, 'Word of the shooting has got back to the regulars in the Dog, Donald. Old Cedric staggered in an hour ago, and now he's the most popular man in the village. Oh, one thing. I overheard some chap talking about seeing someone in the woods on the Saturday afternoon a week back. I didn't catch all of it, but I thought you'd better know.'

'That's interesting. Saturday afternoon is when Verlinden might have . . .' He paused. 'I wonder if I should pop in and have a word?'

'The bloke doing the talking was a big, bald-headed chap.

A farmer. He was in his tractor when he "saw someone", he said.'

Maria said, 'Are you disappearing again?'

'I won't be long. Fifteen minutes, if that.'

'Tell you what,' Albert said to Maria. 'I could take you and Charles home and come back for Donald later. It's only three miles to Meadford. Would that be all right, guv?' Albert asked Charles.

'Of course, if Donald is agreeable to being left in a draughty village pub for half an hour,' Charles said with a wink at Langham.

'I think I might survive.'

Lord Elsmere crossed the room, drink in hand, and touched Langham's elbow. 'A quiet word, Langham, if I may.'

'By all means.'

He drew Langham to one side. 'I've been giving this a bit of thought and I've come to the conclusion that, considering what a foul-up the local constabulary made of finding the painting, I have little faith in Montgomery and his men in nabbing the killer any time soon. I was wondering . . . You and Ryland seem pretty sound chaps, and I like the way you recovered the painting – put the inspector's nose out, and no mistake. Now I have a proposition: I'd like to hire you to look into this business, find out who the ruddy hell did for Verlinden, and I'll make it worth your while. What do you say?'

'Well . . . I'm gratified by your confidence. I think Ralph would be agreeable.'

'That's settled, then. Now, I was thinking of going to lie down for an hour before dinner. I don't suppose your party'd care to stay on and dine with me?'

'I think the plan was to push off and have dinner at Charles's.'

'Absolutely fine. I'll see you around the place, Langham; keep me updated, what?'

'Will do.'

Elsmere crossed to the little group beside the fire and said his goodbyes. When he'd departed, Langham joined Maria and the others, wincing.

'Bad news, my boy?' Charles said.

'Lord Elsmere's asked me and Ralph to investigate the case.

Thing is,' he went on, pulling a face at Maria, 'we were due to get back to London in the morning . . .'

'But I have the obvious solution,' Charles said, beaming at them. 'You and Maria shall stay on for another day or two, and while you and Ralph play at detectives, I shall go a-house-hunting with Maria. What could be more perfect, my dear?'

'But what about . . .?' Maria began.

'Molly has the keys to the agency,' Charles interjected. 'She can open up in the morning and man the barricades until we return.'

'If it's all right with you, Charles,' Maria said.

'All right? It's perfectly splendid!'

'Drink up, then,' Albert said. 'I'll drop you at the Dog on the way, Donald, and come back for you in half an hour.'

They finished their sherries, said goodbye to Major Rutherford, and took their leave.

Langham climbed from the Daimler and watched its tail lights disappear into the darkness.

The sun had long since set and the stars were incandescent overhead. He paused beneath the creaking sign of the Dog and Gun and stared up at the sweep of the Milky Way: that was something he rarely saw in London, the massed stars, or the twinkling beacon of Venus just above the treetops to the south-east.

An icy wind was blowing in from the north-east, across the fens, and he shivered and pushed through the door into the snug.

Half a dozen regulars sat over their beers in the tiny room. A wireless played dance band music, turned low, and a fire blazed in the grate. Conversation abated temporarily as he ordered a pint of bitter; then it resumed at a lower, more circumspect volume. That was another thing he'd have to get used to in the country, he thought: the suspicion of outsiders.

He hitched himself on to a high stool along the bar from a hefty, bald-headed man he took to be the farmer Albert had mentioned. He was speaking in lowered tones to three other men, pint mugs in hand.

'Nasty do to happen in Neston,' the farmer was saying. 'Still, what you expect wi' foreigners about the place?'

'According to old Cedric,' a thin-faced character piped up, 'there weren't much of him left. Shot a dozen times, he was.'

Langham took a draft of ale, wiped his top lip, and said, 'Three times, actually.'

The effect of his words was startling. An immediate silence settled over the room – and on the wireless even Edmundo Ros's *Nightingale* segued into a diminuendo.

The quartet of locals at the bar turned and stared at him, and two drinkers at a table beside the fire lowered their pints in anticipation of yet more entertainment.

'And how would you know, *actually*,' the bald-headed farmer said, laying sarcastic stress on the last word.

Casually, Langham slipped a hand into his jacket and came out with his agency accreditation, which he showed to the four. 'Langham. I'm working on the case for Lord Elsmere.'

'Well, I'll be . . .' the farmer began. 'You'll be having a drink, sir?'

'These are on me,' Langham said, sliding a ten-shilling note across the bar to the overweight landlord. 'Six pints, and whatever you're drinking.'

'That's most kind of you, sir. I'll have a half of mild.'

Pints in hand, the locals stared at Langham; even the pair at the table had sidled up to the bar.

'Old Cedric said he'd been shot a dozen times,' the farmer said, 'as if a machine gun'd done for him.'

Langham smiled. 'He was exaggerating, but it wasn't a pretty sight.'

'But it were the Dutch chap, right?' the farmer asked.

'That's right, Patrick Verlinden. Did you know him?'

'Not that well,' the ferret-faced fellow said. 'No one could rightly say they knew him well, for all he was in here most nights. Drank by 'isself, he did. Had his pints then off he went. Hardly spoke to no one, that's right, ain't it?'

The others assented to the truth of this.

'Do you know if Verlinden was here on the night of Saturday the seventeenth?'

Ferret Face nudged the farmer. 'What'd I say, Lionel?' He looked at Langham. 'We all wondered where he was when he didn't turn up. See, he might miss a day or two during the week, but he was in here every Saturday night regular as clockwork.'

'That's right,' Lionel said. 'Regular as clockwork.'

A red-faced local said, 'So you reckon that's when he was shot dead, right? That Saturday night?'

Langham took a couple of inches from his pint. 'It's certainly a possibility. What I need to know is, did anyone see anything that Saturday? Anything at all suspicious?'

'Funny you should ask that, Mr Langham,' Ferret Face said. 'Lionel, you said you saw someone in the woods that night, didn't you?'

The bald-headed man nodded. 'That's right, only it weren't rightly the night. Late afternoon, more like.'

'Do you know what time exactly?'

'I were in the top field, harvesting the beet. I were about to call it a day, so it'd be knocking on, getting darkish, say four.'

'What did you see?'

'Not much – someone in the woods near the big house. Only they weren't coming along the path like you'd do if you were walking into the village, see? They were a little way off the path, moving back and forth. Strange, I thought. Looked like they were searching for something.'

'Searching?'

'Well, scratching around in the undergrowth.'

'Did you see who it might have been?'

Lionel pulled a face. 'It were getting on dusk and I was half a field away, and to be honest I didn't pay it much notice.'

'Any idea if it was a man or a woman?'

'At the time I assumed it was a bloke, but to be honest, what with dark setting in, I couldn't be too sure.'

'And did you hear any gunshots, at all? Three gunshots?'

'I didn't, but then I wouldn't, would I, on account of the tractor engine.'

'That's very interesting, thank you. You don't mind if I pass your name on to the investigating officer?'

This could go one of two ways, Langham thought: if Lionel were one of those people with an innate suspicion of the police . . .

But he needn't have worried. The farmer puffed out his chest and said, 'Don't mind at all. Lionel Chivers, High Wood Farm. But tell the chap he'll find me in here most nights.'

'Thanks, I'll do that.' Langham drained his pint and bought another round.

'This Verlinden chappie . . . Did he have any enemies in the village, get into any scraps with locals, anything like that?'

'Not Verlinden, no, sir,' said the red-faced man. 'Quiet as a church mouse.'

'Do you know how he got on with his fellow residents up at the manor?'

Ferret Face sniggered.

'What?' Langham asked.

Lionel said, 'Well, Mr Langham, we know how he got on with *one* of the residents.'

Langham sipped his pint. 'And who might that have been?'

'He were knocking off young Dudley's missus-to-be, he was. That Esmeralda woman. Seen 'em in here, whisperin' sweet nothings. I was surprised she'd look twice at a bloke like that, what with his scar and his limp. She usually goes for more toffee-nosed types.'

'So you could say she's liberal with her favours?'

'Aye, you could say that,' Lionel said, 'or you could say she's a damned whore.'

'Steady, Lionel,' Ferret Face said. 'You talking about 'is lordship's future daughter-in-law, you are.'

Lionel mimed spitting. 'You know no one respects his lordship more than I do, but his son deserves better than that flighty piece.'

'So . . . who else has she been seeing?' Langham asked.

'Don't rightly know his name,' Lionel said. 'Some big-wig from Bury way, I heard.'

Langham looked around the group. 'Does anyone know who he is?'

His question was met with frowns and a round of negatives.

'Poor Dudley is who I feel sorry for,' the red-faced man said. 'Here, you don't think it were Dudley shot Verlinden, do you? Getting his revenge on Dutchy for seeing his woman?'

Lionel laughed. 'There'll be a lot more shootings around here if it was Dudley,' he said.

Langham looked at his watch. It was forty minutes since he'd entered the Dog and Gun; Albert would be waiting.

He drank up and slipped another ten-shilling note across the bar. 'Have a few more on me,' he said, and took his leave to a chorus of thanks.

In the warmth of the Daimler, wending their way through the darkened country lanes, Albert asked, 'Hear anything useful?'

'I'll say,' Langham said, and gave Albert the run down.

'And I was wondering,' he went on, 'if you could do something for me? How often do you frequent the Dog and Gun?'

'Couple of times a week, sometimes more. Depends if I'm passing. Why?'

'I wonder if you could pop in a bit more often, keep your ear to the ground? Specifically, I'd like to know the name of the big-wig, a fellow from Bury St Edmunds, who Esmeralda Bellamy was seeing – and might still be seeing, for all I know. And anything else you can glean about the residents of the manor. Think you can do that, Albert?'

Gripping the wheel, the young man nodded. 'You can rely on me, Donald.'

That evening, before dinner, Langham got through to the police station at Bury St Edmunds and left a message for Inspector Montgomery concerning Patrick Verlinden's non-appearance at the Dog and Gun on the night of the seventeenth.

Then he rang Ralph at home.

'Don, what's this in aid of on a Sunday night?'

'Would you believe murder?'

'Blow me down! What the ruddy hell . . .?'

For the next ten minutes Langham told Ralph about the discovery of Patrick Verlinden's corpse and finished by recounting Lord Elsmere's request for them to investigate the killing. He arranged to meet Ralph at Neston Manor at eleven o'clock the following morning.

'I'll be there, Don. Good work.'

'See you tomorrow,' Langham said.

He left the library and joined Maria, Charles and Albert for dinner.

FOURTEEN

From the journal of Major William Arthur Rutherford.

A few days after my contretemps with Patrick Verlinden, something unpleasant occurred at the manor. Teddy was quite beside himself, and the rest of us were in something of a flap, too . . . But I get ahead of myself.

I was expecting another visit from Verlinden on Tuesday or Wednesday, but to my relief there was no sign of the young man. I say 'to my relief', but in a way I wanted to know what he might have been planning. This not knowing, this 'limbo of uncertainty' as they say in bad thrillers, is making me nervous.

Last Thursday I completed my usual perambulations without seeing a soul, and was about to retire to my rooms to read Wellard's life of General Patten when I came across Benson in the entrance hall. He'd just got off the telephone and looked drip-white: Miss Miles was there too, standing against the wall with a hand to her mouth. I thought someone had fallen ill, and my immediate thought was that Teddy had taken badly in the night. Benson reassured me on that point, however. He said that he had been just about to summon me. 'His Lordship requires your presence in the library, Major Rutherford.'

Wondering what the deuce all the kerfuffle was about, I limped along the corridor to the library, knocked and entered.

Teddy was sitting before the hearth, holding his head in his hands. He said nothing, but indicated the bare chimney breast, and the gesture was eloquent enough.

Teddy's treasured Gainsborough was gone.

There was nothing much I could say to console my old friend, but I reassured him that the police would sort the whole thing out.

They arrived an hour later, led by a small, bald-headed, bustling inspector in a sharp suit, and I didn't know whether he reminded me of a spiv or a bookmaker's runner.

Detective Inspector Montgomery and his deputy Halliday questioned Teddy in the library, and then came along to our respective rooms and gave us the third degree.

Apparently the painting had been taken at some point during the night, but as there was no sign of a break in, suspicion was falling on the residents of the manor.

Later that afternoon, as the day was drawing in and I was contemplating making myself something to eat, I heard a tap at the door. This is it, I thought to myself, Patrick Verlinden come to antagonize me further.

To my delight, it was not Verlinden but Miss Miles.

She'd come to tell me that Teddy had invited everyone to join him for dinner in the great hall that evening. That cheered me up no end. I hadn't fancied dining alone, after what had happened, and I didn't like the thought of Teddy eating all by himself upstairs in his rooms, either. We'd break bread together this evening; a trouble shared, et cetera . . .

I prevailed upon Miss Miles to stay a while and share a little sherry. She's a sweet child and caring. I understand that her father died just before she came here. My heart goes out to her. She's the daughter I would have liked to have had.

Oddly enough, conversation got round to my long life and the fact that I'd never married. Perhaps I was feeling sorry for myself, and maudlin, what with the worry of the Verlinden business and then the theft of Teddy's picture. I told Miss Miles that I'd been wedded to my regiment, and that in my humble opinion army life had precluded marriage. 'Not fair, if you ask me, dragging a member of the fairer sex hither and yon from pillar to post around the Empire.' Apart from which, I'd never met the right woman, not that I mentioned this to Miss Miles.

She left to dress for dinner and returned for me at a little before seven. My gout was playing up, and when she saw me limp to the door, she suggested I avail myself of my 'buggy', as I call it. Not long after I'd arrived at the manor, five years ago, I had a pretty bad fall and broke my ankle, and Teddy dug out an old bath chair that had belonged to some Victorian ancestor and insisted I take it. But I told Miss Miles I was fine and followed her to the great hall.

I do enjoy the occasional dinner with the other residents, though the theft put something of a damper on that evening's proceedings.

I was pleased to see that Patrick Verlinden was not dining with us.

Dudley asked his father whether the young man would be joining us, and Teddy said that he'd been invited, but had repaired instead to the Dog and Gun.

Dudley muttered something along the lines that he spent too much time drinking himself senseless. 'It will get to the point,' he said, 'where he'll soon be unable to discharge his duties around the place.'

'You're too harsh on him,' Esmeralda snapped. 'He's perfectly entitled to the occasional drink. If you'd undergone what he had during the war . . .' She smiled, having successfully delivered her barb.

Dudley winced and attended to his soup. The woman had hit a sore point: Dudley had pushed a pen as a clerk attached to some strategic planning office in Whitehall during the last shindig.

'I didn't invite you to dine with me,' Teddy said, glaring at Esmeralda, 'so that I could listen to your bickering. As you're no doubt aware, during the night the manor was burgled and the Gainsborough stolen.'

Dudley asked, 'What did the police say?'

'I can't say they've been too helpful. The inspector chappie, Montgomery, rules out the idea that someone broke into the place—'

'But he can't be suggesting . . .?' Dudley began.

Old Teddy sighed. 'I think that is precisely what he is

suggesting. That someone resident at the manor was responsible.'

'But that's preposterous!' Esmeralda exclaimed.

'You mean to say,' Dudley said, 'that he thinks one of us . . .?'

Teddy silenced him with a raised hand. 'At the moment, I gather the impression that the little inspector thinks that I was responsible for my own painting's removal, let's say . . . for insurance purposes.'

'But that's patently absurd!' I said.

'I know it is,' said Teddy, 'and you know that. But the important people we need to convince in this matter are the police and the insurance company.'

'But if they don't believe you . . .?' Miss Miles said.

'Then they'll refuse to pay out, my dear, and things will have gone from bad to worse.'

Dinner continued and the wine flowed, but even the fruit of the vine failed to cheer his lordship; in fact it made him even more melancholy and withdrawn.

Over port I suggested he come back to my rooms for a little nightcap – an invitation he would have accepted with alacrity on any other occasion – but he pleaded exhaustion, excused himself, and limped off to bed.

So I drank alone that evening, considering the events of the day.

To be continued . . . as they say.

FIFTEEN

An iron-hard frost had descended in the night, freezing the land all the way from the Wash to the Thames estuary, and the countryside around Neston Manor seemed stunned into lifeless submission. The rolling farmland was a dozen shades of frozen pewter and a golden sun burned low on the horizon.

Langham arrived at Neston Manor at ten o'clock and parked

in the drive. There was no sign yet of Ralph's Morris Minor. The police scene of crime van stood before the gatehouse, and half a dozen men in boiler suits passed in and out of the building, their breaths clouding the air.

Inspector Montgomery huddled under the archway, out of the bitter east wind, smoking a cigarette with the collar of his greatcoat turned up.

'Thanks for the message last night,' he said as Langham joined him.

'It appears that Verlinden might have been shot on the Saturday,' Langham said. 'It's not conclusive, but as Miss Miles saw him set off along the east path just before four, and he never made it to the pub . . .'

'That looks the favourite,' Montgomery agreed. 'I had the surgeon's report this morning. He was shot from a range of four or five feet, twice in the chest, and then in the head. The first shot would have done for him, apparently.'

'So the killer was making sure?'

The inspector nodded. 'The second shot was to make sure. But the third, to the head? Just to make *absolutely* sure?'

'Or . . . the killer was enraged, and the third shot was the result of pure anger?'

Montgomery shrugged. 'The surgeon puts the time of death between Saturday morning and Monday, but let's work on the assumption that he was killed on Saturday around four, shall we?'

'And the weapon?'

'Esmeralda Bellamy's shotgun, and the spent cartridges found in the undergrowth near the corpse are the same as what Esmeralda used to pepper her last sculpture.'

Montgomery finished his cigarette and flicked it across the drive. 'According to Esmeralda and Dudley, they were still in town at four on the Saturday in question, though I have men checking that.'

Langham stared across at the barn. The big, green-painted, timber door was secured with a padlock. 'But if Esmeralda did shoot Verlinden,' he said, 'why was she so stupid as to use her own weapon?'

'In my experience, Langham, killers often don't think things through logically beforehand. What if Esmeralda snatched up the shotgun in anger, followed Verlinden, and shot him in the heat of the moment?'

Langham frowned. 'I don't buy it. Think about her motive. If she wanted his share of the painting, then the killing wasn't a spur-of-the-moment thing, but pre-planned. Surely she would have thought things through and elected *not* to use her shotgun?'

'Always assuming, of course, that that was her motive – it might not have been.'

'Of course, she might not have killed him,' Langham said. 'Someone could always have used her shotgun with the intention of incriminating her.'

Montgomery laughed. 'You're spouting theories like a detective in one of your thrillers, Langham. Me, I'll see where the evidence leads, and then speculate. Boring, but it gets results.'

Langham smiled to himself. He refrained from pointing out to the inspector that his methodology had proved signally lacking in the instance of the missing painting.

Montgomery indicated the gatehouse. 'Come inside. I want to show you something. At least we'll get out of this bloody wind, though it's not much warmer indoors. I don't know how Verlinden could live in such a dump.'

Langham followed the inspector into the gatehouse and surveyed the living room-cum-kitchen. Two policemen were kneeling on the floor, one before the bookcase, the other beside the magazine rack, going through the paperbacks, newspapers and periodicals in painstaking detail. Sounds of movement overhead indicated that the bedroom and bathroom were being similarly searched.

The stench of soured milk and mildew was overpowering.

'What do you notice?' Montgomery asked.

'The almost complete absence of personal effects,' Langham said. 'I commented on it to Ralph the other day.'

'Other than a photograph of Verlinden with some of his flier chums,' Montgomery said, 'there's nothing. We've been through the place with the proverbial t-c: not a letter, official document, proof of identification – nothing.'

'What about on the body?'

'Nothing, Langham. Not a thing. He was a foreign national, so I assumed he'd have a passport, but we haven't found one.'

'Bank details?'

'No sign of anything. I haven't questioned his lordship about it yet, but I suspect he was employing Verlinden on the sly, slipping him a few quid a week and no questions asked. We found a bit of loose change around the place, and fifteen bob in change in the body's trouser pocket.'

'He certainly lived the frugal life.'

'I have a contact in C Division in London checking with the customs people for any record of his coming to Britain, but that might take days. Also, someone is liaising with the RAF regarding Verlinden's service records. But again, that might take a while.'

'All told, a bit of a mystery man.'

'My guess is he led a pretty sad, lonely, nomadic existence. After the RAF he lost his way, never settled, moved from one place to the next and made ends meet with menial jobs and petty crime sprees.'

At the sound of a car engine, Langham looked through the filthy window, expecting to see Ralph's clapped-out Morris Minor. Instead, Elsmere's maroon Wolseley, with Benson behind the wheel, drew up outside the manor. His lordship unfolded himself from the passenger seat and slowly climbed the steps to the entrance.

'I think I'll go and beg a hot drink,' Langham said, 'and have a word with Elsmere while I'm at it.'

He left Montgomery in the gatehouse and crossed the driveway.

Benson was assisting Elsmere from his bulky overcoat when Langham pushed his way through the solid oak door.

'Langham,' his lordship said, 'you look frozen to the bone.'

'It's perishing out there.'

'Don't I know it? I've just been into town and the wind is cutting. What about a spot of tea?'

'I wouldn't say no.'

'Benson, be so good as to bring tea and crumpets to the drawing room, there's a good chap.'

Benson departed and Elsmere led the way along the dimly lit passage to the west wing. As they went, Langham regarded Edward's stooped back and grey hair, considering the revelation that, back in the thirties, Elsmere had bankrolled a chapter of Mosley's Blackshirts. He wondered if Elsmere still had the same political leanings, or if the passage of time had tempered his views.

After the Arctic conditions prevailing in the gatehouse, the warmth belting from the fire in the drawing room came as a welcome relief.

They settled themselves into armchairs. 'Been thinking over what's happened here recently,' Elsmere said. 'The business of the theft, and Patrick . . . And you know, I can't help feeling guilty.'

Langham was surprised. 'Guilty?'

'Must admit, when it clicked that Patrick was behind the theft, my first reaction was anger. I gave the chap a job, a roof over his head – and this is how he repays me. Attempts to steal my favourite painting. Then he goes and gets himself shot dead, and I started to look at things through his eyes . . . Do you understand?'

'I think so.'

Benson entered the room pushing a tea trolley. He poured Darjeeling into bone china cups, and Langham took his before milk was added. He helped himself to a couple of the buttered crumpets heaped on a serving plate and sat back in the armchair.

When the butler departed, Elsmere went on, 'There he was, a war hero, living on the breadline, grubbing around for menial work. I paid him a pittance, really, and let him live in a box hardly fit for a dog.' He took a great chunk out of a crumpet and looked across at Langham, chewing. 'Is it any ruddy wonder the chap thought he'd help himself to the painting?'

Considering Elsmere's reactionary views regarding Suez the other day – and his political affiliations back in the thirties – Langham was surprised at his sudden fit of conscience.

He sipped his tea and set the cup aside. 'We're trying to ascertain if Verlinden had a bank account. We haven't come across any details, bank books, et cetera, and we were wondering if you had any idea?'

'Odd you should mention that. I wanted to pay him by cheque when he started here, but he said he didn't have a bank account and didn't care to open one. I thought it odd at the time and paid him cash in hand every week.'

'Would you mind telling me how much you paid him?'

'Not at all. Four pounds a week, and an extra five shillings if he did a half day at weekends. He was happy enough with the arrangement.'

'Did he ever speak to you about his past, his experience with the RAF?' Langham bit into a crumpet.

'I happened to see that photo of his when I was looking for him one day. I asked him about it, and imagine my surprise when he told me that one of the chaps in the photo was him. I wanted to know more, of course; I asked him where his squadron was based.'

'Did he tell you?'

'Not that I recall. Said something along the lines of the south of England, which told me nothing. Then I made a silly gaff and asked him why he no longer flew – many RAF pilots went into private aviation after the war. He just pointed to his leg and said that that was the reason. Exit Edward with egg on his face.'

Langham smiled. 'I wonder . . .'

'Go on.'

'It's just that if he were injured in the war so badly that he couldn't fly, wouldn't the government have paid him a pension? I must admit I don't know how things stand in that regard. I'll look into it.'

Lord Elsmere was staring at him. 'You mean to say, that the chap might *not* have served with the RAF?'

Langham shrugged. 'Or he *was* drawing a pension and he was squirrelling it away for a rainy day in a bank account he told no one about.'

'Interesting,' Elsmere said. 'More tea?'

'I don't mind if I do – and these crumpets are rather good.'

Replenished, Langham pulled a piece of paper, folded into four, from his breast pocket and spread it on his lap. Over breakfast he'd sketched a plan of the manor house, ground floor and first floor; now he set it on the coffee table.

'I'd like to get some idea of where everyone is staying in the house. I don't suppose you could sketch in the rooms?'

'By all means. Now let me see . . .'

Langham passed Elsmere his retractable Parker pen and his lordship pored over the plans. 'Miss Miles and the major are here, in neighbouring rooms in the west wing, ground floor. Esmeralda has her rooms above them, here. Benson is beside the library in the east wing. My room is here, on the first floor of the east wing, and Dudley is along the corridor from me.' He drew in the rooms and corridors missing from Langham's rough sketch and added the initials of each room's occupant.

'Thank you, that's excellent.' Langham regarded the drawing. 'Now, the various exits. Front door, here. And I take it there's a tradesman's entrance?'

'There, next to the old kitchen. And there's also an old door in the east wing, along the corridor past the library, though that's rarely used these days.' Elsmere sketched in the two remaining doors and returned the pen.

Langham stared at the completed ground plan. 'I take it you have the key to the east door in your possession?'

'It's actually kept on a hook beside the door itself. As I never use the door these days, I really don't want to haul the key about with me. It's ancient and weighs a ton.'

Langham finished his crumpet and drained his tea. 'You don't mind if Ralph and I spend an hour or two poking about the place, do you?'

'Be my guest. Anything to assist your enquiries. And now, if you'll excuse me, I think I shall go and lie down before lunch. Will you be joining me for a spot of fare?'

'I thought Ralph and I would nip down to the Dog and compare notes a bit later.'

'Capital idea. I've heard old Reg keeps an excellent pint. Good luck – and keep me posted.'

Langham was standing before the fire, warming himself and contemplating snaffling the last crumpet, when the sound of a grumbling car engine announced the arrival of Ralph's Morris Minor.

He crossed to the window and knocked on the mullioned glass as Ralph climbed out. He saw Langham's beckoning gesture and gave a cheery salute.

Several minutes elapsed before the drawing-room door opened and Ralph peered in, his querulous expression turning to one of relief as he beheld Langham. 'So this is where you've been hiding!'

'You've been so long I thought you'd got lost.'

'I ruddy well did. Took a wrong turning and found myself in a kitchen the size of a barn. It's so dark in this place it's a wonder anyone finds their way about. There I was, looking for a light switch, when I remembered there weren't any.'

'Positively medieval, as Maria said yesterday.'

Ralph looked around the room and his gaze fell on the remains of morning tea. 'So while I've been freezing to death in the old jalopy, you've been filling your face?'

'There's a crumpet left. Help yourself. I'll call for the butler to fetch another cup if you'd care for some tea.'

Ralph advanced on the coffee table. 'Don't bother him. I'll use your old cup and drink from the other side.'

Langham poured him a cup of tea, adding milk and three sugars. Ralph sat in the armchair recently vacated by Elsmere and sucked at the beverage. He indicated the ground plan on the coffee table. 'Been doodling?'

'Getting a few things straight in my head. I wanted to know where all the residents are situated. The place is like a warren, as you've found out.'

Ralph gestured with his half-eaten crumpet. 'So give me the gen about yesterday.'

Langham recounted the interviews, adding his own thoughts and opinions as he went along. As well as bringing Ralph up to speed, he found that going over the facts of the interrogation helped him to clarify a few details to his own satisfaction.

'Crikey, Don. How do you remember all that malarkey?'

'I suppose it comes from scribbling so much dialogue in my books. I rehearse it all when I'm in the bath or out walking, then remember it when I'm writing.'

Ralph drank his tea. 'The more I hear about this Esmeralda character, the less I like her.'

'Join the club. She's a prickly individual. You know, I pride myself on getting along with most people, but from time to time you come across characters who, with the best will in the world, you take a dislike to. And I'm sure the feeling is mutual with Esmeralda. I suppose I should take it as a compliment that I'm disliked by such a thoroughly bad lot.'

'Do you think *she* might've killed Verlinden?' Ralph said. 'Done him in for his half of the cash from the painting?'

'Esmeralda claims she was in town at the time – the police are checking her story. But why would she be stupid enough to use her own shotgun?'

Ralph peered at the ground plan. 'So where was everyone else at four o'clock on Saturday afternoon?'

'His lordship was here, in his upstairs room in the east wing, taking a snooze. Major Rutherford was here, in the west wing, enjoying a pre-prandial snifter. And Miss Miles was next door, here, listening to the wireless. It was she who saw Patrick Verlinden leaving the gatehouse just before four. She was making herself a cuppa and happened to look through the window as he crossed the drive towards the woods.'

'And shortly after that someone followed him into the woods and did the business.' Ralph examined the plan. 'Thing is, they were taking a hell of a risk, weren't they? I mean, they might have been seen as they crossed the drive to the woods.'

Langham shook his head. 'Ah, but I don't think they left by the front entrance. There's a little used exit in the east wing, here' – he prodded the plan – 'which lets straight on to the edge of the woodland. The killer could have left by this door and remained unseen. Drink up and we'll go and have a shufti.'

Ralph slurped the last of his tea and Langham pocketed the ground plan and led the way from the room.

They made their way back to the entrance hall, then took the dim corridor leading to the east wing. A cold draught blew around their ankles, and Langham wondered if the temperature was much above zero. They came to the library and walked on, the floorboards creaking underfoot.

They came to a T-junction in the corridor. Langham consulted the ground plan, grateful that Lord Elsmere had added corridors as well as rooms. 'This way,' he said, taking the right turn.

The passage mounted two steps and turned left, and twenty yards ahead was the side door, a blackened timber slab a little over four feet high.

Hanging on the bulging wall next to the door was a pitted iron key resembling a medieval instrument of torture. Little wonder Elsmere deigned not to carry it around with him.

Langham inserted the key into the capacious keyhole, rattled it around for a while, and finally managed to unlock the door. He pulled it open with an effort, its hinges creaking in protest.

A flagged pathway ran down the side of the house, and beyond it was a tangle of shrubbery. They turned right, towards the front of the house, and emerged at the edge of bare woodland.

'So our killer waits till Verlinden enters the woods and follows,' Langham said, 'slipping into the cover of the shrubbery and remaining unseen from the house.'

They did the same, walking single-file down the narrow path. A razor-sharp wind whistled through the trees. Langham turned up his collar. The winter sun, shining through the stark treetops, was bright but offered little warmth.

They approached the place where Patrick Verlinden met his end. Langham indicated the stand of ferns, stepped off the path, and stared down at the dark earth and disturbed leaf cover.

'The police surgeon says Verlinden was shot at close range, just off the path. I suspect the killer followed him this far, then called out. Verlinden turned, the killer approached, and before Verlinden could run, the killer raised the shotgun and fired from four or five feet away. Verlinden staggered back through the undergrowth and the killer advanced, stood over him and administered two more shots, one to the chest and one to the head, removing half the skull in the process.'

'Bastard meant business,' Ralph murmured.

'I'll say.'

Ralph knelt beside the disturbed ground. 'And then the killer covers the corpse with dead leaves.'

Langham nodded. 'The ground being too hard to bury it.'

He looked through the trees to the south and made out a

field. 'There was a farmer in a tractor a few hundred yards away. I spoke to him in the Dog last night. He saw someone poking around here at four o'clock on the Saturday in question. Our killer. Sadly, he couldn't identify the figure – couldn't even say if it were a man or a woman – and thought little of it at the time.'

He knelt beside Ralph and picked up a handful of leaves. 'I suspect the killer hoped the body might go undetected for a while. He or she thought without old Cedric's lurcher.'

They climbed to their feet and stared around them at the undergrowth.

'Esmeralda Bellamy's shotgun was left lying around in the barn, but the cartridges were taken from Lord Elsmere's gunroom, which was unlocked. Looks as if it were an inside job.'

'So if Esmeralda and Mariner's alibi stacks up,' Ralph said, 'the killer can only be one of three people. Lord Elsmere, Major Rutherford, or Rebecca Miles.'

The two men stared at each other and laughed.

'You thinking what I'm thinking, Don?'

'What, that I don't believe any of the three could have done it?'

Ralph nodded. 'Lord Elsmere? Motive? None as far as we know. Major Rutherford? Christ, the old fellow's gaga as well as infirm. Could you really see him following Verlinden all the way out here? And, again, why? So far we can't pin a motive on him. And then we come to the beautiful Rebecca Miles . . . No, I can't believe she'd do such a thing.'

'Why's that?'

'From what I've seen of her, and from the little I've spoken to her, I get the impression that such a killing would be beyond her.'

'For what it's worth, I agree.'

'So where the ruddy hell does that leave us?'

Langham looked at his watch. It was just after midday. 'It leaves me in sore need of a pint and a pie.' He pointed through the trees to the village nestling in the frosted countryside. 'The Dog and Gun beckons.'

'Lead the way, Cap'n'

They stepped back on to the path and followed it through

the woods and down the hill beside the beet field. Ralph looked up into the pearly sky and shivered. 'Looks like snow.'

Little Neston was quiet, with few people abroad; lights shone behind the windows of thatched cottages, and the shops they passed – a newsagent's, a baker's and post office – were bereft of customers.

'I just hope,' Ralph said as they approached the Dog and Gun, 'the police can scupper Esmeralda's alibi and prove she was back in time to do the dirty.'

'And everyone'll be happy. Order is restored, the innocent are reprieved, and the witch will burn.'

Ralph looked at him. 'You come out with some odd stuff at times, Don.'

Langham pushed open the door to the snug. 'Age before beauty, sir. After you.'

The fire burned in the hearth and the wireless played dance music just like the night before; the only difference this time was that today they were the only customers in the place.

Langham ordered two pints of bitter and asked the landlord if he served food.

'We do a nice steak and kidney pie, sir, baked fresh today in the village.'

Ralph rubbed his hands. 'A Kate and Sidney for me, landlord.'

'Make that two,' Langham said, and carried his beer to the table beside the fire.

'How's the house-hunting coming along?' Ralph asked. He took a mouthful of beer and said in an aside, 'It's a decent pint.'

'Charles took us on a conducted tour around a few villages on Saturday, and very nice they were too. But we haven't actually viewed any houses yet. Charles and Maria are taking a day off today to look at a few potential properties.'

The landlord delivered their pies, ovals of golden pastry sitting in tinfoil dishes on bare dinner plates. What they lacked in presentation they more than made up for in quality.

'Excellent,' Langham said, chewing a mouthful. 'It'll be worth moving from London for the pies alone.'

'But you'll miss the city, Don.' It was more a statement than a question. 'And how will you adjust to country life? Not much to do out here in the sticks.'

'Do you know something, I think I could live on the moon so long as I was with Maria. I wake up in the morning and thank my lucky stars. I feel like pinching myself to make sure it isn't a dream.'

'Aye,' Ralph said, looking reminiscent. 'I remember those days.'

Langham finished his pie and washed it down with a mouthful of ale. 'Drink up, Ralph, and we'll have one for the road. Then it's back to the manor for a natter with whoever's at home.'

Ralph was about to go to the bar when the door opened, admitting a swirl of icy wind and a flurry of snow. A young woman stood hesitantly on the threshold, staring in at them. Langham was unable to tell if her red eyes were a result of the cold, or tears.

She appeared reluctant to enter the premises and lifted a hand in a timid wave. 'Could I have a word?'

Langham gave Ralph a look. 'Of course.'

'Not here,' the woman said, beckoning.

Langham climbed to his feet and crossed to the young woman.

'You're Mr Langham, right? My friend said you were working on the investigation up at the manor. I was in the bakery – that's where I work – and I saw you pop in here. I'm on my dinner break, see, so I thought . . .'

Langham touched her elbow. 'Slow down. Take it easy, and tell me . . .'

The young woman's voice caught on a sob. He was sure, now, that she'd been crying.

'I need to talk to you. It's terrible, what happened to Pat. But he was frightened, see. He was desperate.'

'Would you like a drink? You'll feel better if . . .'

She glanced around the snug as if it were the anteroom of hell itself. 'I can't come in – if my mum got to know I'd been in here . . . She didn't know about me and Pat, you see.'

'Is there somewhere we might talk?'

She sniffed back her tears. 'Back at mine. Just across the green. You don't mind, Mr Langham?'

'Of course not.' He gestured to Ralph and they followed the woman from the pub.

SIXTEEN

They crossed the village green, through a flurry of snow, to a terrace of tiny cottages. The woman unlocked the front door of the end dwelling and ushered them into a sitting room equipped with flimsy utility furnishings, a scruffy sofa drawn up to a beige tiled hearth, and a small fold-down dining table before the window.

The woman was in her mid-twenties, with a thin, pinched face and lank auburn hair. She had the appearance of someone who, with an improvement of diet and a pay-rise of a pound a week, might have been able to make herself look very pretty. As it was, she appeared impoverished and harried.

Langham and Ralph stood uneasily by the door, staring at her as she strode back and forth before the hearth, still bundled up in her wet raincoat.

She sat down on the sofa, rocked forward and held her head in her hands, sobbing.

Ralph indicated the armchairs on either side of the fireplace. They sat down, and Langham ventured to touch the woman's shoulder. 'You and Patrick . . .?'

'I can't believe it!' she wailed. 'I heard from Mr Greaves at the bakery just this morning. He told me Pat was dead, shot dead. It was all over the village. Everyone who came in to the shop was full of it. "Here, Dora, have you heard about the murder?" How do you think that made me feel, Mr Langham? Everyone talking about it as if it were a serial on the wireless, and no one knowing that me and Pat . . .' She sobbed again and pressed her hands to her face.

Langham murmured, 'Dora, you said that Patrick was frightened, desperate. If you could just explain . . .'

She removed her hands from her tear-streaked face and stared at the bevelled sunray mirror above the mantelpiece, her gaze distant. 'I liked him as soon as I saw him, Mr Langham. He came into the bakery this summer and I thought, he's a nice-looking chap, despite the scar. He hardly said anything then, but he'd come in a couple of times a week for a Cornish and we got talking. Then he asked me out to the pictures in town, only I said no because of my mother. She didn't like me going out with strange men, and if she'd got to know he was a foreigner . . . But then I told Brenda, she's my best friend, and Brenda said next time to tell my mum I was going to the pictures with her. So when Pat came in and asked me out again, I said yes . . .'

'How long ago was that, Dora?'

'Three months back. August. Would've been our anniversary next week.' She sniffed, composed herself, then went on, 'I loved him, Mr Langham. He treated me ever so good. We even went to a restaurant one time. And now and again he came back here . . . But we couldn't let anyone know, Mr Langham, for fear of my mum finding out. She didn't hold with foreigners. She even thought Londoners were odd.'

Langham smiled. 'Some people are like that.'

'But Pat was a good man, for all he liked a drink. He didn't cause no trouble, just sat in the pub with his pint and minded his own. He had a lot to dwell on, you see, with what happened in the war. He was a war hero, Pat was. He told me about his time in the RAF, but he never mentioned the crash.'

'You said he was frightened?' Langham said gently.

'I could tell something was wrong. He was always quiet like, but this time he was even more withdrawn. First, I thought it was me, he didn't like me any more. But he said he loved me.'

'Did he tell you what was worrying him?'

Dora ran her knuckles back and forth across her lips, nervous. At last she nodded. 'Someone was threatening him, but he didn't know why.'

Langham exchanged a glance with Ralph. 'Threatening?'

'He had this note. He showed me. It worried him sick. He told me he didn't know what it was about, but he thought it was from one of them up there.' She gave a nod in the direction of the manor. 'He said they didn't like him, all apart from his lordship who was a decent chap, he said.'

Langham perched on the edge of his seat. 'Do you know what was in this note?'

She nodded decisively. 'He left it here, said he didn't want it up at his place, reminding him.'

'Do you still have it?'

She crossed to a small chest of drawers and pulled out the top drawer, withdrew a small blue envelope, and returned to the sofa. She sat staring down at the envelope with tear-filled eyes, then passed it to Langham.

The address was typewritten: Patrick Verlinden, The Gatehouse, Neston Manor, Little Neston, Suffolk. In the top right-hand corner was a cancelled two-penny stamp.

Langham removed a sheet of light blue paper from the envelope and unfolded it.

> Verlinden, I know all about you and your lies. I'll be in touch.

The message, like the address, was typewritten.

He passed the sheet to Ralph, who examined it and murmured, 'The o is filled, Don, and the drop on the y is broken.'

Langham peered at the postmark, but it was smudged and undecipherable. He looked at Dora. 'Do you know when he received this?'

'A fortnight ago, on the Monday. I thought he'd been acting strange for a couple of days. I asked him what was wrong, and on the Wednesday he showed it to me.' She stared down at her hands, then whispered, 'And that was the last time I ever saw him.'

He returned the sheet to the envelope. 'Can I take this with me?'

'Of course. I don't want it sitting there like . . . like I don't know what. And to think, whoever typed *that* . . .' She looked up at him. 'I was wondering, you see, if whoever sent him that horrible note might have, might have . . . you know . . .'

He reached out and took her cold hand as she broke down and wept again.

'But who could have done that to Pat, Mr Langham!

Why would someone have shot him like that? He didn't deserve that. He was a war hero. He was a lovely, quiet, gentle man . . .'

Langham squeezed her hand. 'If it's any consolation, Dora, he wouldn't have felt any pain; it would have been over very quickly.'

Her eyes widened, pathetically hopeful. 'It would? He wouldn't have suffered?'

'Not at all. The police surgeon told me he would have died instantly.'

'But I've been thinking about it over and over, and imagining him lying there, all alone in the cold, bleeding to death and suffering . . .'

'It didn't happen like that, Dora. It would have been . . . instant. You can rest assured that he wouldn't have suffered.'

'That's good to know, Mr Langham, thank you.'

He slipped the envelope into his jacket pocket. 'Did Patrick ever talk to you about his past?'

'Not much. Just . . . just that when the Nazis invaded his country, he had to get out. So he came here. He wanted to do his bit, and he'd learned to fly in Holland, so he volunteered for the RAF.'

'Did he say what he did immediately after the war?'

She shrugged, looking disconsolate. 'Odd jobs, he told me. He couldn't walk far, and he couldn't really lift anything very heavy, and he got these blinding headaches from time to time. He told me he just drifted from job to job – and . . . and' – she smiled through her tears – 'and that got me worried, because I thought he'd drift again, leave the manor . . . But he said he was settled there, said he loved me.'

'You said that Patrick thought the note might have been from someone up at the manor?'

'Well, he did wonder. He didn't really like that lot, you see – apart from his lordship, and that artist woman.'

Langham said, 'Esmeralda?'

'That's her. He said she was decent enough. I was jealous at first, you see, because he went to the Dog and Gun with her once or twice. But he said she might be able to help him earn some money. So you see, I had nothing to worry about, what with Esmeralda being engaged to his lordship's son and all.'

Langham leaned forward. 'Did Patrick mention *how* she might help him earn some money?'

She shook her head. 'He said it was early days, but I wondered if she might have him working for her in that barn of hers.'

He shot Ralph a look, then said to Dora, 'I'm glad you had the sense to contact us.' He tapped the letter in his pocket. 'This might prove very helpful.'

She looked at the clock on the mantelpiece. 'Crikey, look at the time! That's nearly my lunch hour gone. I'd better be getting back to the bakery or Mr Greaves'll be wondering where I've got to.'

She smiled from Langham to Ralph. 'It's good to talk to someone. You see, I couldn't tell anyone about Pat and me. You'll do your best, won't you, to catch . . .?'

Langham rose to his feet. 'We'll do everything we can, Dora. Now, is there anything else you think might be relevant?'

She pinched her bottom lip between her teeth, and Langham received the distinct impression that she was considering whether or not to tell him something else. In the end she shook her head and smiled at him timidly. 'I don't think so, Mr Langham, but if I do . . .'

They thanked her and took their leave.

'Well,' Langham said as they headed back across the green, 'what do you make of that?' He turned his collar up against the wind and the driving snow.

'Poor kid,' Ralph said. 'Do you think Verlinden was going behind her back with that Esmeralda woman?'

'More likely he and Esmeralda were prospective business partners – planning the theft of his lordship's painting.'

'And his claim that he didn't have a clue what that note was all about? Another lie?'

Langham nodded. 'I'm pretty sure it was. Mark my word, there was more to our Mr Verlinden than meets the eye.'

A green Morris Commercial bus ground along the lane, its tyres churning through the slush. It drew to a halt ten yards ahead of them and three passengers alighted.

One of them, Langham saw, was Rebecca Miles, weighed down by a bulging canvas shopping bag.

'Pick your tongue up off the floor, Ralph, and close your mouth.'

'But you have to admit she's just a bit gorgeous. Lordy, what's a woman like her doing in a place like this? She ought to be in the movies.'

Ralph increased his pace and caught up with her. 'Need a hand with that, luv?'

She turned and gave a dazzling smile. 'Oh, Mr Ryland, Mr Langham. Why, yes. Thank you. It is rather heavy.'

Ralph took the load and they fell into step with the woman as she walked from the village. She wore a scarlet crocheted hat which set off her pale complexion and made her look even more gamine than usual.

'Just been into town?' Ralph asked.

'I pop in every Monday to do a little shopping. Sometimes I stay and have a late lunch, but as the weather forecast was rather bad . . .'

'You don't own a car?' Langham said.

'I never learned to drive,' she said. 'I wouldn't trust myself to be in charge of so much hurtling metal. I must admit I'm a bit of a daydreamer.'

The snowfall increased, suddenly reducing visibility to twenty yards. They came to the beet field, and Langham paused. 'Should we take the shortcut, do you think, or continue the long way round on the road?'

'I usually take the road, but as I have my boots on . . . we could take the shortcut. I don't mind about . . .' She trailed off, her cheeks colouring.

Langham said, 'Then let's take the shortest route, shall we? I don't like the look of this snowstorm.'

They leaned into the wind and took the footpath beside the field. The ground was frozen solid, so they didn't have to worry about getting their footwear muddied. They came to the woods and Langham led them into its minimal cover.

'I keep thinking about what happened here,' she said, 'and I still can't really believe it. I was wondering . . .'

Langham looked over his shoulder. 'Yes?'

'If it were the work of a madman, Mr Langham, then everyone might be in danger.'

Ralph was shaking his head. 'Shouldn't worry yourself about that, Miss Miles. I think whoever killed Verlinden was after him and only him.'

'But who would do such a thing? Patrick was a quiet, inoffensive young man.'

They came to the stand of ferns where the Dutchman was shot dead and passed by without comment.

As they were emerging from the woods, with the looming shape of Neston Manor obscured by snow falling from a milky sky, Langham fell into step alongside the young woman and asked, 'How's the book coming along, Miss Miles?'

She smiled. 'Very slowly, as it happens. What with all this business . . . I haven't really been able to concentrate.'

'Do you write longhand?'

'Yes, I don't own a typewriter. I shall employ someone to type up the manuscript when I'm happy with it.'

Langham frowned. 'Pity. I'm looking for someone with a machine I could borrow for ten minutes. I have a letter I'd like to get off this afternoon.'

'The major has a portable typewriter. He uses it to write up his journal. I'm sure he'd be more than happy to let you use it. If you're lucky, you'll catch him in time to join him for an afternoon dram. He'd appreciate the company.'

'Excellent. I'll pop in now and have a word.'

Miss Miles turned to Ralph. 'Would you care for a cup of tea, Mr Ryland, as thanks for carrying my groceries?'

'Why, that's kind of you. I'd love a cuppa.'

She led the way into the manor and through the maze of darkened passageways to the west wing. As they came to her door, she pointed further along the corridor to a small, blackened door identical to hers. 'That's the major's room. Just knock; he'll be delighted to see you.'

She unlocked her door and stepped aside to allow Ralph to enter with her shopping.

Langham continued to the major's door and knocked.

SEVENTEEN

He heard the old soldier on the other side fumbling with a key. The door swung open and the major peered out at him.

'Ah, Langham, isn't it? What can I do for you? Come in, come in . . . Looks as if you've been out in it. Wicked weather. Come and warm yourself by the fire. And you'll join me in a peg or two? I was just about to indulge.' He led Langham into a cosy, beamed sitting room and waved his walking stick at the open fire.

'Draw up a seat and get warm, Langham.'

'Why, that's kind of you. I don't want to intrude . . .'

'Intrude? On what, my boy?' the major said, shuffling over to a drinks trolley and pouring two measures of Scotch.

'Do you know something – it might be old age, but I got it into my head that you and the little chap were working in films or some such. Then yesterday Miss Miles mentioned you were detectives.'

'That's right. Lord Elsmere called us in to investigate the missing painting, you see, and didn't want everyone to know.'

'Aha! Hence the cover story,' the major laughed.

Langham eased himself into a comfortable armchair and looked around the room. Two walls were entirely lined with old books. A big desk sat in the middle of the room, with a bulky typewriter in pride of position. Beside it sat a pile of typescript.

'I don't do anything these days that could be called important,' the major said, 'certainly nothing that can't be interrupted. Work on my journal every so often, but I've got less and less to record these days.'

He tottered across to Langham, passed him a tumbler of whisky, and sank into the opposite armchair.

'Suppose you've come to quiz me about young Verlinden, hm? Been thinking about it, and all I can assume is that he got into an argument with a local. They all have guns round here, y'know? Everyone hunts these days, not just the gentry.'

'I suppose there are some hotheads in the village.'

'Not that I'd know, as I rarely get out,' the major grumbled, 'but every place has them. Just young Patrick's luck to pick a fight with the wrong kind.'

Langham smiled. 'That's quite possible,' he said, sipping his whisky. 'My word, that's excellent.'

The major laughed. 'You get to my age, young man, and you think what the hell! Why stint? How long have I got left? Might as well enjoy the best while I can.'

Langham raised his glass. 'Admirable sentiments, Major.'

The old soldier gazed across at him with watery eyes. 'You know something, Langham? The older one gets, the less one is interested in filthy lucre. There was a time, not so long ago, when I bought the *Financial Times* every morning and spent an hour checking my portfolio. Had quite a few stocks and shares a few years ago. I'd watch 'em go up and down like a gambler watching the fortunes of his horse in the Derby! It came to rule my life, I'll tell you. All I could think about when I woke in the morning was how the dashed things were doing. Thought of nothing else.'

'But no more?'

The old man smacked his lips around a mouthful of single malt. 'No more, Langham. How much longer have I got? I won't see another year out. Blasted money's not important to me any more . . . I say, be a hero and refill this, will you? And help yourself while you're at it, young sir.'

Langham took the major's glass, refilled it, and added a finger to his own. He returned to the fire.

The major clutched his drink. 'Where was I?'

'The diminishing importance of filthy lucre,' Langham reminded him.

'And you know what made me realize what a fool I'd been?'

'The wisdom of years?'

The old man creased his lips in a thin smile. 'Nasty business. Five years ago. Whiff of a scandal. More than a whiff, in fact. Got me fingers burnt. Frightened me to death. Don't like to talk about it. Brings back unpleasant . . .' His eyes misted over. 'Less said, the better, what? Let bygones be bygones?'

'Quite,' Langham said, intrigued.

'Still, old Teddy was a lifesaver. Veritable rock. Came to me rescue, offered me this place. And I'm happy here, damn it. Never happier! I have me books, me whisky, and a pretty young filly next door who looks in on me from time to time . . . What more does a man need, Langham?'

'Not much, Major, I must admit.' Langham drained his glass and gestured across at the bookshelves. 'That's a pretty impressive collection. Mind if I take a look?'

'By all means, Langham, and if there's anything that takes your fancy, feel free to borrow it.'

Langham crossed the room and stood before the floor-to-ceiling bookshelves. The volumes were almost all military history, along with a few big-game hunting memoirs and manuals on hunting and fishing.

On the top shelf, spanning the width of the wall, Langham noted more than fifty volumes bound in calfskin.

'Ah,' the major said from his chair, 'you've spotted me memoirs! They go right back to 1899, Langham, when I was mixing it with the Boer. I started scribbling me thoughts out there – long evenings, y'see, not much to do – and continued ever since. At the end of every year I take the typescript up to a fellow in Holborn and have 'em bound. It'd be nice if one day a historian would edit the lot into a single volume, what? That'd open a few eyes, I'll tell you!'

Langham turned to the desk and pointed to the pile of typescript.

'And these are your latest entries?' he asked.

'That's right, just a few idle thoughts.'

Langham stared down at the topmost sheet and read a few lines.

He leaned against the bookshelf, marshalling his thoughts.

Every letter o in the line was smudged, and the drop of the letter y was broken.

He looked across the room to the old man, feeling a little sick. The major sat back in the chair, his thin legs crossed, the half-full tumbler of whisky clutched in the varicose claw of his right hand.

Why the hell, he asked himself, would Major Rutherford have sent Verlinden the note now sitting in his pocket . . .?

Verlinden, I know all about you and your lies. I'll be in touch.

He took another look at the typescript, as if doubting the evidence of his eyes. But there it was, in black and white: the filled in o, and the broken drop on the y . . .

The major turned his head and peered at him. 'As I say, I don't have as much to say these days, and to be honest I don't like using that infernal contraption. Much prefer me own portable.'

Langham stared across the room at him. 'What?'

'I said, I much prefer my own machine, but I took it into the mender's last week and still haven't got it back. I had to borrow that brute.'

Langham smiled to himself, his faith in the crusty old soldier restored. 'So . . . who does this one belong to, Major?'

'Mentioned at dinner one evening that mine had conked out, and Dudley said Esmeralda had an old machine I could borrow. She was away at the time, spending a few days in London. Dudley hauled it here the very next day. Dashed clunky contraption, what? But beggars can't be choosers, as they say.'

'So this belongs to Esmeralda?' Langham said.

'And the sooner I get my own back, the better!'

Langham turned to the bookshelf and indicated the bound journals. 'Would you mind terribly if I . . .?'

'Help yourself, Langham,' the major said.

Langham selected a volume whose spine was embossed with MCMLV – last year – and pulled it from the shelf. He opened it at random and read a page. He saw with relief that the letter o was pristine and the drop on the y unbroken.

He returned the volume to its shelf.

'Now you'll join me in another, won't you, Langham?'

'I'm afraid I must be getting off, Major, but thanks all the same.'

'In that case,' the major said, 'be a hero and top me up, would you?'

*   *   *

He left the major to enjoy his whisky and wandered back through the house. Benson apprehended him in the entrance hall. 'Mr Ryland is in the drawing room, sir. He asked if you would care to join him.'

Langham thanked the butler and made his way to the drawing room. He found Ralph enthroned before the fire like the lord of the manor, a plate of buttered crumpets on his lap and a teacup gripped in his right hand.

'Do you know something, Don? I could get used to this. First time I've been waited on by a butler.'

'It's a different world, isn't it?' Langham sat down and poured himself a black tea.

Ralph peered at him. 'You look puzzled. What gives?'

'While Major Rutherford plied me with whisky, I managed to get a gander at the typescript of his latest journal entries.'

'And the o and y don't match, right?'

'Wrong. They do match. The note sent to Patrick Verlinden was typed on that machine.'

Ralph lowered his cup and looked incredulous. 'I don't believe it! Surely the old boy wouldn't have . . .?'

Langham raised a hand. 'Just what I was thinking. Then he told me that he'd borrowed the typewriter – from Esmeralda.'

'That's more like it! Esmeralda I *can* see trying to blackmail Verlinden – previous form and all that.'

'That was exactly my thinking at first,' Langham said. 'But consider this. If she did shoot Verlinden, so she could get *all* the money when she sold the painting, then why would she have sent Verlinden the note? "I know all about you and your lies". We thought the note a prelude to blackmail, but why would she have considered blackmailing someone she intended to murder? So if she did write the note, then it's unlikely she would have killed him. Do you get my logic?'

Ralph finished a crumpet and set the plate aside. 'OK, how about this. She intended to blackmail Verlinden and sent the note to put the frighteners on him. A couple of days later he nicks the painting, or rather hides it. Her way of looking at it is that sooner or later they'll sell the painting and halve the proceeds – then she'll blackmail him, anonymously, of course, and fleece him of his ill-gotten gains.'

'But . . .'

'Hear me out,' Ralph said. 'Then she has a better idea. She needn't go through with the risky business of blackmailing him and arranging to collect the money – she'll just shoot the poor blighter dead and cop all the dosh.'

Langham pulled a face, staring down at his tea. 'I suppose it's a possibility. That's always assuming, of course, her alibi doesn't hold and she did arrive back here in time to pull the trigger.'

'Either way, Don, she's a bad lot. There she was in the Dog and Gun with Verlinden, speaking sweet nothings into his ear, while planning either to blackmail or murder him.'

Langham finished his tea. 'I don't suppose there's anyone else who could have used her typewriter to write the note, is there?'

'How about Mariner? He'd have access to her rooms. He might've typed it while she was working . . . But that's a bit farfetched. It's Esmeralda who has previous when it comes to blackmail, not Mariner.'

'So assuming you're right,' Langham said, 'and Esmeralda sent the note, then changed her mind about blackmailing him and settled on killing him instead . . . I wonder what she'd found out about him? And how? What did she know about him and his lies?'

Ralph wiped his buttery chin on a napkin. 'How about we ask her outright?'

'Tell her we know about the note, and her plans to blackmail Verlinden, and see how she reacts?'

Ralph nodded. 'Just after I'd said goodbye to Miss Miles, I saw Esmeralda enter the house and go upstairs, presumably to her room.'

'And speaking of Miss Miles,' Langham said, 'how went your little tête-à-tête?'

Ralph smiled. 'Very well. She was interested in the agency and our work. I told her that most of our time was taken up with routine stuff like trailing unfaithful spouses and insurance frauds. Then I asked her about her life before coming here.'

'What did she say?'

'She worked in London as a secretary after doing a shorthand course, and then nursed her father. When he died and she inherited some money, she decided she'd had enough of the Smoke. Oh – and I found out what she's writing.'

'You asked her outright? She seemed coy on the subject the other day when I brought it up.'

'I did ask her, but she just waved, said "some novel" and changed the subject. Then she went to powder her nose – and I took a quick peek at a big notebook on her desk.'

'You underhand little sneak!'

'Can it, Don. Anyway, it looked like a thriller about some girl in Nazi Germany, being chased through the streets of Berlin. I just read a few lines, then I heard a tap running in the bathroom so I nipped back to my chair.'

'She didn't see you?'

'No fear.'

Langham's thoughts returned to Esmeralda Bellamy, and he finished his tea and said, 'Right, let's go and see what Esmeralda has to say for herself, shall we?'

EIGHTEEN

They made their way through the house to the entrance hall and climbed the staircase. Langham was in the process of taking the ground plan from his inside pocket when he heard a door slam on the landing above, followed by a volley of angry voices.

Ralph pulled a face. 'Sounds like Mariner and Esmeralda, going at it hammer and tongs.'

'I've had quite enough . . .' Esmeralda cried.

'Where the hell are you going?'

'Anywhere but here!'

'Esmeralda! Come back!'

She cried, 'Not in a million years . . .'

A figure appeared on the landing and tore at speed down the staircase. Langham and Ralph pressed themselves to the wall to prevent being skittled as a fuming Esmeralda, struggling with two suitcases, stormed past.

She strode across the hall and slammed the front door behind her.

'Exit aggrieved party,' Langham said. 'And so much for our plans to put her on the spot.'

Dudley Mariner appeared above them, gripping the gallery rail and staring after Esmeralda like a ship's captain incredulous at the mutiny of his crew. He tore along the landing, swung himself around the carved bollard at the stair-head, and tapped at speed down the stairs.

Langham watched him cross the hall and run out into the drive, leaving the front door wide open; an icy wind whistled into the house.

They exchanged shrugs and made their way down to the entrance hall.

Mariner tramped back into the house, looking woebegone.

'She's gone,' the young man said disconsolately. 'Taken her clapped-out Hillman and scarpered.'

'You look,' Langham said, 'as if you need a drink.'

Mariner summoned a smile. 'Do you know what, I think I do. Care to join me?'

'A small one for the road, then,' Langham said, and he and Ralph followed the young man back to the drawing room.

Mariner crossed to the drinks cabinet with the air of a condemned man and poured three drams. They seated themselves before the open fire.

'We've all experienced it, haven't we?' Mariner said. 'The rows, the recriminations, the lover running off . . .' He looked up and smiled bleakly. 'But it doesn't make it any easier, does it? It doesn't stop that terrible, hollow, sick feeling right here.' He lodged a fist in his solar plexus.

'What happened?' Ralph asked.

'This time?' Mariner said. 'Oh, it was all my fault, of course. For being so weak, so . . . what were her exact words? So "spineless and ineffectual".'

Langham sipped his whisky, a response redundant.

'Things between us have always been a bit rocky,' the young man went on. 'She's the strong one, the one who gets things done. You slip into roles, don't you? You adapt to your partner, take the course of least resistance. I thought that was what she wanted, to be in control, in power.'

'Perhaps,' Langham ventured, 'that's what she did really want, despite her calling you what she did.'

Mariner smiled bleakly. 'When we met, Langham, I thought she was attracted to something in me; my personality.'

'But now?'

He gripped the glass in his fist, staring bitterly at the drink. 'But now I realize the truth – when we got together, she thought she was hitching a ride on the gravy train. That's one thing I've come to understand about Esmeralda. Her materialism; it's all about acquiring money.' He sighed. 'I suppose it stems from when she was a kid and had nothing. She was brought up by her father during the Depression, and now she's compensating. Her childhood poverty has made her selfish and grasping.'

'So when she got engaged to you,' Langham said, 'she thought she'd inherit . . .?'

Mariner nodded. 'All this. The house, grounds, the title, and the respect that goes with it all.'

'It must have been a bit of a shock when she learned the truth,' Ralph said.

'Listen, it was a hell of a shock for me, I can tell you.' He finished his whisky and refilled it from the bottle he'd brought to the coffee table. 'A top up?'

Langham placed a hand over his glass. Ralph shook his head and said, 'I'm driving back to London pretty soonish.'

'Do you know,' Mariner went on, 'everything started to go wrong from the day my father's painting went missing. That's when the rot set in.'

Langham looked at the young man. 'But surely you knew about the state of your father's finances before then?'

'Ah, but that's the thing, Langham. I didn't. Call me a naive fool, but I lived in blithe ignorance of how parlous things were. Oh, I knew Pater didn't have tens of thousands to fall back on, but I thought he was reasonably comfortable. I assumed I'd be inheriting the house and land, with funds set aside to cover the death duties. Imagine my shock when he broke the news last Monday.'

'Last Monday?' Ralph said, exchanging a glance with Langham.

'He brought me in here, poured me a drink, and told me that things were looking pretty grim on the old finances front. Long and short of it, he was penniless, though he was looking into ways of making things a little easier for me when he shuffled off. He was obviously referring to the deal with Carnaby and Wentworth, though as that was still under negotiation, I think he didn't want to tell me about it until it was a done deal.'

'I was under the impression that you knew about your father's situation long before last Monday.'

'You'd've thought so, wouldn't you, what with my managing the estate. But you see, it was always my father who controlled the purse strings. Oh, I knew things were tight, but I never guessed . . .'

Langham hesitated, then said, 'I hope you don't mind my asking, but did you tell Esmeralda the news?'

'It's strange, but a part of me, some buried part of my consciousness, was reluctant to do so. It was as if a part of me knew how she'd react but didn't want to admit it to myself.' He nodded. 'But yes, I told her the very same day.'

'And you think that's the reason she . . .?'

'Yes, I do. Her little performance just now was the upshot. There she was, thinking she was all set to become the lady of the manor, set for life – if not rolling in it, then at least reasonably well off. The truth came as a shock, and her walking out has made me realize that, to her, I was never anything more than a milch cow, there to be used.'

'I'm sorry,' Langham murmured.

'When I told her, she was obviously shocked. I said we'd find some way around it, muddle through. I said' – and he laughed as he recalled this – 'I said that at least we'd have each other! And the other day, when my father announced the rescue package from the property company . . . I thought that this might swing things, make her a little more amenable.'

'And what was her reaction to your father's announcement?'

'She wasn't impressed. She didn't want to be the wife of a farmer on a pittance, living in a small apartment. She wanted the works, the title *and* the estate *and* the riches. So she worked herself up to that little performance, called me spineless and left.'

Ralph asked, 'Do you know where she might have gone?'

Mariner shook his head. 'No, no idea at all. She has no one, no family. No one . . .'

He finished his drink and stared into the empty glass, then looked up and smiled at them. 'I'm sorry. This is the last thing you probably wanted to sit here listening to.'

Langham said, 'Not at all. And it does you good to talk, you know?'

'I suppose I'd better go and tell Pater what's happened.'

'Do you think she might . . .?' Ralph began.

'What, come back?' Mariner asked. 'Oh, I don't think so.' He reached into his pocket and pulled out a ring. He held it up before him. 'She left this, you see. Well, she flung it at me. It's only paste – I couldn't afford anything better. I said it was temporary, until my finances improved, and then I'd buy her a diamond ring. But that's the kind of woman she is, gentlemen: had the ring been diamond, she would have taken it with her.'

Mariner made to rise, but Langham said, 'Oh, one small thing. I understand you loaned Esmeralda's portable typewriter to the major a while back.'

Mariner grinned. 'And did I earn myself a tongue-lashing when she got back from London!' he said. 'She told me I wasn't to give her things to anyone without her express permission. Hey-ho . . .'

He sighed, nodded a terse farewell, and left the room.

They sat in silence for a while, staring at the fire.

Ralph pulled his notebook from the breast pocket of his jacket and leafed through the pages. 'So the painting is taken a week last Wednesday,' he said, 'Patrick Verlinden is murdered most likely on the following Saturday, and on the Monday Esmeralda finds out she isn't coming into a fortune.' He looked at Langham. 'Significant?'

Langham gazed across the room; outside, darkness had fallen, and the tiny mullioned panes were being gradually covered by snow.

'I wonder . . .' he said.

'Go on.'

'If Esmeralda thought she was coming into money through Mariner, why plan to steal the painting – or murder Patrick Verlinden? Why go to the risk of doing either?'

'OK,' Ralph said, 'perhaps she knew beforehand what the financial set-up was – perhaps she'd found out that his lordship was on his uppers, which was why she planned the theft and, later, the murder.'

'I suppose that's a possibility.'

Ralph smiled to himself. 'Christ, Don, imagine how she must be feeling. At one point months back she thinks she'll eventually be rolling in it. Then she thinks she'll at least have the proceeds from the painting. And now she has sweet bugger all! What's it called?'

'Poetic justice?' Langham said. 'We'd better inform Montgomery of the latest development, though where she might have skedaddled to . . .'

'What next?' Ralph asked.

'We really need to know whether Esmeralda and Mariner's alibi for the Saturday early evening holds water. Until then we're stymied.'

Langham crossed the room to the window and peered out. The snow was six inches deep and falling fast.

'You said you were planning to drive back tonight?' he said.

'That's the plan.'

'Think again. Come and look at this.'

Ralph joined him and whistled.

'How about coming back to Charles's tonight?' Langham suggested. 'He'll be more than happy to put you up. We'll have dinner and a drink and see what the conditions are like in the morning. I was planning to drive to London tomorrow and follow up a couple of leads.'

'I'll do that. I can't say the idea of driving in this appeals much. I'd better phone Annie to tell her what's what.'

It was still snowing, five minutes later, when Langham left Neston Manor followed by Ralph in his Morris Minor.

Charles flung open the door and cried, 'But look at you! And Ralph – what a pleasant surprise!'

'Ralph intended to drive to London, but I persuaded him otherwise. Room at the inn?'

'By all means. The more the merrier. I'll show you to your room, young man, then you can come down for drinks. Maria and I returned early this afternoon, but Albert shot off at two, engaged on a little sleuthing mission on your behalf, Donald.'

'I saw the Daimler parked outside the Dog and Gun as we were passing,' Langham said.

'Albert cooked a hotpot this morning and left it in the oven. He said he'd be back at six thirty.' Charles consulted his watch. 'And it is now six – time, I think, for the first one of the evening.'

Maria was in the library, poring over a manuscript, when they entered. 'Put aside work, my dear,' Charles carolled, 'and tell Donald all about the properties we've discarded today. Scotch or gin and tonic, Donald?'

'I think a gin for a change,' Langham said. 'I've been enjoying a tot or two of Scotch this afternoon. But these houses . . .'

Maria, seated before the blazing fire, looked wonderful in a green pleated skirt and a white bodice with pearls. 'Charles and I have toured more villages than I can name.'

'But not Spankington Wallop?'

'We couldn't find it, sadly. But we did come upon a Lesser Piddlethorp, which made me wonder where Greater Piddlethorp might be. We looked at a few houses for sale, and the odd thing was that the houses I liked were in villages I didn't care for . . .'

'And houses you didn't like the look of,' Langham laughed, 'were no doubt in villages you liked?'

'Such is life!' Charles declared. 'But it means only that you will have to spend another weekend with me before Christmas, scouring the area.'

Conversation moved on to other things, and at one point Langham asked Charles if he was aware of Lord Elsmere's political affiliations back in the thirties.

Charles pulled an exaggeratedly glum face. 'I heard rumours, my boy, and once or twice, when Teddy was in his cups, he let slip views which I found unsavoury in the extreme. Why do you ask?'

'He mentioned it the other day. You see, between the three of us, he knew Ralph's father.' He recounted what Ralph had told him about his father being the branch secretary of the British Union of Fascists back in the thirties. 'Quite understandably, Ralph cut up rough about it and didn't say much.' He sipped his gin. 'But I'd be interested to know if Elsmere still holds these views.'

Charles pulled his chin. 'Do you know something, I think he regrets his involvement with Mosley. He's mellowed with age and doesn't like his past being raked up.'

'Well, he was half-cut when he mentioned Ralph's father.' He fell silent as the door at the far end of the room opened and Ralph joined them.

Presently Charles's housemaid announced that Albert had returned and that dinner would be served in five minutes.

They filed into the dining room to find Albert entering from the kitchen bearing a huge terracotta tureen and looking more than a little pleased with himself.

'Have I been busy this afternoon!' he said, ladling out bowls of rich broth with beef and dumplings.

'Charles mentioned you were on the case,' Langham said. 'We'll have to put you on the agency's payroll.'

'You will when I tell you what I've found out.'

'But first,' Charles said from the head of the table. 'A toast to house-hunting friends and unexpected guests!'

They drank. Ralph smacked his lips. 'Don't go a bundle on red wine normally, Charles, but this is a drop of all right.'

'A Montrachet '34,' Charles said. 'One of the finest, I do believe.'

Maria sipped her wine and smiled across at Langham. 'How is the investigation proceeding, Donald?'

'To be honest we could do with a lead,' he said, looking across at Albert. 'I'm all ears.'

The young man gulped down a mouthful of hotpot and dabbed his lips with a napkin. 'Well, there I was, enjoying my second pint in the snug and nattering with a couple of locals when this chap walks in. Knew right off he's a flatfoot. I can sniff 'em a mile off. Thick-set young chap, beady eyes, balding . . .'

'Sounds like Montgomery's chap,' Ralph said, 'Detective Sergeant Halliday.'

'So he walks up to the bar and has a quiet word in old Reg's shell-like, and then him and Reg disappear into a back room. They're in there about ten minutes – I can hear the sound of their voices but I can't make out what they're saying. There I am, sitting at the bar nodding and smiling at what some farmer is telling me about bleeding foxes, when all I want to do is hark at what the tar-bender and flatfoot are yawping about. So, after a half hour the copper pops out the back room and off he toddles.'

'And you're none the wiser?' Langham asked.

Albert pointed across the table. 'But that's where you're very wrong, Mr Donald. Very wrong indeed. 'Cos old Reg likes a gossip as good as the next man, and he's not one to keep a secret. So he tells us that the rozzer wanted to know if young Dutchy, this Verlinden chap, was in the Dog on Saturday evening, and who else was in the place from four o'clock onwards.'

'We know Verlinden never reached the pub,' Ralph said, 'but who *was* there?'

Albert beamed. 'None other than his lordship's son, Mariner, is who.'

Langham lowered his glass. 'Mariner? But he and Esmeralda were in town, or so they said, until about five-ish.'

Albert shook his head. 'No, they weren't. They got back to the manor around three thirty 'cos one of the locals said they saw Mariner's Vauxhall drive through the village around then. And then some time after four, he turns up at the Dog and has a quiet Scotch in the lounge. Old Reg told us that Mariner, never the happiest, looked particularly miserable that night, had a face like a slapped arse, he said. He ordered a single whisky, sat by hisself in the corner, then drank up and left just after five.'

'This puts a different complexion on the issue,' Langham said.

'So if Esmeralda was back at the manor by three thirty,' Ralph said, 'she could have taken her shotgun from the barn and followed Verlinden into the woods.'

'She could at that,' Langham said. 'But what about Mariner?'

'Come again?' Ralph said.

'If Mariner got to the Dog at some time after four, *he* could have followed Verlinden into the woods, couldn't he?'

Ralph pointed at him with his fork. 'And his motive? Did he suspect Esmeralda and Verlinden were having an affair?'

'I honestly think Mariner's too naive to have suspected,' Langham said. 'No, but I have another idea . . .' He sat back, took a mouthful of wine, and said, 'I've been mulling this over for a while, going through the residents one by one and ascribing motives, however far-fetched.'

'And?'

Langham smiled. 'And this one is pretty far-fetched – in fact, all the way from France.'

'You're talking in riddles, my boy,' Charles said.

'One of the big mysteries of this whole affair is Patrick Verlinden, agreed? Where he came from, what he – a war hero, if you believe what he claimed – was doing odd-jobbing for a pittance at the manor. Now recall the other day when it came out that Lord Elsmere had a son way back in the twenties, whom he'd heard had been killed in France during the war?'

'Go on,' Ralph said.

'What if – and this is merely a suggestion – what if this son, James Edward, actually survived the war? What if Patrick Verlinden and James Edward were one and the same person, come to claim what he saw as being rightly his?'

He looked around the table at a phalanx of incredulous expressions.

'Well, blow me down,' Ralph said, sitting back in his chair.

'But . . .' Albert said, struggling to find a reasonable objection, 'wouldn't he have come straight out and told his lordship who he was?'

Langham shrugged. 'How do we know that he didn't? Lord Elsmere might have been a little reluctant to mention the fact. Or maybe Verlinden was playing his cards close to his chest and biding his time, for whatever reasons.'

'And then,' Ralph said slowly, 'Dudley Mariner finds out who Verlinden really is, sees the danger of being disinherited, and decides that young Verlinden must be got rid of?'

'And remember, we found out today that when Verlinden was killed, Mariner thought he was still due to come into a decent inheritance.' Langham spread his hands. 'But I'm the first to admit that all this is highly speculative. He might be as innocent as the driven snow. But it's worth our consideration.'

Maria said, 'You said that Lord Elsmere had *heard* that his son had been killed in France? He didn't know for sure?'

'He heard, a year or two after the war, that James Edward had been killed along with his mother in an air raid on Paris in 'forty-four.'

'I wonder . . .' Maria began. She touched Langham's hand. 'I could phone my father in the morning. He must have contacts at the embassy here who would know how to go about finding out if the boy and his mother *were* killed then.'

'His lordship's first wife, Gloria, married an American millionaire by the name of Dowling at some point in the twenties, so presumably mother and son would have taken his surname.'

'I'll contact my father and see if he can suggest anything,' she said.

Ralph laughed. 'At this rate, Don, we'll be employing more detectives than there are suspects, what with Dick Barton here,' he went on, pointing at Albert.

The young man held up a big hand. 'Oh – I learned something else at the Dog today,' he said. 'Don, you asked me to find out the name of this big-wig Esmeralda was knocking off.'

'Dick Barton indeed.' Langham laughed.

'I got talking to this farmer about Esmeralda, and he said she was leading Mariner a right dance and seeing this bloke up beyond Bury St Edmunds.'

'Did the farmer know his name?'

'He's a chap called Wallace Pitt-Lavery. A Tory councillor, due to stand in the next parliamentary elections. Ex-RAF. Squadron leader, by all accounts. Apparently he lives in the big house next to the church in Middle Langley, a village a couple of miles north of Bury St Edmunds.'

'Albert,' Charles said, beaming at the young man, 'I'm proud of you! Is there no end to your talents? Valet, chauffeur, mechanic, cook, boxer, private eye . . .'

Albert gazed across the table at Charles like the proverbial tomcat who'd snaffled the cream.

'I wonder . . .' Ralph said. 'Don, what about we take a mosey on up to Middle Langley first thing, on the off chance that Esmeralda's holing up there?'

'Good idea,' Langham said. 'I was going to drive into London in the morning, weather permitting, but that can wait until the afternoon.'

'And now,' Charles enquired, 'who's for dessert? And I see that one or two glasses are looking *outrageously* empty.'

NINETEEN

Langham set off immediately after breakfast the following day, keeping his speed under forty miles an hour so as not to lose Ralph who was following in his Morris Minor. The snow of the night before had ceased, but it still covered the land to a depth of six inches, and weak sunlight illuminated the rolling fields.

Maria and Charles were spending another day in the country, reading manuscripts; they planned to return to London and the agency in the morning.

Langham had passed a restless night going over the minutiae of the case. Unlike Ralph, he was far from convinced that Esmeralda was the guilty party. A woman as organized and determined as she was, he reasoned, would hardly plan to blackmail her victim and then, quite arbitrarily deciding that she wanted *all* the proceeds of the art theft, change her mind and murder him.

At the same time, he couldn't envisage the ineffectual Mariner shooting Verlinden – even if he had feared being disinherited. As for Lord Elsmere, Rebecca Miles, and Major Rutherford . . . He had yet to discover motives that might place them in the running as suspects.

They arrived at Middle Langley just before ten o'clock and parked beside the stocks on the green. It was a pretty village,

its thatched cottages made more picturesque with the addition
of snow. With its Saxon church, ancient graveyard, and lack of
new buildings, the place might have remained unchanged for
the past two hundred years.

Squadron leader Pitt-Lavery's residence was a foursquare
Georgian pile situated next to the church.

'Look,' Ralph said as they passed the church. 'Isn't that
Esmeralda's Hillman?'

The car stood in the driveway, its roof and bonnet covered
in snow.

Ralph laughed. 'I'll enjoy seeing her squirm when I tell her
we know she was back at the manor by three thirty that Saturday
afternoon.'

'I just hope the squadron leader's amenable to playing host
to a couple of down-at-heel gumshoes,' Langham said, pushing
open the wrought-iron gate and leading the way up the flag-
stoned path to a white-painted front door. He dropped a heavy
iron knocker three times and arranged his tie.

The door opened and a small, grey-haired woman in her
sixties smiled at them uncertainly. 'If you're door-to-door—'
she began in Lowland Scottish tones.

Langham was swift with his accreditation. 'Detectives
Langham and Ryland,' he said, producing his most charming
smile. 'I wonder if I might speak to Esmeralda Bellamy?'

'I'm afraid she's stepped out to the village, but she'll be back
presently.'

'Then could we possibly speak to Mr Pitt-Lavery?'

The woman – presumably the housekeeper – relented and
led them along a hallway to a spacious drawing room. 'If you'd
just wait here, gentlemen. Now who should I say?'

Langham repeated their names and the woman departed.

He crossed the room to the window and stared out over a
long back garden. Snow had started to fall again and large flakes
adhered to the glass, obscuring the view.

'Bloody hell!' Ralph said.

Langham turned. 'What is it?'

'I don't get it,' Ralph said, scratching his head. 'Coincidence,
or what? Come and have a look at this.'

Ralph was standing before a sideboard on which sat a dozen

framed photographs; on the wall above it were more black and white photos. All of them portrayed uniformed airmen, either singly or in groups. A large portrait in pride of position on the wall showed a distinguished-looking young man with a long face and receding hair, in the uniform of a squadron leader.

'I reckon that's our man, Squadron Leader Pitt-Lavery,' Ralph said, pointing to the photograph. 'But take a look at that . . .'

With a flourish he indicated a black and white snap on the sideboard. The photograph showed half a dozen men standing in front of a Hurricane. 'My word,' Langham said.

'It's the same one as Patrick Verlinden had at the gatehouse,' Ralph said, 'except this one shows a bit more of the plane in the background. And look – the tall geezer on the left: it's Pitt-Lavery.'

'And the chap third from the right is Patrick Verlinden,' Langham said. 'So they knew each other during the war.'

Ralph nodded. 'I think this might be the break we've been looking for, me old mucker.'

The door opened and Wallace Pitt-Lavery entered the room, looking a little older, and more distinguished, in the flesh. He was tall and angular and wore a dark suit and tie. He introduced himself and they shook hands.

'I understand you wish to speak to Esme?'

'That's right,' Ralph said, showing his accreditation. 'We're investigating the death of Patrick Verlinden, and we'd like to ask a few questions. Did Miss Bellamy happen to mention . . .?'

'She told me all about the dreadful affair, and of course I'd read about it in the local paper.' He gestured to a sofa and two armchairs before an open fire. 'Won't you take a seat? Esmeralda should be back shortly.'

Pitt-Lavery folded himself on to the sofa, crossing his long legs. Ralph sat in an armchair. Langham moved from the sideboard and sat side-saddle on the arm of the unoccupied chair.

'It must have come as a shock,' Ralph said, 'knowing Patrick Verlinden as you did?'

'I'll say. Bolt from the blue. Esme phoned me the day the body was discovered.'

'When was the last time you saw Verlinden?' Ralph asked.

Pitt-Lavery considered the question. 'That must have been about six months ago, when he left here.'

Ralph looked surprised. 'Left here?'

'That's right. Patrick worked for me for a few months earlier this year. He lodged in the summer house at the end of the garden and did odd jobs around the place. The thing was, there wasn't enough work to occupy him full-time, so he had to look elsewhere.'

'What struck us as strange,' Langham said, 'was why a man with his credentials – a war hero, after all, injured in action – should have been reduced to working as an odd-job man.'

Pitt-Lavery blinked, smiling uncomprehendingly from Langham to Ralph. 'War hero? Where on earth did you get that from?'

Gesturing towards the sideboard, Ralph said, 'But you knew him during the war . . .'

'During the war?' Pitt-Lavery assumed an expression of amused puzzlement. 'Whatever are you talking about, Mr Ryland? I first met Patrick Verlinden when he knocked on my door back in March, looking pathetic and begging for work. I took pity on him and found him a few jobs to do, as I mentioned.'

Langham moved to the sideboard and returned with the group photograph of the airmen. He passed it to Pitt-Lavery. 'The young man, third from the right? Isn't that Patrick Verlinden?'

Pitt-Lavery took the picture. 'No, of course not. That's Mike Naylor.' He passed the photograph back to Langham. 'I don't know where you picked up your information, gentlemen, but I can assure you that Verlinden was no pilot. He told me he was injured in a German air raid on Rotterdam at the start of the war.'

Langham replaced the photograph on the sideboard and returned to the armchair, this time dropping into the seat and staring across at the ex-squadron leader. Pitt-Lavery, for his part, was looking more than a little bemused, shuttling a quizzical look between the two detectives.

'So if Verlinden worked here as an odd-job man,' Ralph said, 'he could have entered the house, and this room, whenever he wished?'

Pitt-Lavery shrugged. 'Of course, when there were jobs that

needed doing. He painted the window frames in here, as a matter of fact.'

'Do you know if any of your photographs are missing? Or might he have taken one for a time and then replaced it?'

'None are missing, as far as I'm aware. But . . .' He hesitated, stroking his long jaw-line. 'But a few days before Patrick left, he was in here polishing the sideboard. He told me he'd accidentally knocked over the photograph you indicated, breaking the frame. He said he'd take it into town to be mended. I told him not to bother, but he insisted.'

Ralph snapped his fingers. 'There you have it! He took the photo and had it copied while the frame was being fixed.'

'Copied?' Pitt-Lavery said. 'But why on earth . . .?'

'He wanted the picture,' Ralph explained, 'to pass himself off as a fighter pilot and a war hero, which he did when he went to work for Lord Elsmere.'

Pitt-Lavery shook his head. 'Well, I'll be . . .'

Langham considered what the ex-squadron leader had said. 'I hope you don't mind my enquiring,' he asked, 'but how long have you known Esmeralda Bellamy?'

Pitt-Lavery thought about it. 'Well, we first met around six months ago – just after Patrick Verlinden left here. You see, Esme came to the house one morning and explained that she wanted to check the reference I'd given Verlinden, who'd applied to work for Lord Elsmere.'

'Ah, she did, did she?' Ralph said, glancing across at Langham.

'Tell me,' Langham said. 'Did you bring her in here?'

Pitt-Lavery nodded. 'Yes, we had tea, as I recall—'

Ralph interrupted, 'And how long after that was it that you and her became lovers?'

Pitt-Lavery rubbed his jaw. 'Well, seeing as you ask . . . It was quite a while. Just a month ago, as a matter of fact.'

From the hallway, Langham heard the sound of the front door opening and closing. 'That must be Esme,' Pitt-Lavery said. 'If you'll excuse me one moment.'

He climbed to his feet and left the room.

'It's beginning to make sense,' Ralph said. 'When Esmeralda came here, checking up on Verlinden, she sees the photo . . .'

'And realizes,' Langham said, 'that Verlinden's story about being a war hero is highly suspect. I wonder if that's when she decided to blackmail him—'

He was interrupted when the door opened and Pitt-Lavery ushered a stony-faced Esmeralda Bellamy into the room.

Perhaps in an attempt to make an effort with her lover, Esmeralda was wearing make-up, which she'd never bothered with when Langham had seen her at the manor. The effect, however, struck him as tragic; she was a plain woman and the application of cosmetics served only to emphasize her ordinariness.

'Gentlemen.' She looked from Ralph to Langham. 'I thought I'd adequately answered all your questions, but evidently not.'

'There are a few outstanding points we'd like to clear up,' Ralph said.

She crossed to the settee and sat down. Pitt-Lavery moved to join her, but Ralph said, 'If you don't mind, sir, we'd like to conduct the interview with Miss Bellamy alone.'

The ex-squadron leader looked at Esmeralda, then cleared his throat. 'Very well. I'll be in the library if you need me, Esme.'

He left the room.

Ralph looked across at Langham and nodded for him to take the lead.

'Now,' Langham said, 'I understand you came here six months ago to consult with Mr Pitt-Lavery about Patrick Verlinden's reference?'

Blowing smoke impatiently, Esmeralda said, 'That's right. I met Verlinden a few days after Lord Elsmere agreed to employ him. I was suspicious of his claims to have flown for the RAF, despite the photograph. I came here and spoke with Wallace, and when I saw *his* photographs' – she gestured across the room – 'I noticed that one of them was almost identical to one Verlinden had on display in the gatehouse—'

'And that's when you decided to blackmail him?'

'What on earth makes you think . . .?' She drew on her cigarette, her hand shaking.

Langham took the notepaper from his inside pocket. He unfolded it and held it up before Esmeralda.

He read the line out loud: '"Verlinden, I know all about you and your lies. I'll be in touch". Of course,' he went on, 'you didn't know *all* about him and his lies, but he didn't realize that. You had him where you wanted him—'

'You have no proof,' Esmeralda began in desperation.

Langham waved the letter. 'Oh, I don't know. This is pretty conclusive, what with the smudged o and the broken y. It was typed on your machine. And taken together with your previous blackmail attempts . . . I should think it'd be pretty damning evidence, myself.'

He stared at her. She was stone-faced, giving absolutely nothing away. He replaced the note in his pocket and sat back.

Ralph said, 'What we'd like to know, Miss Bellamy, is when you decided not to blackmail Patrick Verlinden, but to kill him? Did you think that it'd be too much bother, as well as being too risky, to extort money from him – so why not just wait till he'd nabbed the painting, then shoot the poor chap dead and get all the dosh from its sale?'

She shook her head, her face still expressionless. 'I didn't kill Verlinden. The idea is preposterous.'

Ralph sat back in the armchair and allowed the uneasy silence to stretch. He even lit a cigarette, taking his time about it, before inhaling a lungful and observing, 'You lied about the time you arrived back at the manor on the afternoon of Saturday the seventeenth.'

A spark of alarm showed in her eyes. 'Lied? I can't recall . . .'

'You told the police you didn't get back from Bury St Edmunds until after five o'clock that day.'

She waved this away, but her smile faltered. 'Four, five . . . It's a while ago now. I can't recall exactly when we might have got back.'

Ralph made a show of consulting his notebook. 'You and Dudley were seen driving through the village just after three thirty. It's estimated that Patrick Verlinden was murdered around four o'clock that afternoon.'

She leaned forward and buckled the end of her cigarette in an ashtray on the coffee table, her fingers trembling. 'It's quite possible we returned earlier than I first thought. I don't wear a watch, you see, and I often have no idea of the time. It was getting dark, and I must have assumed that it was later than it actually was.'

'Or you knew very well what time it was,' Ralph said, 'and arrived home well before four, when you knew Verlinden set off through the woods for the Dog and Gun. So you took your shotgun from the barn, followed him and did the business.'

'No!' she cried. 'I wouldn't . . . I would never kill anyone!'

Ralph sat back. 'It looks bad, Miss Bellamy. It looks very bad indeed. You have a previous conviction for blackmail, you write a nasty note to Verlinden and you're seen conspiring with him in the Dog and Gun. Then his body turns up, shot with your own weapon . . . *and you lie about where you were at the time of the shooting.*' He shook his head. 'Oh, it looks very, very bad to me.'

Ralph looked across at Langham and nodded.

Langham climbed to his feet. 'We'll make our own way out,' he said, and left the woman sitting very still and staring blankly at the fire.

'Well,' Ralph said as they stepped from the house, 'what did you make of that?'

'It seems so obvious she shot Verlinden that I'm not at all sure she did.' He shrugged. 'It seems a big step to take, from being a blackmailer to a killer.'

Ralph smiled. 'That doesn't mean to say she didn't make that step, Don.'

'No, you're right. It doesn't.'

They arrived at their cars parked beside the village green.

'I think I'll pop in and see Montgomery,' Ralph said. 'Bring him up to speed and give him Esmeralda's note.'

Langham took the envelope from his pocket and handed it over. 'And then?'

'I'll motor down to the manor and have a word with Mariner about his scuppered alibi. You?'

'London-bound. I want to follow a couple of leads on Major Rutherford and Rebecca Miles.'

Ralph looked up into the sky, scowling at the falling snow. 'I'll probably take up Charles's invitation to stay another night. See you back there tonight, Don.'

Langham saluted, slipped in behind the wheel of his Rover and set off for London.

TWENTY

From the journal of Major William Arthur Rutherford.

Last Friday, the 16th, I rose late to find that a pipe under the sink in the kitchenette was leaking. I managed to stem most of the flow myself, swaddling the affected length with rags, then had breakfast and promptly forgot about the dashed thing. I should have told Benson immediately: I blame old age.

On my morning walk around the drive, I saw Inspector Montgomery and his deputy drive up and speak with Esmeralda and Dudley in the barn; then Montgomery crossed to the gatehouse, and through the window I saw him pacing up and down in the front room, giving young Verlinden a grilling. My turn next, I thought as I made my way back inside.

At eleven, tired of Wellard's life of General Patten, I left my room and summoned Benson to serve me tea and crumpets in the drawing room, with the morning paper. I'd scarcely been there ten minutes when Miss Miles joined me, which was more than pleasant. I rattled the *Telegraph* at her and asked what the deuce the politicians were playing at these days, which elicited a somewhat forbearing smile from the girl. I am under no illusions: she must think me a reactionary old fogey, which I suppose, from her up-to-the-minute and progressive point of view, I am. But she's rather sweet in her tolerance and doesn't hold it against me.

We had polished off the last of the crumpets when the door opened and Teddy limped in, accompanied by an officious-looking young man in a sharp pinstriped suit. Teddy looked like thunder, and the young chap's lean face was set in stone.

Teddy introduced us, brusquely, to Mr Williams of the

something-or-other-insurance company and looked at the debris of our elevenses. I got the message and said we were just leaving. On the way out, as Benson was entering the room, I belatedly mentioned the leaking pipe; Benson said he would inform his lordship at the first convenient opportunity.

As I was passing through the entrance hall, on my way back to the east wing, who should come down the staircase but young Verlinden. I must admit that the affair of the stolen painting had pushed the unpleasantness of our previous meeting to the back of my mind – but the sight of the young man, and the mocking smile he gave when he saw me, turned my stomach. Just what on earth did he want? He brushed by me without a word and left the house.

Miss Miles touched my arm and asked if I was all right, bless her. I assured her that I was fine, other than a little gyp in the old foot, thanked her and limped back to my room.

I spent the rest of the afternoon reading, and at three indulged in a couple of fingers of whisky. There is nothing like the balm of a single malt to keep the worries of the world at bay.

When a knock at the door sounded around four o'clock, I blithely assumed it was Inspector Montgomery, come to question me about the missing painting. Imagine my displeasure, therefore, when I opened the door and Patrick Verlinden walked in as brash as you like, carrying a toolbox.

'I have come to mend the pipe, Major,' he said as he pushed past me.

'You've no need,' I told him. 'I've fixed it myself.'

He ducked under the lintel to the kitchen area, opened the door under the sink and knelt to inspect the pipe.

He laughed. 'Do you call that fixed, Major?'

He pulled out the sopping rags I'd bound around the pipe and deposited them in the sink, giving me his best lopsided grin as he did so.

He opened his toolbox and busied himself with his head stuck in the cupboard.

I wanted to leave him to it, retire to the library and wait until he'd finished the job. But at the same time something counselled me to remain where I was. I possess nothing of great monetary worth, but I have several items of sentimental value around the place. I wouldn't have put it past Verlinden to help himself to whatever he fancied.

I returned to the fireside, poured myself another Scotch, and tried to read.

That was impossible, of course; how could I concentrate on General Patten's push across Europe when Verlinden was banging about under the sink? I wanted nothing more than for him to finish the job as quickly as possible and get out. I might have known that I was hoping for too much.

The noise stopped a while later, and an odd silence ensued. I turned in my armchair and stared into the kitchen. He was leaning back against the sink, wiping his dirty hands on one of my clean towels and staring at me in silence. That stare, with his drooping left eye, and the sardonic twist to his mouth, made my stomach turn.

'I have fixed the pipe,' he said.

'Thank you,' I replied. 'Now, I was about to take a bath, so . . .'

He tossed the towel on to the draining board but made no move to leave. 'I was hoping that you might be a little more grateful for what I have done, Major.'

'I said thank you—'

'I was hoping that you would offer me a drink. I see that you are drinking whisky. I like good whisky.'

'As I said, I was about to draw myself a bath.'

He limped from the kitchen. The sudden movement, after his inactivity, startled me. He crossed the sitting room and paused before my books. He stood there with his hands on his hips, staring up at the titles.

I took a mouthful of whisky. To my annoyance, I found that my hand was shaking.

'You have many fine books, Major.'

I made no reply.

I was tempted to reach out and pull the tasselled cord that would summon Benson, but something stayed my hand. While a part of me wanted nothing more than to ask the butler to eject the young man, I felt that there would be something submissive about the action, and I have never been one to have others fight my own battles.

I watched him. He stepped forward, reached up and ran the fingers of his right hand across the spines of the books at chest height. 'They must be worth quite a bit, Major?'

I said nothing. My grip tightened on my glass. I was trembling with rage and, I admit, fear – and I despised myself for it. Why, I'd faced down threats from armed men in the past without so much as batting an eyelid. So why was I letting Verlinden intimidate me so?

'And these,' he went on, indicating the top shelf, 'must be your journals.' He looked over his shoulder and smiled at me without the slightest warmth.

'Now, I wonder . . .' He reached up and touched the journals one by one. '1948,' he said, ''49, '50 . . . Am I getting close?'

I managed to say, 'Don't know what the ruddy hell you're driving at.'

'Don't you, Major? Now, where was I? 1950 . . . Ah, '51. An interesting year, was it not?'

'I've no idea what you mean.'

'Well, let me see . . .'

He reached up and pulled down the journal marked MCMLI. He leaned back against the bookshelf, flicking through the volume with little care. He stared down at the typewritten pages, frowning, and pausing in his riffling to read the occasional passage.

By this time I was shaking with rage. My journals were private; the repository of my innermost thoughts and feelings. To have this young lout leering at them was tantamount to sacrilege.

'Ah . . .' he said, looking up at me. 'August . . . This is what I was looking for.'

'What do you want?' I cried, my voice breaking.

He ignored me, reading page after page, his narrow brow furrowed with concentration.

At last he stopped reading, looked up, and snapped the covers of the journal shut.

'I am disappointed, Major, that you decided not to write about what happened back in August, 1951 . . .' He shrugged. 'But then again, perhaps that was wise of you.'

I keep my loaded service revolver in the drawer of the table beside my armchair. I was tempted to open the drawer, produce the gun, and tell Verlinden to get out.

He dropped the journal on my desk, making me jump, then moved from the bookcase. He sat down in the opposite armchair and stared at me.

He rested his elbows on the arms of the chair and steepled his fingers before his chest.

'I know everything that happened back in '51, Major. Everything . . .'

He went on to describe, in sickening detail, the one incident in my life of which I am deeply ashamed – and I have no desire to compound my pain here by recounting what he said.

Suffice to say that he finished with, 'And now, Major, I must decide what to do next.'

I managed to say, 'What do you mean?'

'I mean, what might your friends here, his lordship and little Miss Miles, think of you when they learn the truth?'

'What do you want?' I all but sobbed.

He smiled. How I was growing to hate that expression! 'I have written up a little account of what happened in August 1951, Major, and I am tempted to post it to his lordship.'

I almost said that he could do that – that no one would believe what he had written. But my fear was that his missive would sow the seeds of doubt in the minds of my friends.

So I said nothing.

'But then again,' he went on, 'perhaps that can be prevented. It wouldn't take much to make me change my mind. Perhaps even as little as one hundred pounds. Not a lot, I think you would agree, to a man of your means.'

I think it was then, as I sat and stared at the young man opposite, that a wonderful feeling of calm came over me as I realized what I should do.

I sat back in my chair and said calmly, 'I cannot lay my hands on that much straight away, Mr Verlinden. I'll go into town next week . . .'

A fleeting look of what might have been relief crossed his face, as if even in his cupidity he had doubted that I would so readily agree to his demand.

'That, Major, is very sensible.' He climbed to his feet, towering over me. 'I will pay you a little visit on Monday afternoon. Until then . . .'

He limped from the room, and I watched him go with a feeling of intense loathing in my belly.

I crossed to the door, locked it, then returned to the fireside.

I poured myself another whisky, a very large whisky this time, and considered what I should do next.

TWENTY-ONE

Langham threaded his way through an obstacle course of desks and busy reporters, dodging overflowing wastepaper baskets on the way. The newsroom of the *Daily Herald* was like a cross between a lunatic asylum and a factory whose sole purpose was the production of noise, the clatter of typewriters competing with the din of shouted voices. It was a miracle that anyone could think straight in such conditions, he thought, still less write legible copy.

He arrived at the reviews desk and slumped into a chair opposite a small, balding man who looked, with his high collar and tortoiseshell glasses, more like a harried town clerk than a senior editor.

Tyler looked up briefly from his typewriter. 'You're a week early,' he grunted.

Langham braved the lion's den of the newsroom once a month for the latest crime releases, then posted Tyler the reviews a week later. In the early days, when the sales of his own books were mediocre, the column was an assured regular income; now, with his books selling well and the film deal complete, he was thinking of handing in his notice. Something, however, some innate fear that the good times might dry up, kept him coming back for more.

He eyed the tottering piles of novels on the desk. 'I'm actually here about something else, but I might as well take a selection.'

He pulled out a few likely looking titles. 'Recall the Gerson murder case a few years ago?'

The editor looked up. 'Vaguely. What about it?'

'I presume the paper reported the woman's release from jail earlier this year?'

'We did – that'd be young Evans. He covered crime back then. Why, you thinking of turning your talents to true crime?'

'No fear. I'm interested, that's all. Thought it might feed into a thriller I'm working on. Evans around?'

'He was bumped up to features in the summer, so you'll find him dossing over there.' He waved his pencil vaguely over his shoulder towards a glass-panelled room in the corner.

'Much obliged,' Langham said, picked up the half dozen hardbacks and crossed to the box room whose door grandly pronounced: *Features Department*.

He knocked and entered, and as the door swung shut behind him the din of the newsroom subsided.

A young man rocked back on a chair, his feet lodged on the desk.

'Evans?' Langham asked, dropping his load to the floor and sitting down. 'Donald Langham, I review for this rag, for my sins.'

The young man smiled, swung his feet from the desk and leaned forward in one easy motion, offering his hand. He wore shirtsleeves and a green knitted tie, pulled tight and dragged to one side like an awry noose. 'Larry. How can I help?'

'Tyler mentioned you worked on the crime desk until summer.'

'I did, for *my* sins, and hated every blessed minute of it. I admit I'm squeamish – more suited to writing theatre reviews than reporting on gangland killings.'

'Rather you than me, but you've landed yourself a cushy number here.'

'I see it as my reward for having to interview Harry the Knife and Scarface Sid. You don't happen to want an introduction to any of these types, do you?'

'No fear, but if I can pick your brain on another matter?'

'Fire away.'

'The Gerson murder case. Tyler said you covered her release.'

'That's right. Did a feature and an interview when the popsie was released from Holloway. Why the interest?'

Langham gave Evans the line about research for a potential thriller. 'Recall much about the case?'

'I'll say. Stuck with me. It isn't every day a stunner beats her husband to death and immediately turns herself in to the police. Of course, the killing happened four or five years ago, back when I was still a cub reporter for the *Barking Chronicle*. Chap called Nicholls covered the case for the *Herald*; he's retired now. But when she was released I read up on his reports, to give me a bit of background for the interview.'

'I understand she was convicted of manslaughter?'

Evans nodded. 'And if it'd been *me* handing down the verdict, old boy, she would have walked out of court scot-free.'

'On account of her being a bit of a looker?'

'On account of her having been beaten black and blue by a drunken lout of a husband. She married a character called Peter Hayley, a small-time crook – but she must've regretted the day she ever clapped eyes on the hoodlum. She stuck it a year, then one night when he started roughing her up, she picked up a clothes iron and beat him over the head. I saw the photographs. Not much left of a skull when a heavy iron comes down on it a few times.'

Langham winced. 'I'll bet.'

'Anyway, the fact that she handed herself in quick sharp, and had neighbours who'd witnessed her beatings, helped her defence. Prosecution wanted to bring a charge of premeditated murder, but her defence got her off with manslaughter. She was sentenced to five years and got out after three and a half.'

Langham stuffed his pipe and lit up. 'You interviewed her just after she was released?'

'And a hell of a job that was, trying to win the family's trust. I played the "now it's time for your side of the story to be told" angle, and eventually they bought it. Gave me a couple of hours one Saturday afternoon, with the proviso that the father was present and that I'd run a rough copy of my piece by him before it went to press. I agreed: I wanted the interview pretty badly. I'd become intrigued by the case, by the woman. I wanted to see how she'd been affected by the ordeal.'

'And?'

'I went down to Peckham and interviewed Janita and her father at their rather bland suburban semi. She was tiny, gamine, and very damned gorgeous. I don't mind admitting I was tongue-tied for a minute or two, and that rarely happens. There she was, looking like a movie star, and all I could think about was how some bruiser used her as a punchbag. And if that wasn't hell enough, followed by three and a half years in the slammer, when she gets out she finds that her father's dying.'

Langham leaned forward. 'Dying?'

'Leukaemia. Months to live. Apparently, her mother was long dead and the father was being nursed by Janita and her sister—'

Langham interrupted again. 'She had a sister?'

'You bet, and if I thought Janita was a corker, you should have seen her older sister. A dead-ringer for Audrey Hepburn.'

Langham leaned back and tried to sound casual as he asked, 'What was the sister's name?'

'Rebecca, and I still regret not asking her out – but, in the circumstances, it didn't seem the right thing to do.'

Evans went on, recounting the interview with Janita and offering his impression of the woman. 'She was strong, Langham. I thought that a stretch inside might have damaged her, but she claimed it had made her even stronger. I tried to get some family background, asked the father about his history – he sounded foreign, and I thought there might be an interesting angle there – but he wasn't having any of it and kept schtum.'

'Do you have any idea what happened to the women when their father died?'

'I heard on the grapevine that the father passed away earlier this year, and Janita emigrated to Canada. What happened to Rebecca I don't know.' He smiled, reminiscently. 'I even went back to the house, meaning to offer my condolences, but I was told by the new owners that the sisters had moved out a week earlier. Just my luck.'

The door crashed open and a short, fat man, built like a middleweight boxer gone to seed, stared from Langham to the young man. 'Where's that damned theatre copy, Evans?'

'On its way, guv!' Evans said, bending to his typewriter.

'I'd better leave you to it, then.'

'No rest for the wicked.' Evans laughed.

'Thanks for the gen,' Langham said, collecting his review copies and making for the door.

'Any time . . .' Evans called, his farewell drowned out by the cacophony as Langham crossed the newsroom.

He returned to his car and sat in silence for a time, considering what Evans had told him as he stared out at the falling snow.

The Carstairs was one of those exclusive gentlemen's clubs which proliferate in central London, a refuge from the woes and worries of the world in the middle of the twentieth century, a haven where like-minded souls retreated to have their prejudices not only maintained but reinforced. Like most clubs of its kind, it appeared unprepossessing from the street: it was when the visitor passed through its portals that he was dazzled by its opulence and deceptive spaciousness. A grand staircase rose from a black and white marble-tiled foyer and a dapper concierge surveyed his domain, and repelled non-members, from behind the barricade of a mahogany reception desk.

Most London clubs catered for a certain clientele, and the Carstairs was no exception: its members were drawn from the armed services above the rank of captain. It was the most conservative of establishments.

Langham had decided, while seated outside in his car, that his only chance of gaining an audience with 'Fat Boothby' was to stoop to deception. To this end he crossed the marble tiles to reception, flashed a smile at the concierge and announced himself as Detective Inspector Langham. With a sleight of hand worthy of any stage conjurer, he displayed his accreditation and returned it to his pocket before the young man had time to blink.

'I wonder if it would be possible to speak with a certain Major Boothby?'

'The major is currently in residence. I will endeavour to ascertain whether he will receive guests. And the nature of your enquiries?'

'They concern a mutual acquaintance, Major William Rutherford.'

The concierge allowed his first smile. 'I haven't had the pleasure of the major's company for some time now, Inspector. Please convey my regards when you see him, if you'd be so kind.'

'I'd be delighted.'

The concierge rang the desk bell and a liveried youth appeared from nowhere: they conferred in a whisper and the youth ascended the stairs while the concierge ushered Langham across the foyer to the guest room.

'Would you care for a drink while you wait, Inspector?'

Langham declined, and settled himself in a plush armchair before an open fire. The room was dark and Victorian, hung with photographs of military battalions and a dozen oil paintings depicting crusty old soldiers. He smiled as he imagined the conversations that must have taken place within these walls, the strategies argued over and the battles fondly recalled.

The main source of light came from the chandelier in the foyer, and this dimmed appreciably as a huge man waddled into the room. Langham could see that Fat Boothby certainly deserved his epithet: he had never seen a man as round in his life. He was as broad from hip to hip as he was tall, and he moved at a laborious pace with the aid of two walking sticks questing ahead of him like the antennae of some purblind insect.

Langham rose as Boothby negotiated a tiger-skin rug before the hearth and slowly squeezed himself into a two-seater settee.

'I'm grateful to you for making the time to see me, sir.'

'Major to you, young man,' Boothby wheezed. His face was as round as a globe, and the profusion of his moustache compensated for the absence of a single hair on his shining pate. 'Army man yourself, I take it, Inspector?'

'Field Security, sir. Captain. Madagascar and India.'

'India, eh? I served with the Fifth Lancers, Delhi, from 1894 to 1914. Time of my life. Salad days, Inspector. Then the Great War . . .' Boothby's gaze misted over. 'You saw action, I take it?'

'The invasion of Madagascar in '42.'

'Good show. My eternal regret – too old for the last one. Would've loved to have mixed it with the Boche.'

Langham smiled. 'Major Rutherford was saying something along those lines just the other day.'

'Ah, old Rutherford. How is the old chap? Bearing up?'

'He seems well, Major, and enjoying life in the country.'

'I miss him, you know? Saw him every day. Dominoes at eleven, a spot of lunch, and then we allowed ourselves a little of the cup that cheers. Speaking of which . . .' He indicated a bell pull beside the hearth. 'Be a hero and give that a tug, would you, Inspector?'

Langham did so, and within seconds a waiter appeared. 'Brandy and soda,' Boothby said. 'Make it a large one. You, Inspector?'

'Not while I'm on duty, Major.'

'Ah, duty,' the major said. 'Rutherford been getting himself into hot water, eh?'

'Not at all,' Langham said.

'So what's this all about?' the old man asked.

'I'm looking into a fatal shooting in Suffolk, Major, and making routine enquiries about the individuals in the vicinity at the time of the incident. I don't think for a minute that Major Rutherford was implicated, but he did know several of the suspects.' He hesitated. 'I understand that the major was involved in some kind of scandal, five years ago, which led to his having to leave London and move out to Suffolk?'

The waiter appeared with Boothby's drink, arranged a small table beside the old soldier and departed.

Major Boothby chewed his moustache and stared testily into

the fire. 'Delicate matter. Swore me to secrecy. Cut him up badly. Tried not to let it show at first, but I could see through his bluster. Known him nigh on fifty years, y'see.'

'I assure you that whatever you say will remain with me.'

'Your lot were involved, Scotland Yard, I believe – but it came to nothing. At least, no charges were pressed.' He looked up suddenly at Langham. 'But you could get all this from the Yard, couldn't you?'

Langham smiled. 'I'm from the Suffolk constabulary,' he temporised, 'and we like to conduct our own investigations. The Yard has enough on its plate.'

The explanation seemed to satisfy the old soldier. He took a mouthful of brandy, then said, 'Old Rutherford made a silly mistake. This was back in '51. Whether it was greed or simple naivety, who's to say? Upshot – lost it all. Or nearly all. Had a few quid stashed away in bonds, and this just about saw him through. But if it wasn't for Teddy Elsmere offering a refuge, it would've been the almshouse for poor old Rutherford.'

'What happened?' Langham murmured.

'Fell in with a bad lot, a con man. Oh, a charmer, but then they always are, aren't they? Chap claimed to be ex-army. Commanded a Gurkha regiment. Talked a good campaign. I heard him meself, in here, recounting how he led a platoon of his little chaps on a raid in Italy. Turned out to be baloney. Chap'd never even seen National Service and the nearest he'd been to Italy was Dover.'

'What did Rutherford . . .?'

'Coming to that, Inspector,' Boothby wheezed. 'Well, the fellow said he was an investment broker, and was on to a sure-fire winner. All he asked of Rutherford was an initial outlay of ten thousand for a return of twenty per cent per annum after a year. He even took the old boy to a plush office in Mayfair, where the deal was signed and Rutherford handed over his life savings.'

Langham whistled. 'Ten thousand . . .'

'Too good to be true, if you ask me. But he didn't, you see. Kept mum.'

'What happened?'

'Chap vanished and the office was found to be empty. Not hide nor hair could be found . . . Perhaps a month after he signed the deal, I noticed old Rutherford wasn't quite himself. Dammit, he looked as if he'd been handed a death sentence. Even missed a few afternoon sessions. So one day I took the bull by the horns and asked him straight out.'

'And he told you what had happened?'

'He prevaricated for a while, but a couple of snifters loosened his tongue and he told me about the ten thousand – and worse. The police had been in touch, dragged him down to Bow station to give him a grilling. Turns out this supposed ex-Gurkha chap was a big shot in gangland London, into every criminal scam you could imagine.'

'My word!'

'Gets worse. Appears the chap had used Rutherford's dosh to fund a drug smuggling caper from Tangiers to France, and when he was caught red-handed he named old Rutherford as being the brains behind the plot. Would you believe it! Touch and go for a while whether the major would face the music, but in the end your boys saw sense and realized he was nothing more than a "sucker", as I think the word is.'

Major Boothby shook his head sadly. 'Never saw a penny of his ten thousand, of course. I tried to jolly him along with the thought that it could have been worse: he might've ended up in gaol. But it was no consolation. Rutherford was a broken man. Then old Teddy Elsmere stepped in with the offer of a place in the sticks, and that was the last I saw of my old friend.'

'I think the major has done his best and put it behind him. He seems to be enjoying life up there.'

'That's good to know, Inspector.'

Major Boothby asked about the crime under investigation, and Langham spent ten minutes skilfully outlining the case without giving away much detail.

He climbed to his feet. 'I'd best be making tracks, Major. Our little chat has been very helpful.'

'Think nothing of it, Inspector. We must stick together, what? Remember me to Rutherford when you get back, would you?'

'I'll do that,' Langham said, shaking the old man's hand.

'Oh, and on your way out, be a hero and tell the waiter to fetch me another one of these, hm?'

The snow had stopped falling by the time Langham returned

to his car, and a bright sun shone in the mid-afternoon sky. Feeling that his time in London had been well spent, he left the capital and drove north.

Over dinner that evening, Ralph recounted his meeting with Dudley Mariner at the manor. He'd questioned the young man about the Saturday afternoon of the shooting, and his being seen driving through the village at three thirty, and later in the Dog and Gun. Mariner claimed he had little memory of what time he and Esmeralda had returned; he thought it had been around five but might have been mistaken.

'He said he'd had a row with Esmeralda over lunch in town and had been in a hell of a mood,' Ralph said. 'He left Esmeralda at the house and went to the pub, had a whisky and left an hour later.'

'So he could have followed Verlinden into the woods,' Langham said. 'Did he say which way he went to the pub, via the lane or through the woods?'

'He claims to have gone the lane way.'

Charles opened a second bottle of wine and they drank in companionable silence for a while, before the housekeeper entered the dining room and murmured to Maria that she was wanted on the phone. She raised her eyebrows at Langham, dabbed her mouth with a napkin, and slipped from the table.

Albert reported that, in the line of duty, he'd spent a couple of hours at the Dog and Gun that afternoon but had learned nothing more of interest. 'I could really get into this detective lark, Donald.'

Langham laughed. 'It isn't all quaffing ale and interrogating locals, old boy.'

Maria returned, looking thoughtful. She took her seat next to Langham and laid a hand on his arm. 'That was my father.'

He set down his glass. 'News?'

'A colleague of his at the embassy contacted someone in the war records department in Paris, regarding the fate of Lord Elsmere's first wife and son. Gloria Dowling was killed in an Allied air raid on Paris in 1944, but there's no record of her son suffering the same fate.'

'So he survived?'

'That's right. And there's more: records show that later in '44, James Edward Dowling joined the Free French army and was involved in the Allied advance across Europe.'

'And after that?'

'After that, mysteriously, all trace of him is lost. There are no records to account for his whereabouts after 1944.'

Langham squeezed her hand, sat back and looked around the table. 'Am I thinking straight, or has the wine, Charles, gone to my head? *Could* James Edward Dowling and Patrick Verlinden have been one and the same person? They would have been roughly the same age, after all.'

'I think we need to get back to the manor in the morning,' Ralph said, 'and have a little word with his lordship.'

Langham raised his glass. 'We do indeed.'

'And now,' said Charles, 'who's for profiteroles with fresh cream?'

TWENTY-TWO

In the morning, rather than drive over to Neston Manor in separate vehicles, Langham suggested he take the Rover. The lanes that wound their way through the snow-decked countryside were deserted; they passed not a single car on their way, just the morning bus trundling towards Bury St Edmunds.

Langham braked on the crest of the lane overlooking the vale in which Neston Manor stood, surrounded by fields and woodland. The tiny figure of Benson could be seen ferrying logs from one of the barns to the house, and even at this hour of the day lights glowed in several of the tiny windows.

Ralph shivered. 'Don't know how you can think of flitting all the way out here. Won't you miss the pubs? And you've started going to the theatre, haven't you? I don't think they perform Shakespeare out in the sticks.'

'Never been big on Shakespeare, the truth be told. And they have pubs in the country. We had a decent pint at the Dog, didn't we?'

Ralph grudgingly admitted the fact. 'But what if you end up in a village without a pub?' Ralph's expression suggested that no worse fate could befall a decent, upright citizen.

'Don't worry,' Langham said, 'a village with a good pub is at the very top of my list.'

He eased off the handbrake and they coasted down the hill to Neston Manor.

The barn door was open and Langham saw Dudley Mariner within. He stood with his back to the opening and he cut a disconsolate figure with his hands in his pockets and his head bowed. Langham wondered if he had come here, where Esmeralda had spent so much of her time, to brood.

Ralph pointed at Mariner. 'I'll just pop over and have a word.'

'See you inside. I'm going to find his lordship. And you never know, if we smile at Benson we might even get morning tea and crumpets.'

Langham climbed from the car and entered the house.

Lord Elsmere was making his slow way down the staircase, gripping the bannister with his left hand and his walking stick with his right. From the look on his face, a controlled wince with every step, he appeared far from well.

'Good morning, Langham. Making progress?'

'Two steps forward and one back,' Langham said, 'but it's always the same in this job.' He hesitated. 'I was wondering if I might have a quick word.'

'By all means. I was just popping along to the library.'

They proceeded along the shadowy corridor and came to the library. Elsmere settled himself in an armchair and looked at his watch. 'Bit early for morning tea. I'm a stickler when it comes to routine, Langham. Morning tea at eleven, and not a second before. Hope you don't mind?'

'Not at all,' Langham said, warming his back at the fire before sitting opposite Elsmere. 'Now, this is rather a delicate matter.'

'Don't stand on ceremony, young man. I never do.'

'It concerns your first wife and your son, James Edward. You mentioned hearing, after the war, that they'd perished in an air raid in France in 'forty-four.'

'That's right, so I did.'

'I wonder if I might ask how you came by this information?'

'Not at all,' Elsmere said. 'Quite by chance, as it happens. Heard it in my club, would you believe?'

'Positive bush telegraph, those places,' Langham said.

'A chappie I knew, a foreign correspondent for one of the weeklies, he was just back from France – this was in '46. He'd bumped into a mutual acquaintance in Paris, and this fellow happened to mention that he'd heard that Gloria and James Edward had died in an air raid – the notorious Allied bombing in 'forty-four. This correspondent didn't know if I was aware of the fact, so he trod carefully when breaking the news. Odd thing was, it was hard to feel the appropriate emotion. So much water under the bridge and all that.'

'That's wholly understandable.'

'Last time I'd seen James, he would have been a year old, maybe less. It hurt at the time, losing my wife and son in one fell swoop, but you get over these things. And then to find that they'd died in the war . . . Well, it wasn't that much of a shock. I felt a little sadness; who wouldn't? Poor chap would've been just twenty-one. But as for Gloria . . . Do you know something – I found it hard to even remember what the bally hell she looked like.' He stopped and looked across at Langham. 'But why're you bringing this up, young man?'

'Because . . . Well, it's come to our notice, in the course of the investigation, that James Edward *wasn't* killed in the air raid, though sadly your first wife was. He survived the attack and joined the Free French Army.'

'Well, I'll be . . .' Elsmere exclaimed. He peered at Langham, wide-eyed. 'You're quite sure about this?'

'We had it straight from the French embassy in London, sir, via their war records department in Paris.'

'So he joined the Free French, did he?' He leaned forward. 'And then?'

'And then the trail runs dry. The last official record has him joining up in '44. After that . . . nothing at all.'

'But if he'd been killed in action . . .' Elsmere began.

'You would have thought that there'd be some official listing of the fact. And because there isn't, it makes me wonder.'

'Go on.'

Langham hesitated. 'This is a long shot, sir – a very long shot. There's probably nothing at all in it, but in this line of work one must be scrupulous and consider *every* possibility, no matter how ludicrous or impossible they might at first seem.'

'I sense what's coming, Langham.'

'Well . . . It occurred to me that there was a remote chance your first son and Patrick Verlinden might have been one and the same person.'

Lord Elsmere sat back and regarded Langham through watery eyes. His long, lugubrious face betrayed not the slightest flicker of emotion. 'I find it hard to believe, Langham. There was not the slightest family resemblance—'

'There isn't always,' he interrupted.

'But look here, if Verlinden *were* James Edward, why would he have kept schtum? He would've told me who he was, surely?'

'Exactly my reasoning, sir. Why wouldn't he?'

'He didn't, if that's what you were thinking.'

'Of course not.'

'I would have told you quick sharp, if it were so.'

'Thing is,' Langham said, 'I was racking my brains trying to come up with a reason why, if he were your son, he *wouldn't* have told you.'

Elsmere stared into the flames and considered the question. 'If he *were* James Edward – though I don't for a second think he was – then he might have been reluctant to broach the subject, perhaps.'

'If he were your son, do you think Dudley might have had some inkling?'

'If so, he never said anything to me about it.'

'If you don't mind my asking, was Dudley aware of your previous marriage and the fact that you had a son?'

'As far as I'm aware, he was. I think it came up once or twice when he was in his teens.'

'Do you know if Dudley assumed that James Edward had perished in the war?'

Elsmere shook his head. 'I'm not at all sure about that. Perhaps if you were to ask him . . .'

'You wouldn't object?'

Elsmere smiled bleakly. 'Langham, when I employed you to get to the bottom of this tragic affair, I did so in the full realization that you might uncover untold cans of worms. Of course I wouldn't object.'

Langham climbed to his feet. 'I appreciate you taking the time to answer my questions, sir. I'll leave you to your book.'

Smiling bleakly, Elsmere picked up a calf-bound volume from a nearby occasional table. 'Dostoevsky,' he said. 'Somewhat appropriate in the circumstances, don't you think?'

Langham smiled, agreed that indeed it was, and took his leave.

Benson was entering the house with a burden of chopped logs when Langham arrived at the entrance hall. 'Would you happen to know if Miss Miles is in today?'

'I believe so, sir. At least, I haven't seen her leave the manor.'

Langham thanked the butler and made his way to the west wing.

He knocked once, waited a minute, and was about to retrace his steps back through the house to look for Ralph when the door opened. 'Oh, Mr Langham,' Rebecca said, clearly surprised to see him.

'If you're busy . . .' he began.

'Not at all. Do come in.' She stepped aside as he entered. 'I was just clearing away a few things.'

A small desk stood in one corner of the room. He made out a large writing pad and a collection of Biro pens in a chipped mug.

'Working on the novel?'

'Trying to. I seem to be blocked at the moment. What do you do when you're . . .?'

'Blocked?' He smiled. 'Must admit, I don't believe in the old writer's block. It's a myth perpetuated by neurotics who really don't want to write – not that I'd call you one of those for a minute.'

She laughed. 'Thank you!'

'If you're finding it hard, just write any old thing, and you'll find that after a time the words will flow. Then you can go back and rewrite the rubbish.'

She smiled. 'I'll remember that. Would you care for something to drink? I was just about to put the kettle on.'

'A black tea would be nice.'

She indicated an armchair. 'Please, take a seat.'

He did so, and she moved to the rudimentary kitchen area at the far side of the room. He watched her as she put a kettle on the stove and prepared a teapot. She wore a knee-length grey skirt and a black cardigan with the sleeves pulled down; her long black hair was tied in a ponytail. She wore make-up, but unlike the effect achieved by Esmeralda Bellamy, Miss Miles's application of cosmetics enhanced her appearance: crimson lipstick and dark eyebrow pencil that emphasized their plucked arch.

He could see why Larry Evans had been so smitten by the woman.

She carried a tray across the room, and Langham took his teacup and saucer.

'I really don't know how to go about this,' he admitted. 'I've been doing a little digging around in London, talking to a reporter from the *Herald*.'

She sat back, crossed her legs, and balanced her teacup and saucer on her knee. 'I think I can spare your concern, Mr Langham. You're wondering why I lied to you?'

He smiled. 'I was going to ask why you'd been sparing with the truth.'

She sipped her tea and asked, 'What did you find out from the reporter?'

'Just that Janita Gerson is your sister – not someone you just happen to resemble, which is what you told me.'

Rebecca stared down at her cup. 'I hope you'll forgive me. I don't make a habit of lying.'

'But in this instance . . .?'

'It was a time of my life that was very painful, Mr Langham. My father was ill for many years, and I nursed him, single-handedly, throughout. Around the time he was diagnosed, Janita met that monster, Peter Hayley.'

She stopped, biting her bottom lip. 'I didn't approve of the marriage from the very start. Janita might have been in her late twenties when she met Hayley, but she'd led a somewhat sheltered life. He was her very first boyfriend and she thought she was in love. He treated her badly, even then.'

'In what way?'

'Oh, he didn't hit her, at first. But he was verbally abusive. And when she announced she intended to marry him, I was appalled, and my poor father . . . He knew he was dying, and the pain was compounded by the knowledge that his youngest daughter was marrying a thug.'

'It can't have been easy for you.'

'After the marriage, Hayley started to beat her. She'd come home, to Peckham, with black eyes and bruises, and try to claim she'd had an accident. She would stay for a day or so, but she'd always go back to him. She told me she loved Hayley. She made excuses for him, said that he was frustrated at being unemployed and penniless – my sister worked as a shop assistant to pay for all his drinking.' She shook her head. 'Love can be a terrible thing, Mr Langham.'

He remained silent, waiting for her to continue.

'After a year of marriage, Hayley came home drunk one night. He attacked her so viciously he broke her cheekbone. She was in hospital for a week, then came to live with my father and me. Hayley came round to the house one evening, begging Janita to give him one more chance. He said he'd change, would get a job and treat her well . . . So like a little fool, she believed him and left.'

She drew a long breath and paused, staring across the room at the window. 'A few days later a police constable came to the house to inform us that Janita had killed Peter Hayley, beaten him to death with a clothes iron.'

Langham just shook his head in commiseration.

'At the time I was convinced that my sister would hang for what she'd done. I . . .' She hesitated. 'I was oddly proud of her. You probably find that hard to believe, Mr Langham, that I could be proud of someone killing another human being . . . But Peter Hayley *deserved* to die. He was an evil, vicious little thug, and my sister had acted under extreme provocation. You can't imagine my relief when she was convicted of manslaughter, and I knew she would be free in a few years.'

He hesitated, then said, 'And yet you changed your name,

assumed a new identity, almost as if . . . as if you were ashamed of what had happened.'

She shook her head vehemently. 'No. No, I wasn't ashamed, not at all. But you must understand . . . All the publicity, the press coverage at the time of the murder, and then the trial, and again when my sister was released. And then shortly after her release, my father died. It was all just too much. Janita emigrated to Canada to start a new life, and . . . and I wanted a new start, too. It was almost as if I wanted to reinvent myself after years of playing nursemaid to my father, and comforting my sister, and not really having a life of my own.' She smiled at him. 'So I changed my surname, left London and came here, to start a completely different life and do something I'd always wanted to do. And then . . .'

'Yes?'

'And then Esmeralda discovered the photo of Janita in an old newspaper and thought it was me, and threatened to tell everyone . . . And when you questioned me' – she raised a despairing hand – 'it was just a lot easier to claim ignorance, tell you that I was no relation. I realize, looking back, that I should have been honest with you. I'm sorry.'

He shrugged. 'No harm done, I suppose. I know now.'

'Will the police . . .?' she said. 'You won't tell them, will you?' She stared at him, her gaze almost pleading.

He hesitated. 'If I were you, Miss Miles, I'd tell Inspector Montgomery yourself. Come clean, as it were. He's a fair man, and if you tell him what you told me, he'll understand.'

She lowered her gaze. 'Thank you. I . . . I will tell him.' She hesitated. 'How is the investigation proceeding, Mr Langham?'

'As I told Lord Elsmere earlier, two steps forward, one back. I think we'll get there in the end, but it might take a while yet.'

He was about to take his leave – and pay a call on Major Rutherford – when a discreet knock sounded at the door.

Miss Miles answered, and Benson loomed on the threshold. 'I'm sorry to disturb you, Miss, but Mr Langham is required on the phone.'

He replaced his cup and saucer on the tray and moved to the door. 'Thanks for the tea. I'd better go and see who that is.'

'Goodbye, Mr Langham. And I will take your suggestion and tell the inspector.'

'Wise thing to do, in the circumstances. Good day.'

He followed Benson along the passage. 'Did the caller say who—?'

'The lady didn't give her name, sir.'

They came to the entrance hall and Benson indicated the phone. Langham picked up the heavy Bakelite receiver. 'Hello?'

A thin voice asked, 'Is that Mr Langham?'

'Speaking.'

'Mr Langham, this is Dora. Dora Simpson. I spoke to you and Mr Ryland the other day.'

'Of course. What can I do for you?'

'It's about . . . about what happened. I need to see you. About Pat . . . See, he told me not to tell anyone, but I've been thinking . . .' She hesitated. 'I need to show you something, Mr Langham.'

'Very well. Are you at home?'

'I will be in five minutes. I'm ringing from the bakery, but Brenda says she'll cover for me.'

'I'm on my way.'

He replaced the receiver and hurried outside.

He found Ralph in the passenger seat of the Rover, writing in his notebook. He slipped in behind the wheel and started the engine.

'Hey, what about tea and crumpets?' Ralph wailed.

'They can wait,' Langham said. 'I've just had a call from Dora Simpson. She wants to see us about Verlinden. She has something to show us.'

'Show us?'

'She didn't say what.' Langham eased the Rover under the arch of the gatehouse and down the lane. 'She sounded upset.'

'We could always have a pint and a pie at the Dog afterwards, Don. I'm famished.'

'Let's do that,' Langham said. 'How did it go with Mariner?'

'Waste of time. I thought I'd better ask him about the possibility that Verlinden was his long-lost stepbrother, but he wasn't having any of it. Said it was impossible. But then he would, wouldn't he?'

'What was he doing in the barn, other than moping?' He slowed down as they came to a bend and turned along the lane that led to Little Neston.

'Throwing away some of Esmeralda's possessions. And loving it. Said he wanted the damned woman out of his life. Only he didn't say "damned". Did you see Elsmere?'

'And Rebecca Miles.' He recounted his conversations with the pair as he came to the village green and parked up.

'So all in all we're getting nowhere fast,' Ralph said.

Along the street, Dora Simpson stepped out of the baker's shop and closed the door behind her. She turned up the collar of her raincoat and hurried across the green, bending into the wind.

'Right, Ralph, let's find out what all this is about.'

TWENTY-THREE

Dora Simpson showed them into her front room which, compared to the sumptuous library at Neston Manor and Rebecca Miles's comfortable sitting room, was poky and impoverished – and bone-chillingly cold. Dora sensed their reaction and pointed to the empty hearth.

'I'm sorry. I'd light the fire, only I'm all out of coal at the moment. It's so expensive these days.'

'I'll say,' Ralph said. 'What do you do for heating?'

'I've just the open fire in here and a two-bar electric fire for the bedroom. Can I get you a cup of tea?'

Langham sat down on the sofa. 'We won't keep you, Dora. Now . . .?'

The young woman remained standing beside the hearth, hugging her thin frame. Her pinched face appeared grief-stricken as she looked from Ralph to Langham.

'I've been worrying about this ever since I saw you the other day. I know I should have said something . . .'

'You can tell us now, Dora,' Ralph said.

'It's just that Pat . . . he told me not to tell anyone. He didn't want none of them nosy-parkers up at the manor sticking their beaks into his business. You see, he gave me something.'

'What was it?' Langham asked.

'I suppose it doesn't matter to Pat, now that he's not here, does it? And if it'll help you with your investigations . . .' She crossed the room to a cheap pine chest of drawers. From the top drawer she took a small, intricately carved wooden box, nine inches square, then sat down on an armchair with the box on her knee.

'Pat gave me this,' she said in a small voice. 'He said it was an early Christmas present. Beautiful, isn't it?'

'It's lovely,' Ralph agreed.

Dora's thin fingers traced the bas-relief of galloping horses that adorned the lid. 'He didn't have much money, but we was in town one day and I saw this in a shop window and I said how much I liked it, then I thought nothing else of it. We were going to the pictures. We saw *Brighton Rock* with Richard Attenborough. In a way, Pat reminded me of Pinkie – Pat was taller, but he had just the same hunted look about him.' She shrugged, and tears fell from her eyes and splashed on the polished wooden box.

'It's OK, luv, take your time,' Ralph said.

Dora sniffed. 'Anyway, a few days later Pat came and knocked at the door. He had something behind his back and he said, "Close your eyes, darling . . ." So I did, and he said, "Hold out your hands", so I did – and he gave me this box. I'll never forget the look in his eyes when he watched me. He was so happy because he was making me happy.'

She wept, and Ralph pulled a handkerchief from his pocket and handed it to her. She pressed it to her face, blotting her eyes and sniffing. 'I'm being silly, aren't I? I thought I'd done with crying. You can never tell, can you? You think you're done, then the awful feelings just come back again.'

'It takes time,' Langham said, inadequately.

'Anyway, Pat came round here one afternoon, says he has something to put in the box, only it's a secret between me and him. I should never tell anyone or let anyone see what it is. So I said of course, and he gave me an envelope.'

She thrust the box at Ralph.

He took it, sat with it on his lap, then hesitantly opened the lid and stared at the contents.

A long manila envelope lay in the box. Ralph gestured at it. 'Can I?'

Dora nodded, nipping her bottom lip between her teeth.

Ralph took the envelope, pulled open the unsealed flap, and tipped out the contents.

'A Dutch passport,' he said. He looked at Dora. 'And that's all?'

She nodded. 'But he didn't want no one at the manor seeing it,' she said.

Langham took the passport and leafed through the light blue pages, wondering at Patrick Verlinden's desire for secrecy.

'Issued back in 1940,' he said. 'And valid for ten years.' He came to the small black and white picture of a young man, thin-faced and scowling.

Dora smiled to herself. 'Pat told me he was only eighteen when that was taken. He'd changed a lot.'

Langham looked at Ralph. 'I wonder why he never had it renewed?'

He leafed through the pages, looking for customs' stamps. He found two: the first denoting entry into France in 1946, and a second stamp, this time British, showing that Patrick Verlinden had entered the country through the port of Dover in January 1949, a year before the passport expired.

As he flicked through the rest of the booklet, something slipped from between the pages and fluttered to the rug. He picked it up, a small slip of pink paper the size of a bus ticket. He turned it over and stared at a row of printed numerals: 1683.

He passed the slip to Ralph.

'Perforated at one end,' Ralph said, 'and look – it's been torn off across the top for some reason.'

Langham looked at Dora. 'Did Patrick ever mention this slip, what it was?'

She shook her head. 'No, he never said anything about it.'

'Yet he kept it in the passport,' Langham said, 'so you'd think it was important.'

Ralph was staring at the slip, his forehead creased in a frown. He looked up at Langham. 'You know what this is, Don?'

'Go on.'

'It's a receipt for a safe deposit box, with the details of the bank torn off – as if he didn't want anyone to know the name of his bank.'

Langham regarded Dora. 'Do you know if Patrick had a bank account? Did he ever mention a bank to you?'

She shook her head. 'He never said anything about any bank. I don't know if he had an account.'

'When you went into town with him,' Ralph said, 'he never slipped into a bank there?'

'No, never. His lordship always paid him cash – Pat liked it that way.'

Langham took the passport, placed the slip back between the pages, then returned the booklet to the envelope. 'Do you mind if we take this with us? We'd better show it to Inspector Montgomery.'

'Take it. It doesn't matter now, really, does it?' She hesitated. 'Do you think it's important, Mr Langham?'

'It's hard to tell, but it might very well be. If we can find which bank the slip is from . . .'

As Langham and Ralph climbed to their feet, Dora remained seated and looked up at them bleakly. 'Do you think you'll ever find out who did it?'

Ralph smiled. 'We'll find the culprit if it's the last thing we do,' he promised.

Langham gestured with the envelope. 'You did the right thing. Patrick would have understood. We'll let ourselves out,' he said, and led the way from the house.

'Why *do* you think Verlinden never had the passport renewed, Don?' Ralph asked as they walked back to the car. 'He could have got it done at the Dutch embassy in London lickety-split.'

'My guess is that it never belonged to him,' Langham said. 'Dora said his appearance had changed a lot. The passport is something else he stole at some point, just like the photo of those airmen he had copied from Pitt-Lavery's original. *That's* why he never had it renewed.'

'So why did he keep it?'

Langham shrugged. 'The only meagre proof of identity he did have?'

'And if it didn't belong to him,' Ralph said, 'that begs the question: just who the ruddy hell is he?'

Langham stopped at a phone box. 'I'd better get through to Montgomery and tell him we're on our way.'

'And while you're doing that,' Ralph said, pointing along the street to the bakery, 'I'll get a couple of pies. Kate and Sidney?'

'And a bottle of dandelion and burdock, if they sell it. See you back at the car.'

Presently, with Montgomery notified and lunch purchased, Langham drove north to Bury St Edmunds.

They found Detective Inspector Montgomery in his office, poring over case notes with the air of a man at his wit's end.

'Oh, it's you two,' he said, looking up.

Langham gestured to the file on the blotter before the inspector. 'Light reading?'

'I'll give you light reading. I can't make sense of this lot. I grilled Dudley Mariner yesterday and went across to Pitt-Lavery's place this morning and hauled Esmeralda Bellamy over the coals. One of 'em did it, but I'm beggared if I can work out which one.'

He stared from Langham to Ralph, then pointed at the latter. 'You've got crumbs on your tie, Ryland.'

Ralph brushed the remains of the pastry from the front of his suit. Montgomery went on, 'Anyway, what's all this about? And why so secretive over the phone?'

Langham tossed the manila envelope on to the desk.

Montgomery tipped out the passport and leafed through it. Langham indicated the pink slip.

'Ralph thinks it might be a bank deposit box receipt.'

'And it might be at that,' Montgomery said. 'Thing is, a bank in town or in London? If it's a London bank it'll be like trying to find a needle in a haystack. Just a tick. I'll ask Ted, the desk sergeant. He's a St Edmunds man born and bred.'

He was gone from the office less than a minute and returned beaming. 'Ted's pretty sure it's from the National and Midland. It's just around the corner. Come on. I'll get Halliday on the way out.'

They left the station with the portly detective sergeant in tow.

Montgomery led the way around the corner and along the busy high street, dodging shoppers and an old man in a sandwich-board proclaiming: The End of the World is Nigh.

The National and Midland bank was a dour, imposing Victorian building; its manager, though not Victorian, turned out to be just as dour and imposing.

He heard Montgomery out with a stolid expression on his slab-like face, agreed that the pink slip had indeed been issued by his bank, then led the way from his office, along a cold stone corridor, and down a narrow flight of steps into the bowels of the building.

They passed a couple of huge vault doors and came to a barred area which reminded Langham of a Wild West jail. The manager unlocked a squeaking swing gate and they passed inside.

A line of black metal safe deposit boxes lined the wall to their right.

'Now let me see . . .' The manager referred to the slip and paced to the far end of the chamber.

Langham looked at Ralph and raised his eyebrows.

The manager said, '1683. And here we are, gentlemen.' He selected a small key from the bunch on a chain at his waist, inserted it into the deposit box's lock, and turned.

The door swung open. A black metal box, with a handle at the front, filled the cavity. The manager pulled the box out and carried it across to a small table near the barred entrance. From a much smaller bunch he took a key, unlocked the box, and lifted the lid to reveal a bulky manila envelope.

He withdrew the envelope and passed it to Montgomery.

The inspector looked around the small group, then opened the envelope and tipped out its contents.

A small black velvet box, which might have contained an item of jewellery, sat on the tabletop.

'Since you found the slip,' Montgomery said magnanimously, 'you can do the honours.'

Langham gestured to Ralph, who picked up the box and snapped open the lid.

'Well, I'll be . . .'

He set the box back on the table and everyone stared in silence at what was revealed.

Detective Sergeant Halliday was the first to find his voice. 'If I'm not mistaken,' he said, 'that's a German Second World War Iron Cross.'

Ralph eased the black cross from the box and weighed it in his palm.

'And what's this . . .?' Montgomery said, pulling a folded piece of paper from beneath the velvet bedding. He unfolded it on the desk: a certificate printed with heavy Gothic lettering.

'My German's not what it was,' the inspector said, 'but it reads something like: "Awarded to Oberleutnant Ernst Paulens, Russian Front, 1941, for bravery in battle".'

'Well, I'll be . . .' Langham said.

'What I'd like to know,' Ralph said, 'is if the medal belonged to Patrick Verlinden – or was it another ruddy thing he stole on his travels?'

Montgomery asked when the medal was deposited, and the manager led the way back to his office. He pulled a ledger from a shelf, consulted the pink slip, and cross-referenced it to an entry.

'Over three years ago,' he said. 'March, 1953. It was deposited by one Patrick Raul Verlinden, then resident at Withens Farm, just up the road.'

In due course, Montgomery having issued the manager with a receipt for the medal, and the medal itself nestling in the inspector's breast pocket, they left the bank and stood in the street outside.

Montgomery said, 'The note Esmeralda Bellamy sent to Patrick Verlinden – what exactly did it say?'

'"*Verlinden, I know all about you and your lies. I'll be in touch*",' Langham said.

'So how about this,' the inspector said, 'Bellamy knew about the medal, and Verlinden's past – or rather Paulens's past – and decided to do what she did best? Blackmail him?'

Ralph shook his head. 'And how did she know about the medal? Sneak into the bank vault when no one was around, open the box, and come across the ruddy gong? It was deposited back in '53, remember? Long before she first met Verlinden, or whoever the hell he is.'

'Very well,' Montgomery said, undeterred, 'she finds out

about his true identity some other way – maybe when he was drunk?'

'It's far more likely,' Langham said, 'that she suspected Verlinden was hiding something when she went up to Pitt-Lavery's place and saw the photo like the one Verlinden had in the gatehouse.'

'Halliday,' Montgomery said, 'get over to Middle Langley and bring Bellamy in for questioning. And while you're doing that, I'm going to fetch Dudley Mariner from Neston Manor.' He looked from Ralph to Langham. 'One of them did it, and I'm going to get to the bottom of their lies about that Saturday if it kills me.'

He shook Langham and Ralph by the hand, thanked them, then turned and tore back to the station with his raincoat tails flapping.

'I think we'd better get back to the manor,' Langham said. 'I'd like to be on hand to reassure Lord Elsmere when Dudley's taken away.'

They returned to the car and Langham drove from the town centre.

'If Patrick Verlinden *was* Ernst Paulens, a bloody Nazi . . .' Ralph shook his head. 'I'm just thinking about poor Dora, and how she'd feel if it got out . . . Stop!'

'What the . . .?'

Ralph pointed across the road at the entrance to a coal merchant's yard. 'Won't be two ticks,' he said, climbing from the car and hurrying across the road.

He was back a few minutes later, looking happy with himself. 'Just ordered a couple of bags of premium grade for Dora. It'll be delivered in the morning, compliments of the Ryland and Langham Detective Agency. A token of our appreciation.'

'You're a good man, Ralph.'

'Well, I feel sorry for the kid, don't I?'

Langham started the engine and drove off.

Inspector Montgomery had not yet arrived at the manor by the time Langham passed under the archway thirty minutes later. He pulled up outside the house and made his way inside, Ralph at his side.

The butler was in the entrance hall, polishing the glass case containing the skeleton of Sir Anthony Edward Mariner.

'Benson, is Lord Elsmere around?' Langham asked.

'His lordship mentioned that he might take a drink with Major Rutherford at some point this morning. I'm not sure where he might be at the moment.'

'Do you know if Dudley is free?'

'I've just served him tea in the drawing room, sir.'

Langham thanked him and led the way to the west wing.

They found Dudley Mariner seated before the fire, staring absently into the flames. He looked up when they entered and sketched a smile. 'Oh, hullo, Langham, Ryland.' He indicated the tea tray. 'Won't you join me? I'll get Benson to bring more cups.'

'We won't stay long,' Langham said, sitting down. 'We'd just like a quick word.'

'How can I help?' the young man asked.

'We just came to tell you that Montgomery's on his way. He's taking you into the station, along with Esmeralda, to quiz you about the Saturday before last.'

'Ah . . . I thought he might be back.'

Langham leaned forward. 'Thing is, why didn't you tell the inspector that you arrived back here at three thirty that Saturday?'

Mariner spread his hands. 'Honestly, I didn't have a clue what time it was. Esmeralda and I . . . we'd argued. I don't know what time it was when we got back. I dropped her here and went down to the Dog for a quick one. And I had nothing at all to do with Verlinden's shooting.' He shrugged. 'That's the truth of the matter.'

'For what it's worth, Dudley, I believe you.'

The young man smiled, bleakly. 'You might, Langham, but will Montgomery? He has me down as a bad lot.' He hesitated. 'I suppose he's told you all about what happened a few years ago, in the City?'

'He did mention it, yes.'

Mariner looked hopelessly from Ralph to Langham. 'It wasn't as bad as he thinks, you know? I mean . . . Dammit, I'm not proud of what I did. I made a terrible mistake, and my God

how I lived to regret it! But I wasn't . . . I'm not . . . a *criminal*.
I hope you'll believe me.'

He leaned forward, staring down at his clasped hands.

At last he went on, 'I got into debt. Gambling – cards. I was
a fool. I should have got out when I could have . . .' He shook
his head. 'But that's wisdom after the event, isn't it? At the
time, you always think that the next session will be the one
where your luck turns, then all will be well. But it didn't happen
like that, and I got further and further into debt.'

Langham asked, 'How much?'

'A thousand pounds.'

Ralph sat back on the settee and whistled.

'So at the company where I worked . . . I saw an opportunity
to . . . to *borrow*, as I thought of it at the time, two thousand
pounds. You see – and this proves what a fool I was – I planned
to pay back my gambling debt with half the money, and then
. . . I know it sounds insane . . . and then I intended to gamble
until I'd doubled the thousand, and then I would pay back my
company.'

'But instead,' Langham said, 'you lost it?'

Staring down at his hands, Mariner nodded. 'I lost it, and
not long after that the firm's auditor discovered what I'd done.'
He was silent for a time. 'I was lucky not to end up behind
bars. I have my father to thank. He paid back the company
what I'd . . . what I'd appropriated, and managed to hush up
the scandal. Christ, you can't imagine how ashamed I was –
especially when I found out, later, how hard up the old man
was. Anyway,' he finished, 'Inspector Montgomery thinks I'm
a crook . . . but I hope you'll believe me when I say that I was
just a bloody stupid fool.'

Langham murmured, 'We've all done things we regret.'

'What makes matters worse,' the young man went on, 'is
that Montgomery seems to think I'm lying about knowing
Esmeralda back then. I think he assumes we were in it together,
that she persuaded me to embezzle the money. He has a witness
who claims to have seen me with someone matching her descrip-
tion, and he's jumped to the wrong conclusion. But I swear we
met for the first time two years ago, when she rented rooms
here.'

The sound of a car engine broke the ensuing silence. Ralph rose and approached the mullioned window looking out over the drive. 'Montgomery,' he reported.

Mariner sighed and pushed himself to his feet. 'I suppose I'd better face the music . . .'

'Stick to your guns,' Langham advised. 'Tell him you had no idea what time it was when you arrived back here that Saturday, and that you went for a quiet drink at the Dog – not exactly the actions of a man who'd just shot someone dead.'

'I'll do that. Thank you. It's good to have someone on my side.'

'I know you didn't do it.'

The young man paused before making for the door. 'You sound as if you do know who *was* responsible.'

Langham hesitated. 'Let's say that I have my suspicions,' he said, and before Mariner could question him further, he led the way from the room.

Langham was about to turn left, towards the entrance hall, when he saw a figure moving unsteadily in the gloom of the corridor to his right. Peering, he made out the tall form of Lord Elsmere staggering towards them.

'Father . . .?' Mariner called out.

Elsmere collapsed against the mahogany wall panelling, and Mariner rushed to his side and held him upright. The old man's usually sanguine face was grey with shock.

'It's the major. I just – I haven't seen him all day,' Elsmere choked, 'so I knocked on his door and . . . and when he didn't reply . . .' He shook his head. 'I opened the door and . . .'

Langham took his arm. 'What?'

'And I found him.' He gestured vaguely over his shoulder. 'The terrible thing is, Langham, we heard something yesterday afternoon. I was in the drawing room with Dudley and Miss Miles . . . and we heard a shot. I moved to the window. There were two locals with shotguns coming from the spinney across the fields. Hunters.' He shook his head. 'I assumed *they'd* fired the shot. I never thought for a second . . .'

Mariner assisted his father to a nearby settle. Langham glanced at Ralph and they made their way along the corridor.

The door to Major Rutherford's room stood open, and

Langham paused on the threshold. The major was slumped in his armchair before the open fire, which had long since gone out.

'Ralph,' he said, 'run along and fetch Montgomery, would you?'

Ralph turned and hurried away without a word.

Langham entered the room and stared down at the old soldier.

Major Rutherford had shot himself through the temple with his service revolver, which had fallen into his lap. The bullet had passed through his head and shattered a hunting print on the wall beside the hearth, the flock wallpaper around it splattered with grey matter and splintered bone.

A trickle of dark blood had congealed on the sallow flesh of the old man's cheek, and his head hung as if he was dozing.

Langham reached out and touched the major's wrinkled hand; he found the flesh as cold as stone.

He stepped away from the corpse and looked around the room, then crossed to the desk and considered the sheets of closely typed quarto lying next to the typewriter – the major's very last journal entry.

Aware of the silence in the room, and the old man's corpse seated before the empty hearth, Langham sat down and began reading.

TWENTY-FOUR

From the journal of Major William Arthur Rutherford.

I am writing this some time after the events of Saturday the 17th of November. On the evening itself, I could not bring myself to describe what I did in the woods at approximately four o'clock that day.

I have killed a number of men in my time, but always in the heat of battle. This was my first . . . execution.

On Friday the 16th, when Verlinden had threatened me and I decided that the young man had to die, Miss Miles called before bedtime to ask if I needed anything. I showed her my right foot – which I had padded with four socks and swaddled with a bandage – and said that I was unable to walk. I asked for two aspirin and a glass of water, and she assisted me to my bed like the angel she is.

In the morning I refrained from taking my usual constitutional, and when Miss Miles called in again, I asked if she might make me tea and toast. Thus I established that I was in no fit state to walk into the woods that afternoon.

Over the years that I have been resident at the manor, I have observed that Saturday is a quiet time in the house: everyone has their particular routine. Teddy always retires to his study after lunch to read until dinner; Mariner and Esmeralda drive into Bury St Edmunds and rarely come back earlier than five o'clock. Miss Miles listens to the wireless in her room, or works on her book, while Benson has the afternoon off and visits his sister in Newmarket. Patrick Verlinden, a creature of habit if ever there was one, never fails to take the shortcut through the woods to the Dog and Gun at four o'clock.

Late that morning I had watched Dudley and Esmeralda drive off to town, and Benson walk into the village to catch the midday bus to Newmarket. At two o'clock, with Miss Miles in her room and Teddy occupying himself in his study, I took the rear exit from the house and made my way around to the barn. It occurred to me as I went that all my plans would be for nothing if, today, Esmeralda had uncharacteristically decided to lock her shotgun away. I need not have worried: it was lying where she had left it on the carpenter's bench. Concealing the weapon under my greatcoat, I returned to the house.

Now I loaded the shotgun with the cartridges I'd taken from the gunroom earlier, then fortified myself with a single whisky and bided my time until three thirty. I secreted the weapon under my coat and made my way along the passage to the east wing. I let myself out of the side door and slipped into the woods, following the path that led to the top field and eventually the village.

A hundred yards into the woods, where the path veers suddenly to the right, I stationed myself beside the trunk of an oak tree and waited for Verlinden to show himself. Though I was concealed by shrubbery, I had a view back along the path along which the young man would walk.

As I waited, I considered the action I was about to take. In killing Patrick Verlinden, was I doing the world a service in ridding it of someone who had shown, by his threats, to little deserve a place in civilized society – or were my motives more base than that? Was I merely taking revenge on Verlinden to vent my anger on someone who had threatened my good name and the equanimity of my old age?

I will let posterity be the judge of that.

The sight of Patrick Verlinden, when he appeared along the path, startled me from my reverie.

He was limping along with his hands stuffed into the pockets of his tatty overcoat, his shoulders hunched as he stared at the ground.

He was perhaps ten yards away when I stepped on to the path and confronted him.

He stopped a few yards from me and looked up, smiling that infuriating, mocking smile of his.

Then he saw the shotgun and the cold light of fear entered his eyes. But the flicker lasted only a second before he laughed.

'Are you hunting today, Major?' he asked.

'You could say that, Verlinden.'

I stepped towards him, lifted the shotgun and aimed it at his chest. Instinctively he raised his hands and backed off.

I had the luxurious feeling of being in command, which more than compensated for the powerlessness I had experienced the day before in my sitting room when I had been forced to listen to his threats.

'What do you want?' he asked.

'Justice,' I said simply, and pulled the trigger. The shot ripped a great hole in his chest, and I fired again.

He staggered backwards through a stand of ferns and toppled to the ground, saving me the necessity of dragging him off the path. I stepped around the ferns, broke the shotgun and reloaded, aimed at his head and fired for a third and final time.

He was surrounded by fallen leaves and leaf mould, and this I used to conceal his corpse from view. He might lie undiscovered for a week or more before passers-by would be alerted by the smell.

I had a shock in store when I returned to the house. As I was emerging from the woods, I saw Dudley's Vauxhall parked before the manor, though there was no sign of Dudley or Esmeralda. I allowed a minute to elapse, and on seeing neither of the pair, took the path around the back of the manor to the barn. After ensuring that there was no one about to observe my actions, I replaced the shotgun on the bench and made my exit.

Then I returned to my rooms and poured myself a double whisky.

There has been no end of activity around the place since that fateful day. It has come to light that Patrick Verlinden was responsible for the theft of Teddy's Gainsborough, further convincing me – if I needed to be convinced – that I did the right thing in shooting him dead. He was rotten to the core, and I am reassured by the knowledge that I have saved other innocent souls from suffering at his hands.

However, the past week has seen a marked decline in my health. The pain in my chest is becoming intolerable, and twice in the past few days I have passed out, waking both times to find myself lying incapable on the floor.

I do not want to suffer a lingering death, the victim of pain and senility. Nor do I want anyone else erroneously charged with the crime I committed. I could live for months yet, in which time the police might arrest the wrong culprit. Suspicion lately has fallen on Esmeralda, and though I have no love for the woman, I cannot see her hang for a crime she did not commit.

I have been reading through my journals, reliving – as it were – my life, and contemplating its worth. I think I have led, on the whole, a worthwhile existence. I have served my country, and served it well, and only in the last few years has adverse fate intervened . . . But the last thing I want is pity. I have always been, I like to think, the master of my own destiny.

Death holds no fear for me. I have looked it in the face more often than I care to recall, and on more than one occasion laughed.

But first, a final large whisky before the warming fire, and then – to misquote Pepys – so to sleep, eternal sleep.

TWENTY-FIVE

A fter today, Langham hoped he would never again set eyes on Neston Manor.

He braked on the crest of the lane and stared down at the house in the vale. No snow had fallen for several days, but the farmland around the manor, and the woods to the east, were pewter-grey with hoar frost. Nothing moved in the winter landscape except for the occasional cawing crow and threads of smoke rising from three of the manor's dozen crooked chimneys.

He released the handbrake and coasted down the hill.

It was three days since Inspector Montgomery had closed the case on the shooting of Patrick Verlinden. Yesterday Langham had received a call from the inspector. He was holding an informal meeting at the manor to tie up a few loose ends, and Langham and Ralph were called to attend.

As it happened, Charles Elder had asked if Langham and Maria would care to stay the weekend: he had three 'perfect houses' lined up for them to view. That morning Langham had driven Maria to Meadford, dropped her at Charles's house, and proceeded on to Neston Manor.

He would be glad to get this business out of the way, forget all about the manor and its inhabitants, and spend a quiet weekend at Elder House with Maria, Charles and Albert.

He rolled through the archway of the gatehouse and pulled

up outside the manor. Ralph had arrived before him; he sat in his Morris Minor, puffing away on a Capstan.

They met on the steps of the house. Ralph took a last drag on the tab-end and ground it out under the toe of his winkle-picker. He pointed across the driveway to the barn. 'Seen that, Cap'n?'

Esmeralda's Hillman stood in the barn. 'That's odd,' Langham said. 'I didn't think she'd show her face here again.'

'Maybe she and Dudley've got back together?'

Langham frowned. 'I'd like to think he had more sense.'

They stepped inside, where Benson was on hand to take their coats. 'If you would care to make your way to the drawing room, gentlemen.'

'I noticed Esmeralda's car,' Ralph said.

'That is correct, sir. She returned yesterday.'

Langham eyed the butler. '"Returned"?'

Straight-faced, Benson said, 'I understand that Dudley and Esmeralda have enjoyed a . . . *rapprochement*, sir.'

'Indeed?' Langham said, and led the way to the drawing room.

Lord Elsmere stood with his back to the fire, sherry glass in hand. He saluted with it as they entered, gesturing to a side table. 'Help yourselves, gentlemen. Glad you could make it.'

Mariner and Esmeralda sat on a chesterfield over by the window, conversing in lowered tones. Mariner looked up and smiled on catching Langham's eye. Esmeralda refrained from acknowledging his nod.

'Who'd've thought it?' Lord Elsmere said. 'Old Rutherford was the last person I would've had down as shooting Verlinden. Still don't know why he did it – I suppose that's why Inspector Montgomery wants to get us all together.'

'Speak of the devil,' Ralph said as a car engine sounded, and through the window Langham saw Montgomery's Humber roll up the drive.

'How about a spot of lunch when the inspector's said his piece?' Elsmere suggested.

They accepted the invitation, and Elsmere excused himself and crossed the room to speak with Mariner and Esmeralda.

The door opened and Miss Miles entered, looking even

smaller than Langham recalled her. She wore a black skirt and a scarlet cardigan and looked as if she had just stepped from a fashion shoot. She took a sherry from the table and joined Langham and Ralph.

'I expect you're surprised to see her back here,' she murmured, shooting a glance across the room to where Esmeralda was speaking with Lord Elsmere.

'Not half,' Ralph said.

'What brought that about?' Langham asked.

Rebecca smiled. 'It's the gossip of the village,' she said. 'Apparently Dudley was in the Dog and Gun last night, blind drunk in celebration. He told the landlord that Esmeralda had contacted him, virtually begging him to take her back.'

'Begging?' Langham said. 'But why on earth . . .?'

'Esmeralda said that she'd "seen through" Pitt-Lavery and was leaving him.' She lowered her voice and went on, 'But apparently the word in the village is that Pitt-Lavery's been deselected as a Tory candidate after a couple of businesses he's involved with have gone bankrupt. There's even talk of the police getting involved.'

'I see,' Langham said. 'So Esmeralda comes back to the manor with her tail between her legs.'

'I'm surprised Dudley took her back,' Rebecca said. 'But he seems ecstatic at her return.'

'What do they say, Don?' Ralph asked. '"Love is blind"?'

'It certainly seems to be in this instance.'

Inspector Montgomery entered the drawing room, dwarfed by the portly Detective Sergeant Halliday. Elsmere greeted them, had Benson fetch tea when the policemen declined sherry, then arranged chairs in a semi-circle around the fire.

When everyone was seated, Montgomery stood before the fireplace and consulted his notebook.

'I won't detain you for long,' he said. 'I'm here to keep you abreast of the investigation, and to tie up a few loose ends. I invited Langham and Ryland along as they were instrumental in getting to the bottom of various aspects of the case.'

Langham sat back in his armchair, looking around the little group. Esmeralda Bellamy, perhaps conscious of wagging tongues, appeared reserved and reluctant to establish eye contact with anyone. Beside her on the settee, Mariner smiled up at the inspector like a conscientious schoolboy. Lord Elsmere was lost in a world of his own as he stared at his sherry, his lugubrious face appearing even more mournful than usual. Seated primly upright on a Queen Anne chair, Miss Miles caught Langham's gaze and smiled.

'I can officially inform you,' Montgomery announced, 'that the investigation into the murder of the individual hitherto known as "Patrick Verlinden" is now closed. The inquest was held yesterday and a verdict of homicide was passed by the coroner, and my case file is with the superintendent as I speak. The young man going under the alias of "Patrick Verlinden" was shot dead by Major William Arthur Rutherford on or around four o'clock on the afternoon of Saturday the seventeenth of November. Major Rutherford's motive for the killing appears to be that he was in the process of being blackmailed by "Verlinden". And it's thanks to work done by Mr Langham and Mr Ryland that we know the reason behind the threat.'

He proceeded to tell the group about Major Rutherford's disastrous financial dealings with a conman in 'fifty-one, and the major's fear that Verlinden might spread the rumour that he, the major, was at the centre of a gangland drug smuggling operation.

'But I can assure you that the major was nothing more than an innocent, if somewhat naive, dupe in a wily criminal scam,' Montgomery said. 'When Verlinden threatened to open the whole can of worms, the major saw red and took drastic and tragic action.'

It took several seconds for the listeners to absorb this, then Mariner said, 'You mentioned that Verlinden was going under an alias? In that case, just who was he?'

'Again, we have Langham and Ryland to thank for this,' Montgomery said. 'Patrick Verlinden was indeed an alias, assumed by a German national by the name of Ernst Paulens. Further investigation has uncovered that during the last war he served as an Oberleutnant in the SS, first on the Russian front and then, after being wounded in action, as a commandant at the concentration camp of Buchenwald. In the spring of 'forty-five, when the allies were advancing across Germany, rather than risk being captured and tried for war crimes, he stole the identity papers of a Dutch national, who'd died at the camp, and fled. He made his way to France, and from there to Britain. Liaising with the Dutch authorities, we discovered that the real Patrick Verlinden was a member of the Dutch Resistance in Rotterdam, captured by the Gestapo in 'forty-three and transported to Germany, where he found himself in Buchenwald and met his tragic end. It's no small irony, my friends, that such a creature as Ernst Paulens should evade justice by assuming the identity of a Resistance hero.' He looked around the group. 'During his time in England, we've discovered that he committed a string of crimes ranging from petty theft to extortion with menaces. And we're pretty sure that that's only the tip of the iceberg.' He sighed. 'It's a pity that the major saw fit to dispense his own summary justice – I for one would have relished getting my hands on Ernst Paulens.'

Langham glanced across at Esmeralda. She had the good grace to look appalled as she no doubt reflected on her dealings with the war criminal. Beside her, Mariner looked on, oblivious to his fiancée's shortcomings.

Across from Langham, Rebecca sat with her hand to her mouth, shocked. She saw him looking at her and in a quick, almost unconscious gesture, pulled down the left sleeve of her cardigan.

Langham sat back, closed his eyes, and considered what Inspector Montgomery had just told the group.

Lord Elsmere cleared his throat and announced that lunch would be served in fifteen minutes.

'Before then,' Montgomery said, 'if anyone has any further questions, myself or Detective Sergeant Halliday will be only too pleased to answer them.'

Mariner approached Montgomery and spoke in lowered tones, while Esmeralda remained seated.

Langham finished his sherry, aware that Miss Miles was watching him.

He smiled across at her and said, 'I wonder if I might have a little word?'

'Why, yes, of course.'

'Not here,' he said. 'Perhaps we could speak somewhere privately – perhaps in your room?'

She nodded. 'Yes, by all means.'

They rose and left the drawing room.

Langham moved to the small window beside the desk and stared out across the frosted driveway.

Behind him he heard Rebecca cross to the fire and seat herself in an armchair.

'The way you were watching me in there . . .' she said in a small voice.

His throat felt very dry. He tried to swallow and did so with difficulty. He felt sick with indecision.

He managed to say, 'I don't suppose I could have a drink, do you?' He remained staring through the window at the bleak winter scene.

'Tea, or coffee?' she asked.

'Do you have anything stronger? A whisky, perhaps?'

He heard her get up and move around in the adjoining kitchen.

'And perhaps you should pour one for yourself.'

He saw her reflection in the window as she returned to the fireside with two glasses. She sat down and placed the glasses on a coffee table. He could not bring himself to turn around and face her.

'When do hostilities end, Miss Miles?' he asked at last.

'I beg your pardon?'

He drew a long breath, then said, 'I killed a man, once, in Madagascar.' He turned and leaned back against the windowsill, staring across the room at her. 'We'd just landed and were pushing towards the town of Diego Suarez. In the advance, one of our men found himself stranded – Ralph, as it happens – pinned down by enemy fire. I went for him, just as a Vichy French soldier crested a hill about ten yards away. Ralph and I were sitting ducks, and without thinking, in the heat of the battle, I opened up with my Sten . . .' He shrugged. 'The soldier died instantly, and I reached Ralph and dragged him back to safety. I was mentioned in despatches – but I assure you that what I did wasn't an act of bravery. It was a "him or us" moment;

had I failed to act' – he shrugged – 'I wouldn't be here today, and nor would Ralph.'

'Why are you telling me this, Mr Langham?' Her voice was barely a whisper.

'I've often pondered the difference between what I did,' he said, 'and what killers do who plan their actions in cold blood – and if there are ever circumstances in which their acts can in any way be justified. I still feel an odd sense of guilt about what I did, even though common sense tells me that I did the right thing. What I'd like to know, what I'd like to be reassured about, is whether there can be acts of cold-blooded, pre-meditated killing which can be *condoned*.'

She sat very still, staring down at the whisky glass clutched in her small left hand.

He crossed the room, sat down opposite her, and said, 'Put your glass down.'

She looked at him, a question in her eyes, and then did as he asked.

He reached out and took her left hand. It was tiny, and very hot. He sat holding her hand for several seconds, his heart thudding, and then, as she watched him with tears pooling in her eyes, he pushed up the sleeve of her cardigan to reveal the gold wristwatch high on her forearm.

'What are you doing . . .?' she murmured.

He reached out and drew the watch down her arm, at once hoping that he would see what he expected to be revealed, but at the same time dreading it.

He stared at the patch of flesh that had been concealed by the strap, then sat back and said, 'Tell me all about it, Rebecca.'

She stared down in silence at the six numbers tattooed on her forearm, the individual numerals inexpertly rendered and blurred: 846776.

'Please, Rebecca . . .'

She looked from her forearm to the fire, then said quietly, 'I've never told anyone about what happened, Mr Langham, not even my sister. Not even . . . not even my father. You see, I didn't want him to see how much I'd suffered. I didn't want to burden him with all that guilt. His last years were terrible enough, without that.'

She fell silent. He waited.

She stared into the fire, tears rolling down her cheeks. As he looked away, she took a handkerchief from the pocket of her cardigan and wiped her cheeks, composing herself.

'My father was born in Yugoslavia,' she said, 'but he became a naturalised German citizen when his family moved there just before the First World War. He met my mother in 1919. She was English and worked as a secretary for a British company exporting machine parts to Germany. She regularly travelled with her boss to Berlin for trade meetings, and while there she met my father who worked as a draftsman for a German engineering firm.' She looked up and smiled. 'I'm sorry if all this is rather long-winded, but I think the background details are necessary.'

Langham nodded and sipped his whisky.

'They met and fell in love, and my mother resigned her position with the British company when they married. I was their first child, born in Berlin in 1920. My sister, Janita, was born three years later. My mother employed an English nanny, and then a string of English and Scottish governesses and tutors.'

'No wonder your English is perfect, Miss Miles.'

She stared at the golden liquid in the glass on the table before her. 'It was an idyllic childhood, Mr Langham. I was so happy. I wanted for nothing, and my mother and father were kind and loving. I suppose that having such a wonderful childhood made what happened later all the more . . . terrible.'

Langham said, 'Your father . . . Gerson. He was Jewish . . .'

She nodded, reached out for the glass and took a quick drink. She remained clutching the glass and stared at him. 'With the rise of the Nazis in the thirties, my father joined the Communist Party. He lost his job. Life was hard, Mr Langham. We moved from place to place, helped by friends and fellow Communists, always in fear of my father being arrested and interrogated, and worse. I don't know for certain, but I think my father was involved in violent opposition to the Nazis; he certainly organized rallies and helped to print and distribute anti-Nazi propaganda. He never spoke about that time to me, not even when he was dying . . . In 'thirty-eight, my mother could take no more and left for England with Janita—'

'But you and your father remained?'

'My father had applied for a passport so that he might flee the country but was denied. I was eighteen. I had wanted to go to university, but with the rise of Hitler . . . that was not an option for Jews. I met a young man, Jerzy, who was a little older than me, a committed Communist and a committed opponent of the Nazis. When my mother and father agreed that she and Janita should leave for England, they insisted that I too should go.' She shook her head and smiled, bitterly. 'It would have been the sensible thing to do, Mr Langham, and I must have broken my mother's heart . . . But I was young and headstrong and in love. There was no way I could leave Jerzy.'

He took a mouthful of Scotch. 'What happened?'

'Shortly after my mother's departure, my father was arrested and interned, and through contacts of Jerzy's I obtained a false passport and work permit. I took on the identity of a French woman who had worked in Germany but who had died a year previously. When the war broke out,' she went on, 'as a foreign national, and an enemy at that, I was forced into slave labour – there is no other word for it. I worked in a munitions factory. I lost contact with Jerzy; in 1942 he had been arrested on suspicion of aiding the Communists, and nothing had been heard of him since then . . .

'The conditions in the factory could have been worse – they needed to keep a reasonably healthy workforce in order to reliably produce munitions – but I saw workers in other factories, Russians and Poles, who were treated worse than animals.' She fell silent, her lips compressed in a bitter line of recollection.

'The consolation at that time came when I heard, through a mutual contact, that my father had escaped from police custody in 1940. He had managed to flee Germany and enter Yugoslavia, where he was fighting with the Communist resistance. Of Jerzy there was no news.'

She took another sip of whisky, staring into the fire.

At last she went on, 'I will never forget to my dying day the morning of my arrest. I was called to the manager's office, where two Gestapo officers were awaiting me. I was taken from the factory to the local Gestapo headquarters and locked in a freezing cell. Had there been the means, Mr Langham, I think

I would have taken my life there and then. I feared being tortured, and feared even more the idea of betraying Jerzy and others . . . I was taken from the cell and questioned. The officer said the authorities knew who I was, and that my current identity was false . . . "I know you are Rebecca Gerson, twenty-four, born in Berlin on the tenth of January 1920 . . . And do you know how I know this?" Oh, his arrogance as he apprehended my growing fear . . . He took great delight in telling me that Jerzy under interrogation – he meant torture – had informed on me, and others, before he was taken away and shot.'

She fell silent, staring into the flames. Then she looked up at Langham. 'You might think that I felt anger towards Jerzy, but I felt nothing of the kind. I knew that, had our positions been reversed, then I would have broken under torture, and "betrayed" even loved ones. I felt nothing but love for the brave, idealistic young man, and a terrible, all-consuming grief . . . and impotent anger.'

Langham felt something constrict his throat. He took another sip of whisky.

'I expected to be tortured, made to denounce my contacts . . . But this never happened. It was September 1944, and even the most zealous Nazi must have known that the war was lost. The names of a few Communists and anti-Nazis active at the height of the war were of little import now. Perhaps this is what saved me – if being sent to a concentration camp can be termed "saved". I was sent briefly to Auschwitz, and then transferred to Buchenwald.'

Langham closed his eyes. When he opened them again, Rebecca Miles was weeping silently.

She pressed the handkerchief to her eyes, took a breath and composed herself.

'I'm sorry,' she said, smiling bravely. 'I haven't spoken . . . I've told no one about . . . about what happened. Speaking like this, it brings back so many memories.'

'You don't have to . . .' he began.

'But I do!' she said fiercely, clutching the balled handkerchief in her fist. 'I *must* tell you, to make you understand.'

She paused, gathered herself, and went on.

'Nothing can describe the horrors of Buchenwald. I wish I could wipe away the memories, wake up one morning and no

longer recall what I experienced there. But perhaps all the
memories are necessary, Mr Langham. We need to remember
what evil really is.' She wiped her eyes again. 'I was lucky, I
suppose. I was young, and reasonably healthy. I was put on
work detail in an armament factory with other young women,
and every day I saw lines of elderly, the infirm and the sick,
herded to their deaths . . .

'The commandant of the sub-camp where I was imprisoned,'
she said in a barely audible voice, 'was a tall young man,
severely thin, who walked with a limp and had a scar disfiguring
his face.'

'Ernst Paulens?'

'Oberleutnant Ernst Paulens,' she said. 'A "war hero", injured
in a skirmish with the Polish Resistance as his division retreated
from Russia, and handed the sinecure at Buchenwald. He was
cruel – that goes without saying. But his cruelty was fuelled
by a terrible resentment. He hated Poles, the people who had
effectively ended his active participation in the war, more
than he hated even the Jews. I saw him beat Polish prisoners
senseless for merely looking at him, and one day . . .'

'You really don't have to go on,' Langham said.

'But I do, Mr Langham! Don't you see? I *must* make you
understand how evil this man was!'

She closed her eyes for ten seconds, then opened them,
nodded to herself, and went on.

'One day . . . one morning . . . I was among a group of
fifty prisoners being escorted from the hut where we slept to
the place where we worked. We passed a great pit dug by other
prisoners. The pit was a mass grave, where every day those
prisoners who had been gassed, shot or otherwise murdered
were tipped. This morning we were told to halt as . . . as Ernst
Paulens ordered two guards to drag a family of three Poles, a
mother, a father, and a girl of perhaps ten, to the edge of the
pit, where they were made to kneel. Later we learned that the
father had attacked a guard and tried to escape over the perim-
eter fence. And as punishment . . .' She looked up from her
drink and stared at him. 'We were forced to watch as Ernst
Paulens approached the kneeling family, casually drew his
revolver, and shot them, one by one, first the child, then the

mother, and then the father, through the back of the head. Then, smiling, he holstered his revolver and strolled back to his barracks, lighting a cigarette as he went.'

Langham finished the whisky. He was conscious of his heart pounding. He stared at the woman, sitting demure and beautiful in an English manor house, and if ever he was aware that appearances were deceptive, he knew it then.

'That happened in March 1945. We knew that British and American troops were approaching, but to be honest by then I had given up all hope of surviving. Many prisoners were transported from the camp, away from the advancing allies, but fortunately I wasn't among them.

'Ernst Paulens disappeared. He was no longer to be seen limping around the camp, yelling orders at the subservient guards and beating his victims. One morning some inmates took over the watchtowers, killing those guards who remained, and later that day an American tank rolled into the camp, followed by trucks driven by cowed soldiers who were unable to take in what they had come upon. A sergeant gave me a bar of chocolate. The look in his eyes . . . Mr Langham, the terrible pity in the poor man's eyes as he stared at me is one of the abiding memories of what the Germans, the Nazis, had reduced me to.' She smiled at him, bleakly. 'And the chocolate made me sick.'

She remembered her whisky and drained the glass in one go.

He poured two more.

'It was several months before the Red Cross could substantiate my claims that I had an English mother, but at the end of 1945 I was issued with new papers and allowed into Britain. I came to London in December to learn that my mother had been killed in the blitz of '41, though my sister had been evacuated a year earlier and had seen the war out with a family in Wales.'

'And your father?'

She smiled, her face animated. 'Imagine my joy, Mr Langham, when I discovered that my father was alive and living in Paris. I was put in contact with him through the Red Cross, and he was allowed into Britain as a Displaced Person in early '46. We rented a small house in Peckham, my father, sister and I, and I found a job as a secretary.'

'And you changed your name, assumed a new identity?'

Rebecca stared at her drink. 'As I said, Mr Langham, I never told my father what I'd gone through in Germany. Oh, I told him about the factory, the forced labour . . . But I couldn't bring myself to burden him with what I'd experienced in the camp. So when I changed my surname . . . I think my father didn't understand: he thought I was running away from my Jewish identity, when in fact I was attempting to escape the horrors of a previous life.'

She paused, then continued. 'I threw myself into my work. I made friends, enjoyed life in London. It is strange, how one survives, how one doesn't allow the horrors to ruin one's life – that would be to allow evil to vanquish hope, wouldn't it? One survives.' She sighed. 'And then Janita married a sadistic, petty crook, and . . . Well, you know what happened then, Mr Langham.'

'And, later, you nursed your father through his final illness.' He shook his head. 'I can't begin to imagine . . .'

'Don't pity me, please!' she said, something like steel in her tone. 'My father died, but at least he saw Janita released from jail, and start a new life, and he saw me in a job I enjoyed, with friends . . . He told us, before he passed away, that my sister and I had made him a very happy man.'

She fell silent, stared down at her glass.

'And then one day just over three months ago I was in Liverpool Street Station, on my way home from work, when I saw a tall man in his thirties limping towards me. The way he limped struck fear into my heart – but imagine my horror when I looked into his face and saw the scar disfiguring his eye and pulling his mouth into a sneer. I felt dizzy. I very nearly collapsed. It was him, Paulens. Ernst Paulens . . . I had no doubt. As he passed me, I turned and followed him, and I was directly behind him when he walked up to the ticket counter and bought a single to Bury St Edmunds. Without really thinking what I was doing, I bought a ticket to the same place and followed him to the platform. I had no idea what I intended – certainly then I wasn't planning revenge.'

'When did you plan that?' Langham asked.

'Not until later, much later. At the time' – she shook her head – 'at the time I just didn't want him to get away. I had vague thoughts of denouncing him to the police. But, to be honest, my head was a blur of conflicting emotions as I boarded the train and took my seat in the same compartment. Again and again I saw him lift his revolver . . . do what he did . . . and then casually light a cigarette as he walked away, smiling. I'm glad there were other people in the compartment with us – an old vicar who said what a fine day it was. I recall thinking, if only you knew . . .

'At Bury St Edmunds Paulens left the station and caught a bus to Little Neston, and I followed him on to it. I sat a few seats behind him and stared at the back of his head for the duration of the journey, hardly believing what was happening. At Little Neston I allowed him to get ahead of me as he limped from the village, and then I followed him along the lane at a distance – and from the crest of the hill I watched him make his slow way to a big house which I found out later was Neston Manor. Still I didn't really know what I was doing there. I returned to the village and found a room at the Dog and Gun for the night and asked about the manor and the people who lived there. Yes, there was a foreigner living in the gatehouse, a Dutch fellow by all accounts, the landlord said, and someone else said that Lord Elsmere was renting out rooms in order to make ends meet.'

'And you decided to approach Elsmere and rent a room?'

'Not immediately. I returned to London in a daze and tried to forget all about Ernst Paulens. I knew I should tell the authorities that a war criminal was living a secret life deep in the English countryside. But then I started having nightmares, and always the same. A man, a woman and a little girl, kneeling at the side of a great pit, and Paulens pulling the trigger . . .' She stopped and stared at him. 'A week later I decided to leave London, move to Suffolk, and rent these rooms from Lord Elsmere.'

'And to kill Ernst Paulens?'

She allowed the silence to lengthen. 'And to kill Ernst Paulens,' she whispered. 'I rang Lord Elsmere and arranged to visit the manor. He showed me around – I was never in doubt about taking the rooms. I moved in a few days later, telling Lord Elsmere and others that I was writing a book.'

'Not a novel,' he said, 'but an account of your experiences during the war?'

She smiled. 'I wanted to understand what had happened to me, Mr Langham, and at the same time to put the events behind me. I wanted to . . . I wanted to write about Ernst Paulens, and what he had done. When I moved here, the very hardest thing to do was to face him, speak to him . . . I alone knew the truth, that the man masquerading as a Dutch war hero was in fact a sadist who had killed untold numbers of innocent people and had been responsible for the deaths of thousands more . . . I was shaking so much the first time I met him that I thought he must realize that something was wrong. I was nearly sick with revulsion . . . but I learned how to hide that revulsion.'

'He even asked you to have a drink with him?'

She shook her head. 'I wanted so much to refuse – yet at the same time I knew I must go through with it. You see, if I wanted to understand how someone like Paulens could do what he did, how someone apparently so quiet and unassuming could commit such acts of appalling evil . . . I had to speak to him.'

'And?'

'And I met him in the Dog and Gun. It . . . it was perhaps the most difficult meeting I had ever endured. I was shaking and stammering like a fool. I was afraid I'd give myself away, though he must have merely thought I was nervous. I had to stop myself from telling him that I knew who he was, that I knew he was an evil killer living a lie . . . He didn't talk about his past, of course, but told me about the books he was reading.' She hesitated, then went on. 'I expected to find that Ernst Paulens was a shallow, egotistical braggart, that his evil was obvious – but what I discovered was even more frightening than that.'

'Which was?'

'That Paulens seemed an ordinary, shy, unassuming young man. He was well-educated, and well-read, and liked Thomas Mann . . . and he appreciated art. He told me that he admired various paintings in the house . . .' She paused and looked at Langham. 'There he was . . . speaking to me about Thomas Mann and art . . . this person who had the blood of hundreds if not thousands on his hands. And I realized that what really frightened me was that he appeared so unaffected by his crimes, as if he felt not the slightest pang of guilt or remorse. That was when my idea of killing Ernst Paulens became a resolution: I *had* to do it. I told myself that I would be doing it not only for all the people he had murdered in the past, but for the many people he might harm in future.'

'And on the afternoon of Saturday the seventeenth,' Langham said, 'you carried through your resolution.'

'I made careful plans. I watched him, and the other residents. Esmeralda always left her shotgun in the barn, as if inviting me to take it. There was ammunition in the gunroom. On Saturdays, everyone went about their business, leaving the manor quiet. And at four o'clock Ernst Paulens always made his way through the woods to the Dog and Gun . . . And this time I was waiting for him.'

Langham leaned forward, shaking his head. 'I can only imagine his reaction when you confronted him.'

She smiled to herself, as if in recollection. 'He was shocked, when I stepped out from behind the tree and aimed the shotgun at his chest.'

He stared at the woman who had so calculatingly killed another human being.

'I'd rehearsed a veritable screed of accusation,' she said. 'I was going to detail his crimes, demand that he beg for mercy, but in the end . . .' She shook her head.

'What happened?'

'Instinctively he raised his hands, and I said, "Ernst Paulens?" And the look of shock on his face when I said his name . . . *that* was reward enough. Then I said, "This is for the Polish family you murdered in March 1944." And I shot him twice in the chest before he could make a move, and then I reloaded the shotgun and shot him again in the head. Three shots, Mr Langham. Three shots. One for the father, one for the mother, and one for the little girl . . . Then I scraped a few leaves over his body and hurried back to the house.'

She regarded Langham, almost defiantly. 'And no matter what happens to me,' she said in barely a whisper, 'I know that I did the right thing.' .

He leaned forward and poured himself another Scotch, and she nodded when he indicated her glass.

She picked it up and stared at the amber liquid. After a while, she said, 'The way you were looking at me in the drawing room . . . I suspected you knew then.'

He took a mouthful of whisky. 'I didn't know. I had an intimation, a vague idea. A suspicion.'

'But how?'

He sighed. 'A combination of several small things, which individually meant nothing but which, taken together, amounted to a suspicion. The way you wore your watch so high on your forearm, and the fact that your family name, Gerson, was Jewish. And something the *Daily Herald* reporter told me, about when he interviewed your sister after her release: he said that your father was a foreigner and was sure that he had a "story" to tell. Then I thought the reason you gave for changing your name didn't quite ring true, that you wouldn't be associated with a sister accused of killing a sadistic husband. But the clincher was when I read Major Rutherford's last four diary entries.'

Her eyes widened as she stared at him. 'And I thought I'd caught his tone very accurately, Mr Langham.'

He smiled. 'Oh, you did. You mimicked his tone, his voice, very well. What you failed to duplicate was the major's syntax. You see, the other day I read a page of his journal from last year, and the prose was decidedly long-winded, with subordinate clause after subordinate clause, and endless parenthetical asides. When I came to read his last four entries, covering the period of the past fortnight or so, I was struck by the marked difference. The tone of voice was similar, but the grammar very different, economical and succinct. I knew that the major couldn't have written the entries, but if he hadn't, who had? It didn't take very long for all my individual suspicions to fall into place.'

She pursed her lips around a mouthful of whisky as she regarded him. 'I didn't implicate the major solely to save myself, Mr Langham. I was aware that Esmeralda was under suspicion, and as much as I don't like the woman, I wouldn't have been able to live with myself if she were to be hanged for the murder.'

'So when you found the major . . .?'

'I was in the drawing room with Lord Elsmere and Dudley when we heard the shot. We assumed it was the hunters in the wood. Only later that evening, when I looked in on the major before turning in, and found him there . . .'

'It was quick thinking on your part, Miss Miles, to consider faking the journal entries.'

She shook her head. 'Not quick thinking at all. At the time, when I discovered him . . . I was shocked, upset. I liked the old man, despite his politics . . . I was truly shocked. I looked for a note, for some explanation. I know he'd always said he'd take the old soldier's way out – but I expected him to have left a note, at least.'

'But there was nothing?'

'Nothing. And he hadn't even bothered to write up his journal for a couple of weeks.' She took a drink, and then went on, 'It was seeing this, and realizing that he hadn't left a note, that gave me the idea. I returned to my room for a pair of lace gloves so that my fingerprints shouldn't be found in case the police became suspicious, then returned to his sitting room, locked the door and began typing. I finished in the early hours, exhausted, then went back to my room and waited for someone to discover the body.' She hesitated. 'If you're wondering, Mr Langham, it *did* cross my mind to consider if what I was doing in framing the major was . . . ethical. But it came to me that many people of his mindset would applaud his killing of an ex-Nazi war criminal.'

Langham smiled. 'An eye for an eye, Miss Miles. Yes, and no doubt the old man would have agreed with that, too.' He hesitated. 'And the scandal the major was embroiled in, back in 'fifty-one? He must have told you all about that?'

She nodded. 'From time to time I would have a nightcap with the major, when I thought he wanted company. Often he was drunk and rambling, and one evening he told me what had happened in '51, the scandal, and his fear that others should get to know and assume that there was some truth in the story that he'd been behind the drug smuggling.' She shook her head. 'When I came to write the journal entries, I used this as his motive for wanting Verlinden dead.'

She drained her whisky, replaced the glass on the table, and stared at him forthrightly. She took a deep breath. 'What now, Mr Langham?' she asked, her voice wavering.

He sat for a time, staring into the fire, and then climbed to his feet. He walked to the door, paused for a second, and turned.

'Will you find Inspector Montgomery,' she asked, 'and tell him everything you know?'

He hesitated, and looked at the small woman perched on the edge of the armchair, her hands clenched in her lap.

'According to Montgomery,' Langham said, 'the coroner is satisfied and the case is closed. As far as everyone is aware, Major Rutherford did the world a good turn when he shot Ernst Paulens. Perhaps, when all's said and done, we should leave it at that?'

She looked him in the eye, her face expressionless; then she dropped her gaze and murmured, softly, 'Thank you.'

He hesitated. 'There is one thing . . .' he began. 'If the major *hadn't* shot himself, and Esmeralda – or someone else – had been charged with the murder—'

She interrupted, 'Then I would have turned myself in to Inspector Montgomery,' she said, 'and faced the consequences. I do not for one minute regret what I have done, Mr Langham.'

He nodded, pulled the door shut behind him, and walked along the corridor until he came to the bathroom.

He braced his arms against the cool porcelain of the washbasin and stared at his reflection in the mirror for a long time.

Then he doused his face with cold water, dried himself, and joined the others for lunch in the great hall.

EPILOGUE

On the last Saturday before Christmas, Langham and Maria had their second viewing of Yew Tree Cottage in the quiet Suffolk village of Ingoldby-over-Water. A low, drifting mist clung to the land and a fine drizzle sifted down from a grey sky – not that this in any way curbed their enthusiasm. The cottage was exactly what Maria had been dreaming of, and Langham had been happy to learn that there was a decent pub in the village.

'I'll leave you to talk things over between yourselves,' Mrs Ashton said as she left the sitting room.

Maria turned to him, beaming. 'Oh, Donald, it's perfect!'

'And at £650, well within our budget.'

'And three bedrooms – a study each! And the garden . . .!'

A long back garden stretched down to a stream overhung with weeping willows. Langham imagined entertaining guests on the extensive lawn and working the vegetable patch at the side of the cottage.

He took her hand. 'Well, what do you think, girl?'

She made an excited face. 'I love it, Donald. Oh, let's buy it!'

He smiled. 'I think we should. There's a bit of work to be done, but nothing drastic, and it's only five miles from Charles.'

'And there's a nice public house a minute away, don't forget.'

'As if I could!'

The Green Man was situated on the village green, just around the corner from Yew Tree Cottage, a traditional oak-beamed and horse-brass hostelry serving Fullers ales and home-cooked food.

'What say we tell Mrs Ashton that we'll be in touch via the estate agent,' he said, 'and then go for a celebratory drink?'

She squeezed his hand. 'Let's!'

They found the old lady in the kitchen, and Maria thanked her for showing them around and said they would be in touch.

'Oh, it will be ever so nice to have new people move into the village,' Mrs Ashton said, not for the first time.

Langham took his coat from the peg in the hall, and Maria pulled on her raincoat and arranged her hat. They said goodbye and stepped out into the drizzle, holding hands as they dashed along the lane to the Green Man.

At the bar, while Maria was settling herself at a table before the blazing fire, Langham ordered a pint of bitter and a gin and tonic and considered recent events.

More than once since the closure of the Ernst Paulens murder inquiry, he had woken from troubled dreams in the early hours. He'd lain awake, considering what Rebecca Miles had told him, and asking himself again and again if he'd done the right thing.

Two days ago Inspector Montgomery had phoned him at the office; Langham had half-expected Montgomery to announce that he knew Miles had murdered Ernst Paulens, and to accuse him of keeping quiet about the woman's involvement.

Fortunately Montgomery had said nothing of the kind. He was phoning as a courtesy, he said, to keep Langham abreast of certain matters.

Police enquiries had turned up the fact that James Edward Dowling, Lord Elsmere's son by his first marriage, had survived the war but succumbed to tuberculosis in Paris in 1948. Montgomery had personally conveyed the sad news to Lord Elsmere, who had taken it stoically.

The inspector had further questioned Esmeralda Bellamy. Under interrogation, the woman had confessed to plotting with 'Patrick Verlinden' to steal the Gainsborough, and she'd also admitted planning to blackmail him about his past. 'She knew he was being cagey about his past and hiding *something*,' Montgomery told Langham, 'and that was enough for her to consider extorting his half of the proceeds from the art theft.'

As no provable crime had been committed, Montgomery had no grounds on which to proceed against Esmeralda Bellamy. 'But I gave her a stern warning and said that I'd be watching her. Oh – and I thought long and hard about dropping the word to Dudley Mariner about what a bad lot she was. I found myself in something of a moral dilemma.'

For a second, Langham had wondered if the inspector was hinting at his own dilemma, but dismissed the idea when Montgomery went on, 'But I decided not to. Mariner and the woman seem to be muddling along, so who am I to muddy the waters?'

Montgomery had attended Major Rutherford's funeral and reported a 'nice touch' from Rebecca Miles: she had dropped a single red rose on to the major's coffin as it was lowered into the grave. He also reported that Miss Miles had recently left Neston Manor to start a new life with her sister in Canada.

Over the course of the past week, Langham had spoken to a few people in London and done a little research. He'd established that one Oberleutnant Ernst Paulens had indeed been in command of a sub-camp at Buchenwald at the end of the war and had been found guilty *in absentia* of appalling war crimes, and that a certain Rebecca Rachel Gerson had been imprisoned there. He had no reason to doubt that what she'd told him at Neston Manor was anything but the truth.

He leaned against the bar, took a sip of bitter while the barmaid poured the gin and tonic, and looked across the room at Maria.

She sat beside the fire, regarding her reflection in her compact and arranging her hair. She saw him looking and gave a dazzling smile.

He ferried the drinks across to the fireside table.

'Here's to our new life in Ingoldby-over-Water,' he said, raising his glass.

'To us,' she said.

She lowered her glass, frowning at him. 'Donald?' She hesitated. 'Are you happy – about moving here, I mean? The thing is, you've been very quiet lately, and I was wondering . . .'

He took her hand, squeezed, then raised it to his lips and kissed her fingers.

'I'm delighted about the move,' he said.

She tipped her head to one side. 'But? Donald, something is troubling you. Ever since the business at the manor . . .'

He sighed. 'Is it that obvious, darling?'

'It's obvious that something is troubling you, yes.'

He stared down at his drink, then looked up at Maria. 'I need to tell someone,' he said. 'I can't keep it to myself. You see, I need to know if I've done the right thing.'

'The right thing?' She shook her head, narrowing her eyes. 'Please tell me, Donald.'

He took a breath and smiled at the beautiful woman sitting across from him. 'Major Rutherford didn't murder Ernst Paulens,' he said, and felt a weight of responsibility suddenly lift from his shoulders.

Warmed by the blazing fire, with the rain lashing down outside, he told Maria all about Rebecca Miles, and the shooting in the woods at Neston Manor, and what had happened all those years ago in a concentration camp in Germany.